LEAVES ON FROZEN GROUND

GUERNICA WORLD EDITIONS 11

LEAVES ON FROZEN GROUND

Dave Carty

GUERNICA
World
EDITIONS
TORONTO—BUFFALO—LANCASTER (U.K.)
2019

Michael Mirolla, general editor
Margo LaPierre, editor
Cover design: Allen Jomoc, Jr.
Interior layout: Jill Ronsley, suneditwrite.com
Guernica Editions Inc.
1569 Heritage Way, Oakville, (ON), Canada L6M 2Z7
2250 Military Road, Tonawanda, N.Y. 14150-6000 U.S.A.
www.guernicaeditions.com

Distributors:
University of Toronto Press Distribution,
5201 Dufferin Street, Toronto (ON), Canada M3H 5T8
Gazelle Book Services, White Cross Mills
High Town, Lancaster LA1 4XS U.K.

First edition.
Printed in Canada.

Legal Deposit—First Quarter
Library of Congress Catalog Card Number: 2019930492
Library and Archives Canada Cataloguing in Publication
Title: Leaves on frozen ground / Dave Carty.
Names: Carty, Dave, author.
Description: First edition. | Series statement: Guernica world editions ; 11
Identifiers: Canadiana 20190049677 | ISBN 9781771833455 (softcover)
Classification: LCC PS3603.A77414 L43 2019 | DDC 813/.6—dc23

Chapter One

I N THE TREES, in the depths of the forest beyond the reservoir, it was always dark, but here in their home it was light, and it seemed to Céline that even as they slept it was light, for that was the belief she held close, and the warmth of her belief protected her from that which she did not wish to understand.

Céline was not superstitious. But on those days when Gaston and Edmund coaxed her into the forest with them she felt uneasy, as if her nerves had been filed to a point with an emery board, for their long afternoon hikes didn't rejuvenate her as they so clearly did for her husband and son. Even on sunny summer days, it was dim and ghostly under the trees. Sometimes she would hear, but not see, large animals crashing away—as if the impenetrable walls of foliage above their heads absorbed light, shedding what remained of the sun's illumination on her apprehensive features. On these occasions she was certain that if her husband and son ventured out of sight she would not be able to find her way home. Yet Edmund, it seemed, had barely learned to crawl before he was crawling into the orchard behind the house and shortly after into the tangled, dark woods that bordered their farm. Which, she was equally certain, was where he had to be now.

Despite the years she'd spent pleading with Edmund to leave a note telling his worried mother where he was going—how many times had he promised?—there was no note. But his daypack was gone from its customary spot in the corner by the back door, and his Day-Glo green Nikes—his school shoes—had been dropped, one resting upon the other, beside it. So she knew where he was: He was *out there*, spearing stumps and other imaginary monsters with the sharpened stick he would have cut from a tag alder switch, combing the dense brush along the creek bottom or the reservoir or God knows where for rabbits and frogs, the spear poised at his shoulder like the lance of an ancient warrior.

Céline crossed her arms, frowning out the window at the barn behind the house and the gently undulating rise of carefully pruned apple trees beyond and then abruptly strode into the kitchen to make a pot of green tea, resting the tarnished copper pot on the front burner of the ponderous and meticulously scrubbed cast iron stove she had insisted Gaston buy shortly after their marriage. The pot, creased and dented from culinary skirmishes long forgotten, began to rock as the tea within started a slow, comforting simmer. Gaston didn't understand, or refused to consider, that children wandered off and got lost every year. In northern Wisconsin, people vanished every *week*. Bad things happened out there: People got lost; they broke ankles; they were crushed by falling trees; they ran into packs of wolves that killed their dogs.

She had finally let Gaston persuade her that it was okay if Edmund didn't make it back in time for dinner, that you couldn't stop a kid from doing what it was in his nature to do. He reminded her how lucky they were that Edmund loved the outdoors at least as much as the computer games every other kid in the country was addicted to, and yes, of course computers were necessary—Céline's part-time job in marketing in Port Landing depended upon them no less than her bookkeeping duties at Gaston's construction company did—but so was having healthy hobbies, like hiking in the woods.

It amazed her that Gaston could be so sanguine about his son's chronic absences. He never seemed to worry that the nine-year-old was off by himself for hours at a stretch, and when, on rare occasions, she insisted Gaston go and find him, he knew in just which swampy bend of the brook he'd be hunting frogs, or in which muddy corner of the shallow irrigation reservoir he would be swimming. She'd finally given up asking and instead had learned, uneasily, to quietly await his return, her arms folded and her back against the butcher-block counter, the tea tapping impatiently at her side. And, as Gaston never tired of reminding her, Edmund always came back, usually an hour or so before nightfall, wet, muddy and thoroughly happy, full of tales of adventure and willing to eat the dinner she'd saved only because she insisted upon it.

Céline poured herself a cup of green tea and her gaze fell again upon the orchard. She saw the neatly pruned rows of apple trees just beyond the barn not as a stand-alone crop but as the backdrop to their farm, as if the trees were a green tapestry hung in a great, vaulted room bordered by the forest to the west and Lake Superior to the east, a mile in distance; and their farm was the hinge point between the two.

Both of her quarter horses, Sir Lancelot and Dutch (for Duchess), were lounging lazily in the corral behind the barn, their eyes sleepy and half-closed in the summer warmth, hardly appearing the high-priced progeny of the selective breeding that had produced them. The horses had long ago stripped the leaves from the few spare limbs that hung over the rails of the corral, but the rest of the orchard was a solid wall of deep, thrumming, pulsing green, alive with the hum of billions of invisible insects. She would, on occasion, throw a saddle on Sir Lancelot and ride alone down the rows of trees, for having a horse beneath her bolstered her courage.

At least she'd shown Edmund how to make a healthy meal. Céline took a measure of pride that Edmund enjoyed the taste of the red-leaf lettuce and organic tomatoes she grew in their garden. He was a muscular little boy and he'd always been a good eater. Her reluctant and increasingly rare hikes with her son and Gaston wore her out—this despite hours of Pilates at the Port Landing Fitness Center—but seemed to tire Edmund not a whit.

Always there was the forest through which her son moved like a small wraith and his love of the wild country which he shared with his father. It was a love she did not understand, so increasingly she waited alone in the moist warmth of the kitchen, studying the extravagant artwork on the coffee cup that Edmund's strong little hands had thrown and painted for her at summer camp when he was seven. She'd thumb through a stack of *Midwest Living* magazines, frustrated at her own inability to stop worrying that this would be the one time he wouldn't return, awaiting the dull thud on the back porch of his feet stomping the mud off the size seven hiking boots Gaston had bought for him.

On certain summer days, unable to contain her thoughts, she found respite from the heat of her kitchen in her horses. Astride Sir Lancelot's broad, muscular back, she felt safe and even adventurous, her hair brushing the limbs above her head as she rode through the orchard, no longer afraid of the creatures she couldn't see, knowing that Sir Lancelot would protect her. Sometimes she would bring Dutch along on a lead, until one day, when the lead was flicked from her hand by an unseen limb, she found that Dutch was perfectly happy to trot beside them, brushing her whiskery nose against her leg like an affectionate colt, her ears pricked forward in eager anticipation.

To Céline, the scent of them, like warm bread from her oven, was not apart from the scent of home, and her love of them—despite their great size—was not apart from the breadth of her embrace. But when the horses were brushed out and returned to the barn, and the bridles wiped clean and hung on the wooden pegs in the tack room, there was still Edmund.

Céline's protectiveness seemed, in equal measure, to amuse and irritate her husband. Gaston had been raised in Port Landing in the seventies, when the town still retained the cadence of the rural fishing village on Lake Superior it had always been (although you could see signs even then of the boutique artists' community it was destined to become, much to Gaston's disgust), and not in Catholic schools in Minneapolis as she had. He had been raised in the very house they were now living in, the house that his Grand-père had built for the first of his three wives when he returned from the Korean War.

The construction company he founded, Vaillancourt Builders, had survived all three brief marriages and the woeful mismanagement of his only son, Gaston's father. Gaston had in turn done a much better job of running the company he'd inherited, although it had taken him years to build it back to the level it had been before his father had nearly run the business into the ground during the boom-and-bust decade of the nineties. Gaston's French-Canadian father had been a heavy drinker, although his mother, a full-blood Ojibway with a graduate degree in chemistry from Madison, had very nearly been a teetotaler.

Yet Céline imagined genetics at play, and the one or two bottles of beer Gaston drank every evening bothered her. She had drunk, by her own reckoning, three glasses of wine in the entire thirty-seven years of her life, the last of which was at their wedding reception fifteen years earlier. Although she had to admit, when Gaston pressed her, that his drinking was reasonable. Hadn't she and Edmund been well provided for? Hadn't he alone been responsible for turning the company around? His parents, he reminded her, had hardly done the same for him. And she would admit again that he was right on all counts. But these conversations settled nothing; instead, they were conversations that left the door open for future iterations on the same theme.

The Vaillancourt farm had become, by the gradual accretion of the barn, corrals, garden, chicken coop and greenhouse, an organic presence inseparable from the orchard and the forest beyond, as if the cluster of apple trees around the house had, over the decades, crept in from the orchard; and the cedar posts in the corral and cedar siding on the barn longed to rejoin the ancestral cedars in the swamps from which they had come. Grand-père had milled the huge beams that supported the roof in their home from old-growth white pines that the early loggers, who had pretty much leveled the Wisconsin forests by the turn of the century, had somehow missed. Floor-to-ceiling windows overlooked Lake Superior and Madeline and Basswood Islands to the east.

Quixotically, Grand-père had ordered the barn from Sears Roebuck, one of the last to do so, and Gaston's father, before his death, had told them of watching the pallets of lumber being loaded on flatbeds and trucked up the hill from the railroad that until the early sixties continued to run through the center of town. Why Grand-père had purchased a mail-order barn, rather than milling the lumber and building one from the trees that hemmed in their property from all sides, he never explained. But perhaps, as Gaston suspected, it was because he wanted to be done with the house and barn his first wife had demanded of him and was anxious to begin planting the orchard, embarking upon a lifelong relationship that, unlike his marriages, fired his passion and consumed most of his free time.

Grand-père's son, Gaston's father, had been indifferent to the fifty-four acres of lovingly pruned and tended Red Delicious, Honeycrisps, McIntoshes, Cortlands, Galas and Honeygolds, but Gaston had inherited his grandfather's passion for the life of an orchardist, and as soon as Edmund was old enough to keep up, he began accompanying his father on walks through the cool, damp shade beneath the leaves, Gaston sometimes packing a rifle on his ongoing crusade to eliminate the bears that ripped entire limbs from his beloved trees. He'd killed only one that Céline knew of, but the photo of the beast, its nose dripping blood, had somehow wound up thumbtacked to the bulletin board in the small grocery store in Port Landing where she did her shopping. Luckily for her husband, who considered hunting regulations a distraction, bear season had been open.

Perhaps, Céline often mused, if she had been raised in the country as Gaston had, she would not feel such unease in the furthest reaches of the woods, with its bears and wolves and other dangerous creatures. Instead, her Minneapolis upbringing included a panoply of girls' sports, which would ultimately earn her a four-year ride to play volleyball for the fighting Cobbers of Concordia College, but precious few camping trips. At Concordia, rather than sign up for any of the dozens of field trips offered, she'd majored in Communications with a minor in Spanish, and her textbooks kept her safely ensconced in the library at her sorority house.

In her senior year she met Gaston, an indifferent student who had been ejected from the baseball team for punching a rival team's third baseman, and who in due time crashed Céline's sorority Christmas party. She loved the powerful muscles spanning his back and his swarthy, almost Latin looks, in stark contrast with her blond, blue-eyed Nordic features, and although he was nearly an inch shy of her five feet, nine inches, she decided to move in with him after graduation. It never occurred to Céline that Gaston was shorter than the dozens of other boys who had been courting her since high school; his strength and confidence radiated power.

Moving to Port Landing had been an adjustment. She adored the house, of course, with its rough-hewn beams and cathedral ceilings, period wallpaper and pine-paneled rooms, the maple butcher-block counters in the kitchen and the oiled cast iron pans suspended from the massive brass rack above the stove, but it took her years to reconcile the beauty of their farm with the drastic loss of shopping, movie theaters and restaurants she had taken for granted in the city. The orchard was planted on what had once been a gently rising pasture, and in October, when the leaves began to turn, the coppery orange-yellow of the apple trees stopped on the precise delineation where the blood-red leaves of the oaks and maples began, which bled in turn into the deep, brooding greens of the spruces and pines beyond them, lending the entire tableau the richness of a luxurious patchwork quilt, their shiny red house and barn cross-stitched to the hem along the bottom edge.

But while the chilly nights and the riot of fall colors energized Gaston and Edmund, quickening the pace of their patrols and infusing their conversations with anticipation, Céline was content to sit on the front porch in Grand-père's maple rocker with a cup of tea and take in the view of the cobalt-blue waters of Lake Superior below. From a safe and protected remove, the blue expanse of the lake and the black woods cloaking Madeline Island held, improbably, a comforting tranquility that grew with her distance from them.

One day, rather than take his customary afternoon hike into the orchard, Edmund hopped in the truck with his father and the two of them made the short drive to town. Céline watched the red Ford splash through the puddles on the gravel road below the house and then disappear into the trees as the TV murmured behind her, then returned to the kitchen. Gaston had not mentioned taking Edmund shopping, and although she had long ago ceased demanding explanations—during the week, her busy husband practically lived in the company's three-quarter-ton pickup, shuttling from one construction site to the next, it was irritating that he hadn't at least offered up some kind of ETA for their return. Dinner would be ready in an hour—he *knew* that—and having her son miss so many of them already was bad enough.

She had hardly taken the casserole out of the oven when she heard Gaston's truck return and pull into the turn-out beside the house, followed by the slamming of doors and Edmund's excited chatter. She placed the casserole on a cutting board and dropped her hot pads on the counter and walked to the window.

Edmund had disappeared under the second-story deck. Céline heard him bouncing around down there, along with some other sounds she couldn't place, but Gaston stood in the sunlight, a grin on his chiseled face, his hands resting casually on his hips. A tiny black puppy darted into view, and on its heels came Edmund with an even smaller, reddish puppy wriggling fitfully in his arms. Edmund beamed with joy, his short arms cradling the tiny creature like a squirming baby, the black puppy racing around his legs and yipping in shrill, excited squeaks while Edmund talked to the pup in his arms as if to a child. Suddenly, with a sharp kick, the red pup catapulted backwards out of his grasp, landing squarely on its head. Céline caught her breath. But then, as if being dropped on its head was all part of the fun, it joined the black pup in its frenetic circumnavigations around Edmund's legs. Céline folded her arms, stepped outside and onto the deck, leaned over the railing and waited.

The sound of the French doors closing behind her briefly arrested the motion of them all: the dogs, Edmund and Gaston. The two puppies stopped as if they'd hit the end of a tether and gazed up at Céline with rapt fascination. Edmund, who was standing directly below her, craned his head back and up, a goofy smile on his face. Gaston grinned.

Céline's eyes settled on the smaller of the two pups, the reddish one, who returned her gaze with star-struck reverence. She sensed intuitively that it was a female, a girl dog (she never could bring herself to call it a *bitch*), and that the larger of the two was probably a male. The red pup had a deep mahogany coat and four delicate white paws, with a splash of white that encircled its muzzle and flowed down its chest like an elegant white cravat.

"We have dogs now?" she said.

"Not just any dogs," Gaston said. "Border collies. Stock dogs." The black pup had begun nuzzling Gaston's leg. Gaston pushed it away with the toe of his boot. "I had buddies who had some when I was a kid. There was a lot of them around here back when there were still guys working livestock. They're a lot smarter than other dogs. They're like ..." The black pup was sitting on its haunches and staring at Gaston as if waiting for an answer. Gaston studied it for a moment, scratching his chin. "They're just really smart," he said.

Céline nodded. "We don't have livestock," she said. "We have chickens."

"Same difference," Gaston said.

"I already got names for them, Mom. Guess what this one's called?"

Edmund had stepped onto the lawn and was trying to coax the red pup to him. He radiated joy, and Céline knew in that moment that any input she might have had with her husband, the kind of mutual decision-making that husbands and wives were supposed to do before buying furniture, or appliances—forget about dogs—had been deftly sidestepped by his unannounced trip to town.

She had never in her life personally owned a dog. Her mother had owned a Cavalier King Charles spaniel, but the sluggish beast had lived on her mother's lap and would have nothing to do with anyone else in the family. Now Céline owned two dogs. She could persuade Gaston, sometimes. She could, sometimes, move Gaston in one direction or another away from one of his intractable positions. But she could not stop her son from loving these ... *collies* ... any more than she could stop him from making expeditions into the forest beyond the orchard. Nor would she try. She had, she realized, been overruled in a discussion she had never had a chance to participate in.

Edmund dropped into a crouch and slapped his thighs and called to the dogs. "Here! Here!" he said. The red pup lowered her nose to the ground but wouldn't let him near her. Finally, he dove for her, launching himself into the air as if trying to field a grounder just beyond the tip of his glove, and Céline marveled anew at her son's easy agility, the sports gene he had inherited from both of them, that innate athleticism. But the pup was quicker still and pranced just out of reach, playfully dropping into a crouch, her small rump in the air, her tail swishing with delight at this new game.

"She came right in last time I called her," Edmund said. He sat on his knees and brushed the grass from his bare legs. "But anyway, that one's Breeze, you know, like when it's just a little bit windy." Céline heard her son's voice rise in pitch, breathless with his excitement. "She's a girl. And the black one's Cloud. That was Dad's idea. He said if one dog's Breeze, then maybe the other one should be like the weather too, sort of related. So it was like, breezes come from the clouds. But it was my idea too; I got to make the final decision. He's a boy."

"Pretty goddamn brilliant, if you ask me," Gaston said under his breath. He gazed across the front yard.

Céline glared at him. "Those are very nice names, Edmund," she said.

Gaston scratched the black stubble on his chin. "They can live in the barn, Céline. I'll build them a box or something in the hay. Barn stays warm all winter, right? Horses do just fine. They don't have to come inside at all."

"Gaston, shouldn't we have talked about this?" Céline saw Edmund's stricken expression, but resolutely braced her arms against the railing. She would not be denied her say. In the blue water beyond Madeline Island, a pair of low-slung fishing boats chugged into the wind, their thin white wakes trailing in the distance. They plied the open water beyond the Apostle Islands in good weather, on the lee side of them in bad. Always there were fishing boats.

"Yeah. Probably. But, you know, Edmund's been wanting a dog forever. I heard about these at the shelter. I wanted to get them before somebody else got them, right? Dogs like this don't show up down there that much. They're purebred, no papers, but that's what the gal said. Purebred Border collies aren't exactly cheap. Not expensive like your horses, maybe, but spendy. All I had to give was a few bucks for shots. They're littermates, you can probably see that, so you can't really separate them at this age. So I got 'em both."

"I see."

"I already agreed that they're my responsibility, right, Dad? I already said that," Edmund said. "Look, Mom! I already got her trained!"

Céline could not ignore how desperately her son wanted the two pups, and how much he wanted her to want them, too. He waved wildly for her attention and then grabbed a stick of kindling from the woodpile and heaved it in a high spinning arc over the lawn. The red pup watched and as the stick began its descent, she sprang. So quick was the little dog that she snatched up the stick on its second bounce. The black pup, Cloud, raced along behind her, his fat, short legs churning in vain, but he was far too clumsy to keep up. He returned to Gaston, as proud of himself as if the entire performance had been his alone. Breeze circled Edmund's legs, holding the stick high, spit the stick at his feet and dropped into a crouch and stared at it, her eyes wide and unwavering. Céline caught herself smiling.

"She even caught it once!" Edmund said. "It was so cool! I mean, I threw it and she caught it in the air before it even hit the ground. This dog is *fast*, Mom. Right, Dad?"

"Fast as your mother's horses, even," Gaston said.

Céline's gaze rose to the trees above their heads. In the winter, after the leaves had fallen, the crowns opened to reveal glimpses of Port Landing through barren, entwined limbs, a snatch of eggshell-white siding on an expensive bungalow in the subdivision far below, beyond that the red neon glow of the perpetually OPEN sign in the window of Happy Jacks Saloon along the docks. But now, at the height of summer, the town, a half mile below their farm, was hidden behind an impenetrable wall of verdant green foliage.

Edmund and Gaston gazed up at her, their eyes raised to where she stood on the long redwood deck above their heads like Caesar on a podium before supplicants, her reflection magnified in the bank of east-facing windows at her back. Edmund's brown eyes were rimmed with worry, and despite her instinct to comfort her son, why, she wondered, were both so keen on her approval now? The decision had been made, and they had made it without bothering to consult her. As if, like the wicked witch of the west, she would raise a gnarled finger and banish Toto from her son's life forever. As if she would break his heart *now*.

Céline inhaled, her nostrils flaring ever so slightly, and gazed at the lake. The wakes from the fishing boats had dissipated and the boats were nowhere in sight.

"They're your responsibility, young man," she said.

Edmund yelped and clapped his hands and as if on cue the two pups began dashing in wild circles around his legs, yipping in delight. Edmund made a goofy little happy dance, unable to contain his delight.

"Wait a minute!" Céline said. "All I said was ... I didn't ..."

But Gaston had already turned, put his hand on Edmund's shoulder, and redirected him toward the barn. The two pups tumbled ahead. She watched them go, her apron furling in the light breeze, Gaston's broad back working under the sweat-stained folds of his cotton T-shirt. Just before they disappeared around the corner of the house, he looked back, caught her watching him out of the corner of his eye, and winked.

Chapter Two

Iɴ Pᴏʀᴛ Lᴀɴᴅɪɴɢ the Fourth of July was ostensibly the biggest holiday of all. It presented itself squarely at the height of summer, when the breezes off Superior were cool and languid—not choked with driving snow as was so often the case during the fall and winter holidays—when vacation time was available to all, coaxing downstate tourists and residents alike out of their cottages and into the streets, compatriots in a brotherhood of spectators in thrall of the fireworks displays over the bay.

Gaston brought his glove with him, a vintage Rawlings Reggie Jackson XFG-12. He'd spent years looking for a miniature version of the deep-pocketed leftie for Edmund, but there were extant no miniature versions of classic baseball gloves for nine-year-old short-stops and he had finally been forced to settle for a Regent knock-off. Edmund didn't care.

"You might want to think about that glove right there," Gaston told Céline on the short drive to the city park.

The Reggie Jackson lay between them. They had driven past the organic berry farm that bordered the subdivision below their home. The view opened onto the approaching town of Port Landing, the water-blackened dock pilings aligned like sentinels along First Street, the tiers of redwood-sided, architecturally-shingled Victorian mansions tastefully hidden in copses of manicured trees, where owners of downstate car dealerships and financial planners paid real-estate brokers a fortune to find them a tiny lot with a view.

"Same glove I played with in high school. Same glove I had that night I met you. Same glove on the back seat on our first date. Probably don't remember that, do you? I *love* this glove. This glove and I go way back."

He poked her playfully in the side.

She slapped his hand away. "I get it," she said. "You and your glove." She rolled her eyes toward Edmund in the back seat. Breeze and Cloud clambered onto his lap, and despite the air conditioning blasting from the vents, he lowered the window. Both dogs were leaning across his lap, their paws draped over the windowsill, their small black noses thrust into the wind, their ears snapping like pennants in the back draft. Breeze squinted and snapped at the invisible bugs that pinged off her nose. Gaston put his hand back on Céline's thigh. Pretty high up.

There was no domesticating this man, Céline thought. Her girlfriends had husbands who came home from work, mixed themselves a drink and quietly got inebriated in front of the TV. Gaston had … a *chin*. It stuck out from his face like the splitting maul he left buried in the stump in the back yard, cleaving the world like the heavy maul cleaved saw logs into kindling. Problems, people and irrelevant objections fell to either side.

She'd fixed them a nice lunch, which she put in the hand-woven wicker basket she'd found for ninety-nine cents at Goodwill. Gaston was appreciative, but he made it clear he and Edmund were going to play baseball at the annual father/son game, and they'd eat when they were through. Too much food in your stomach made you heavy and slow. But they'd have to pull Edmund away from his dogs if they were to play at all.

* * *

Céline had never seen anything like it. The three of them—Edmund and the two dogs—seemed to be perpetually in orbit, each around the other two. The dogs were half-grown now, still pups, but it was clear that Cloud would be a third larger than Breeze, who was already pushing twenty pounds. Céline was still trying to reconcile the hit to their budget from the food they consumed: The pups were ravenous as wolves and went through a twenty-pound bag in two weeks. Both dogs were healthy and impressively strong, with dense coats and clean white teeth.

Gaston hammered together a crude carriage from an ancient Radio Flyer wagon that had belonged to his father, and while Céline watched in amazement, Breeze set her small shoulders into the harness and towed Edmund back and forth across the yard while Gaston roared with laughter. Cloud, always the shy one, was hesitant and intimidated by the noisy contraption, and preferred, instead, to stand in Gaston's protective shadow and watch the show, his ears pricked with delight at the goings on.

Edmund's routine had changed on the very next day following Gaston's arrival with the two mewling puppies: Where before he had dumped his books by the back door before heading outside on a hike, now his first stop was to the barn to summon his dogs, if, as was increasingly the case, they weren't already waiting for him at the end of the driveway. Céline was getting used to the hair, which was everywhere: on the rug in the living room, on the tile floor of the kitchen, on her clothing. She didn't like it, but, as Gaston had pointed out, her horses had hair too, and she had to admit that after an hour of currying Sir Lancelot and Dutch, a deeply soothing activity she thought of as a kind of active meditation, she was just as covered with the stuff as Edmund was after a romp with his two dogs.

* * *

There were already dozens of people milling around the city park, and men and their sons were converging on the baseball diamond. Edmund swung open the back door of the truck and the two dogs, as if shot by a cannon, catapulted outside, followed by Edmund, his right hand thrust inside his glove.

"Edmund, will you stick around for a little bit? Please?" Céline said. Breeze was already crouched at his feet, poised for a game of fetch. Edmund whipped a baseball across the parking lot. The little red dog was after it in an instant.

"Aw, let him go," Gaston said. "Game doesn't start for an hour. Let him burn some of the stink off. Kids need to run around."

Céline turned to usher a parting reminder to Edmund, to stay within earshot where she could reach him, to stay out of the bog behind the outfield fence, to control his dogs, but he was already gone. She spied him halfway across the park, running toward a group of boys in the distance, Breeze prancing along beside him with the baseball in her mouth. Edmund bounded across the grass like a fawn. Céline, despite her own considerable abilities, had never considered herself much of a runner. But Gaston, who at forty still spent three or four nights a week pumping iron in the basement, could still pound out a mile on the high school track in under seven minutes, which, once a year, he did, just to prove that he could.

Gaston and Céline wandered down to the dugouts hand in hand. The sun soaked through her blouse and warmed her bones, easing her reserve, allowing her peevishness at her wayward son to dissolve into the peaceful, overarching solace of family. She moved closer to Gaston, leaning into him, feeling his solid heft against her bare shoulder. Gaston had put on weight during their marriage, but not much, nothing like the husbands of some of her girlfriends. Still visible beneath the tanned skin, like boulders just below a dark current, were the powerful muscles developed over two decades of weight lifting, muscles that allowed him to casually throw a half dozen wet two-by-fours over his shoulder on his daily deliveries to the Vaillancourt Builders construction sites.

He often complained of missing the hard, physical labor he'd done working for his father during his summers home from college. Since he'd taken over the company, he said, he never got to *work* anymore. But this was news to Céline: Whenever she visited him at a construction site, she invariably found him down in a ditch manning a shovel or up on the deck with a framing hammer in hand, his worn leather tool belt cinched around his waist.

The dugouts were built from concrete block with tin roofs, and the insides and outsides had been painted and spotlessly scrubbed by the Port Landing Jaycees. But after a heavy rain the drains sometimes backed up, necessitating a quick clean-up detail. Gaston leaned over and poked his head into the shade under the roof, and then backed out. A bald man with a mop emerged, nodded, and somberly extended his hand.

"Radcliff!" Gaston said. "Good to see you. How the hell are you?" Céline dutifully extended her hand and he shook that, too, averting his eyes.

Radcliff was as tall and narrow as Gaston was compact and wide, and like many balding men, he compensated for his lack of hair above with a full beard below. Yellow teeth glinted unevenly from behind a dense, grizzled mustache.

Radcliff and his wife, Sally, lived in a rented bungalow several miles down the road in Washburn, and every morning he climbed into his wheezing Chevy Apache and chugged into Port Landing, where he had, over the decades, crewed on a succession of dilapidated fishing boats. Gaston had told Céline, only half-joking, that Radcliff had been fishing since birth. No one who knew Radcliff doubted it. Radcliff, in the only windfall of his life, had inherited his father's skiff, but somehow, in a long ago financial misappropriation, had lost it. The Radcliffs and their only child, a tall, frail boy about Edmund's age, eked by on a diet of smoked whitefish and herring, venison, and all they could raise in their overgrown garden. Some of Céline's friends in the Rotary drove to Washburn and delivered a care package of food and clothing to the Radcliffs each Christmas.

Gaston and Radcliff had maintained a casual friendship since high school, where they'd played on the same baseball teams. According to Gaston, Radcliff had been a pretty fair right fielder, with a long wind-up but a rocket-like delivery to second base. Radcliff was also a charter member of the monthly poker games the two sometimes attended, which ostensibly were open to any Port Landing High School graduate, but which were, Céline suspected, more of an excuse to drink free from the encumbrances of wives and kids. In any event, she couldn't imagine Radcliff saying much of anything. Gaston occasionally tried to talk him into taking a job as a company laborer, which would have paid him more than he ever made as a fisherman and eventually provided minimal health care for his family, but Radcliff, Gaston had snorted, had only furrowed his bushy brow and shaken his head. When Gaston pressed the issue, he shook his head all the harder.

Gaston and Radcliff had disappeared inside the dugout, so Céline shaded her eyes and tried to locate her son. She spied him with another boy and the two dogs walking the perimeter of the bog behind the outfield fence (she had known this would happen), scanning the shoreline intently for empty mussel shells, bits of colored stone, rifle casings or whatever else he could find to stuff in his pockets (and later forget). Even at this distance she could see the mud splattered on his bare legs. Now they wandered down the length of the fence toward her: Edmund wearing his glove, Breeze prancing about his knees begging him to throw a ball for her to retrieve. When they approached, she recognized the other boy and folded her hands and grinned.

"Why, hello, Tony. It's nice to see you. Where's that mother of yours?"

Tony shrugged and scraped his toe in the dirt and his pale, freckled face flushed with embarrassment. He had a shock of white-blond hair and was nearly a head taller than Edmund, who had been his best friend since kindergarten. Tony Trumbo's father, Lloyd, worked for Gaston as a project foreman. The two families were not close, but they often rubbed elbows at social functions. Céline had always enjoyed the company of Tony's mother, Gail, who had an earthy sense of humor and was fun to be around.

Céline had wondered openly about Tony to Gaston. Why was the boy so shy? Was his father like that, too?

"Man, you're really something," Gaston had said, shaking his head. He had returned from lifting weights in the basement and the veins stood from his arms like pulsing blue tracks. He fished a beer out of the refrigerator, flicked the tab into the garbage bucket under the sink and pressed the cold can against his cheek. "I really wonder about you sometimes, Céline. I mean, can't you figure it out? You scare the shit out of him. You're too pretty. Half the guys in Port Landing get like that around you."

"Oh. Well." Céline could think of nothing else to say. Tony was what, nine? Edmund was nine, so he must be nine, too. She had that kind of effect on *children*? Sure, she knew all about men; there had been men hovering around her since high school, some more annoying than others, but … a nine-year-old? The thought flustered and embarrassed her. She cast another glance at Tony, who smiled shyly and looked down. The dogs flopped into the grass. Cloud rolled on his back with a beatific look of contentment, a wide toothy dog grin. Breeze lay by his side, panting in the warm air.

Edmund slid his hand into his pocket, and Céline saw the mischievous look on his face an instant before he yanked a night crawler out of his pants and tossed it at his mother's knees. Céline shrieked and jumped straight backwards, and Edmund laughed so hard he began to wheeze. Tony joined in, glancing at Céline out of the corner of his eye, his face beet red, the two of them feeding off each other's slapstick antics. In the next instant Breeze hopped on the night crawler, and after poking it with her nose once, she gobbled it down, prompting melodramatic exclamations of disgust from both boys. She stared at them, chewing contentedly. Cloud trotted over for a look but Breeze growled under her breath and he dropped his head and slunk away, casting back a lost, forlorn look.

"Do you really think you should be throwing worms at your mother?" Céline said, trying to be stern. But the question struck her as so inane that as hard as she tried to contain herself she began to laugh almost as hard as the boys. Behind them, Gaston and Radcliff watched, Gaston, as always, shaking his head and grinning.

* * *

Céline took a seat in the bleachers just above the dugouts and was joined by several other wives. Radcliff sat beside her only after she'd repeated her invitation. He leaned back, his bony fingers clasped around one knee, and gazed at the lake. He answered her questions politely when she spoke to him but did not venture conversation otherwise. Puffy white clouds hovered in the blue sky above Madeline Island and several sailboats darted along the shoreline like brightly colored minnows in random schools, solemn and directionless. Radcliff's son, Bobby, was prone to asthma attacks and couldn't risk playing baseball. He spent the summers holed up in the Radcliff's rented shack in Washburn with a vaporizer running around the clock until the cool weather of fall, when the pollen and dust damped down enough for him to return outside and resume a semblance of a normal life.

It was a beautiful afternoon. This had always been what Céline loved most about Port Landing: the summer afternoons. The sun warmed her skin and gave it a delicious bronze glow. She leaned against the bleacher behind her and unbuttoned the top button of her blouse, tugging it open for just a little more sun, as much as she dared, as much as was proper. Around her, other women were doing the same.

Out on the diamond, the game lurched, inexorably, from one inning to the next. The Jaycees had launched a relentless, heroic assault on the weeds in the infield, but in the humid, verdant summers of northern Wisconsin, the weeds were edging ahead, and the groundskeepers were reduced to mowing it short and leaving it at that. Kids in oversize ball caps and huge mitts were posted at each position, and the unwritten rule was that the youngest among them could be accompanied by their fathers. One infinitely patient soul had volunteered to pitch for both teams, and lobbed a baseball over the plate again and again.

Edmund was halfway between second and third, and poised beside the dugout was Gaston, his hands cupping his mouth, yelling something to his son. Edmund stared at him and then took two steps down the baseline. Gaston nodded, mouthed the word "good," and folded his arms. Edmund smacked his glove and said something to the batter. The chatter of the other boys on the infield rose in unison as a boy from the opposing team walked to the plate. The boy took a few choppy practice swings, then stepped into the batter's box and waited for the first pitch, his helmet nearly covering his eyes and tottering about his small head like a bobble toy on a spring. He swung hard but undercut the pitch by six inches and the umpire gently signaled a strike. The crowd murmured and a woman in the stands behind Céline cupped her hands around her mouth. "Just meet it, Jared. Just meet it," she said. Everyone nodded in agreement.

The pitcher held up the ball so Jared could see it, then gently lobbed it in underhand. This time, Jared caught a piece of it, and the ball took a few bounces across the infield and dribbled into left field, just beyond the third baseman's reach. The boy seemed dumbfounded by his hit and for a moment seemed unsure of what to do, but in the next instant the spell was broken and he dropped his bat and began sprinting for first.

Céline spotted a reddish blur out of the corner of her eye, and before she could turn, before she could even focus, she knew exactly what it was. Breeze streaked across the outfield with lightning speed and scooped up the ball, then turned and began trotting to Edmund, who had buried his face in his glove. The third baseman made a dramatic lunge for her as she passed, but she sidestepped his flailing arms, looking back over her shoulder to see if he would follow her, then resumed her stately trot to Edmund, as every adult in the stands and the fathers of the boys on the field and even the boys themselves convulsed with laughter. Breeze trotted to Edmund, dropped the ball at his feet, and then backed off a step, watching intently, begging him to throw it for her. Edmund threw the ball back to the pitcher.

Gaston stepped forward and called for a time out. He and the other men on the field huddled with the umpire, and when they'd finished, the ump signaled them to resume the game. The boy would be safe on first. Gaston threaded a piece of rope through Breeze's collar and walked her off the infield and gave her to Céline, then turned and strode back across the infield.

It was then Céline sensed a change, an imperceptible stilling of breath. Gaston had tucked his white T-shirt into his jeans, giving him a crisp, military bearing. Céline saw the women around her watching him, saw them shift in their seats and even saw one touch her hair. Then he stepped back into the shadows beside the dugout and the moment ended as unremarkably as it had begun. The chatter resumed as if nothing had happened as indeed nothing had. But Céline understood.

She had long ago arrived at a state of uneasy acceptance: that which attracted her attracted other women as well. Gaston, with his compact, powerful frame and square chin, his perpetually unshaven jaw, his straight black hair pulled into a ponytail and his dark, piercing eyes, wasn't as handsome as he was rugged, but his perpetual grin was like leavening in a cake, a lightening of his strong features that lent an improbable buoyancy and mischievousness to everything about him. Men, by and large, enjoyed working for him. Women found ways to be near.

Gaston did not go out of his way to discourage the attention. But, as far as Céline knew, he had never strayed, nor had he ever given her reason to believe that he had any inclination to do so. On some nights, at dinner parties among friends or at one of the chamber functions they attended throughout the year, she would excuse herself from whatever conversation she was involved in and glide across the floor to where her husband was expounding upon some aspect of the booming construction business and hook her arm through his: *mine.* In heels, she loomed two inches above him, and where other men might have found this unsettling—although Céline couldn't imagine herself *unsettling* anybody—to Gaston her height was an unending source of self-deprecating jokes about the size of his equipment vis-à-vis hers. The more this embarrassed her, the more it delighted him that she was embarrassed. She'd finally had to set a boundary: at least not in front of Edmund. Please.

The game dragged on for several more innings and then, as much for a lack of momentum as a conclusive score, sputtered to an end. Céline gathered the few articles of clothing she'd brought for her son and met Gaston and Edmund by the bleachers. They ambled to the parking lot, the dogs tumbling ahead. Lights were blinking on over Port Landing and the town took on a cheerful postcard glow. Gaston put his hand on Edmund's shoulder and Edmund gazed up at him in worship and awe, as sons do before their own incipient awareness of separateness comes to fruition. She shaded her eyes and scanned the diamond. The other fathers were already leaving, their sons at their sides or running ahead, dispersing across the gravel parking lot and climbing into cars and trucks. It had been a pleasant afternoon. Edmund had been so cute, standing at shortstop and pounding his oversized glove exactly as Gaston had shown him.

Breeze bounded toward Edmund, a baseball in her mouth. Cloud preferred to trot quietly beside Gaston, ready as always to do his bidding. Gaston paid no attention to the dusty little dog, and Céline wondered if he even knew the half-grown pup was around. Gaston, who saw dogs as animals to be tolerated, not catered to, no less than her horses or the flock of Banties in the coop he'd built for her, acknowledged their occasional usefulness, while otherwise ignoring them as long as they behaved themselves.

Edmund's life, on the other hand, seemed to revolve around animals. In so many ways, in his temperament, in his surprising strength, in his endless teasing, he was his father's son, but in this he differed. There was a sensitive side to Edmund, a receptiveness, that yearned for the receptiveness and softness he found in her. As a child, he'd spent hours at her side making clay animals while she happily labored to throw pots on the wheel in the continuing education building attached to the high school. He made all kinds of things: globs of clay that he called "bunny" or "horsey" or whatever else he'd seen on their farm that day. It struck her as odd that she couldn't remember if he'd ever made a glob called "doggy," but it didn't matter now; he had two of them.

From the moment Gaston brought the pups home from the pound, Breeze was Edmund's alone. She had given herself to him, co-opting his affection as matter-of-factly as she had settled into the straw dog bed Gaston had put together between two bales in the corner of the barn. Cloud was happy to follow along on Edmund's swimming trips to the half-hidden irrigation lake past the orchard, but while Breeze churned ahead of the boy through the water, towing him while he grasped her collar, Cloud would paddle out a few yards and then return to shore, barking anxiously at being left behind but too timorous to swim out to meet them. Cloud was never the initiator, never the bold one.

Céline had noticed something else in the preceding weeks: Increasingly, wherever Gaston went, Cloud followed, always on the periphery, always watching. Sometimes the perpetually dusty pup—his black coat seemed to attract every speck of dirt in the yard—would simply sit and observe; but at other times he would lean timidly against Gaston's legs, his head lowered in supplication, furiously wagging his tail. In return, Gaston, his mind occupied with the day's project, rarely gave him more than a cursory pat before shooing him away. Yet even this perfunctory gesture of affection delighted the little dog and he would kick up his dirty white paws and dance in happy circles.

They walked to their truck. A father of one of the other players handed Gaston a beer. He took a long draught and the cold flushed his dark skin, bringing color to his cheeks. He slid his fingers down Céline's wrist and closed them around her hand and she moved into him, her breast brushing his shoulder. Breeze pranced in circles, proud of the baseball she held in her mouth. They loaded the dogs in the back seat, Edmund clambering in last, Breeze leaping into his lap the moment he clasped his seat belt. Céline gazed at her husband over the top of the truck, and he held up a finger, beckoning her to listen. From somewhere far across the lake, she heard the deep bellow of a freighter, faint and clear.

Chapter Three

CÉLINE STARED AT the driving rain, worried about her son. A few times every summer, this happened. He had disappeared several hours earlier with a wave and a grin and no particular itinerary. But she had a pretty good idea where he'd gone: to the orchard. Or he was somewhere in the forest that lay beyond.

Céline marveled at the force of the storm. It had come howling in off the lake and flung itself at their home in violent waves, as suddenly and as unexpectedly as a head-on collision, and in its brief, unmitigated fury, seemed determined to wash their house, their barn, their chicken coop, Gaston's shop and everything else they owned down the two-lane blacktop into Port Landing. She had seen nothing like this, ever, growing up in Minneapolis.

But the summer storms never lasted long. They spent their wrath in a few short minutes, and then, even as water was pouring in rolling sheets off the eaves, the first rays of sun would peek through the clouds, splitting open the dark, brooding canopy and revealing slivers of a faultless blue sky.

Gaston stood behind her, rocking forward on the balls of his feet. "He'll be fine," he said. He cradled a cup of coffee in his hands.

"I know."

"He will. Nothing's gonna happen to him up there. He'll get a little wet, is all. Probably think it's a big adventure." He peered at her over the top of his cup, then gazed out the window. It was still raining, drops slamming into the window like shotgun blasts.

Céline spun around. "How can you not worry? I mean, he could drown up there or something. He's *ten*. You know what rain like this does to the creek."

The brook that ran through their orchard, a rivulet that on most summer days she could easily hop across, tripled in size during storms like this; she had seen it happen too many times not to think it wouldn't happen this time, right now.

Gaston wiped his mouth with his fingers and set his cup on the windowsill and folded his arms. In the corner, a trickle of rainwater seeped under the glass. It advanced down the sill in fits and starts, hesitantly, as if unsure of the force of gravity, until it found the edge and pooled, spilling on the rug and forming a small, dark wet spot.

"I am worried, a little. I'm just not like you. He's got a raincoat. He knows the way home. He knows how to stay dry. I showed him how to do all that stuff plenty of times. He knows how to take care of himself. I mean, he's pretty damn self-sufficient for a kid his age. Better than some adults I'm not gonna mention. He's probably waiting it out under a lean-to like I showed him. Probably curled up nice and cozy with the dogs. Kids like him, this is *fun*."

Céline was unconvinced. She sensed his exasperation with her, but what kind of mother would she be if she didn't worry about her son? She'd always had reservations about Gaston's hands-off approach to parenting. But there was no debating him on the merits. Gaston had covered all the bases, and she knew that what he told her was true. Edmund loved being outdoors, in all kinds of weather. Most of all, he loved showing his father that he was a competent woodsman, that he'd taken to heart that which Gaston had shown him, that he could, in the teeth of a raging summer gale, take care of himself. Computers and computer games held a certain attraction, of course, but usually only on days when he was stuck inside, or after he'd returned from his explorations.

Céline knew that Gaston was proud of his son's passion for the wild places she was reluctant to go. Edmund was, he had often said, very much like himself as a boy of the same age. He'd explored the same orchard, mounted day-long expeditions into the same woods.

Gaston's father had not gone with him. He had been a drinker and found the wild interior of saloons more to his liking. But his grandfather, Grand-père, had shown him what to do. Grand-père had shown him how to navigate the woods and deal with inconveniences like bears and rainstorms. Grand-père had given him the rifle that still hung above the back door, and Gaston kept the bore swabbed and the chamber loaded.

Céline's gaze rose to the rifle then returned to the window. The rain would be letting off soon, a culmination she sensed more than saw. And then, suddenly, it was over. The sun broke through, pushing the angry dark clouds back across the lake, revealing a sparkling expanse of quiescent blue water. Céline put her fingertips on the windowsill and leaned forward, peering at the orchard for a sign of her son. In that moment the back door flung open and Edmund strode in, soaked through, his wet boots dripping mud and water on the tile entryway. Behind him, Breeze and Cloud peered around his legs, desperate to be invited inside. Both dogs looked like drowned muskrats.

Gaston stared at the ceiling, then exhaled with a quiet sigh and poked her in the ribs. He walked to the kitchen and refilled his cup.

"Where have you been?" In her relief, it was all Céline could think of to say.

Edmund was grinning. "It was so cool!" he said. "I was walking through the woods, up by the reservoir. And then the storm hit! We knew we were in big trouble, Mom, so I got under a big old blowdown, like a bear. And I started a fire and I used that fire starter stuff Dad gave me and I put the space blanket over the dogs and me. I got a little wet, but I was pretty comfortable. The dogs stayed pretty warm too, I think. Cloud doesn't like the thunder, but I wasn't scared at all. I knew you'd be worried, Mom. Dad said you get worried about stuff, but I was okay."

Céline shot Gaston a sideways glance. He ignored her. He drew up a chair and began nodding along with Edmund's story, leaning forward, his elbows on his knees.

"You built a little teepee with kindling, right?" Gaston said. "Like I showed you."

Edmund nodded vigorously.

"Yup," Gaston said. "That always works. And you stocked up on firewood, right? Enough to get you through the night if you had to?" He glanced at Céline, then back at his son.

Edmund nodded again. "There was lots of dead wood on the blowdown. I could have stayed there all week."

Gaston turned toward his wife and nodded once, curtly, as if it were settled. Céline bit her tongue. She had no idea why crawling under a rotten log full of bugs and God knows what else was "cool"— Edmund was drenched, no matter what he thought he was—but then, she had never understood anything at all about the strange dark woods beyond their farm that her son and husband found so fascinating. Edmund's cheekbones had finally begun to show through the chubbiness that he'd had since he was a toddler, and it struck her, then, that her son would become a man who looked just like his father, with the same broad chest, the same powerful legs, the same square jaw. And the same inexplicable love of being wet and dirty.

Edmund began removing his rain-drenched boots, slamming his heel into the tile in an effort to yank one of them free. He crossed one leg over another and tugged mightily at the stuck boot. Slowly, with a wet, sucking sound, it slid free. His sock slid off his foot and landed in a sodden heap on the floor.

"Can Breeze and Cloud come in? Just for a little bit? They got pretty wet out there, Mom. I'd be a lot wetter if it weren't for them. It's like, they got wet so I could stay dry. We were like a team." From the kitchen window, Céline saw the back ends of both dogs poised outside the door, their tails wagging expectantly.

Céline put her hands on her hips. "Well ..."

"Uh-uh," Gaston said.

"Why, Dad? I won't let them get anything wet."

"You mean like this?" Gaston picked up one of Edmund's soggy socks. Water drained from the toe and puddled on the tile below. He dropped it and it landed with a sodden plop. "You know what your mother's rules are. No dogs in the house. They'll be fine in the barn.

You can take a towel and dry them off, okay? You know what Mom thinks about dog hair."

Céline rolled her eyes. Somehow, she knew the dog issue would get back around to her. It was true, she didn't like dog hair. Who liked dog hair? Even people who *loved* dogs didn't like dog hair. Not a single one of her friends liked dog hair, and almost every one of them had a dog. But she could have learned to live with it. And it wasn't like she didn't like dogs, per se. She thought they could be cute at times, like little furry horses. Especially Cloud, with his sad brown eyes and perpetual eagerness to please. Breeze, well … Breeze had a mind of her own. Not unlike Edmund.

But still. She remembered their what, their argument? No, it hadn't really been an argument. She had simply expressed a perfectly valid reservation about dogs living in the house, which, Céline reminded herself, she had every right to express, and Gaston had unilaterally decided, *ex cathedra*, that the dogs would *never* live in the house. That was his way of meeting her halfway. She didn't recall saying she *refused* to let them live in the house, only that she had reservations. But that's the way it always was with Gaston: black or white. There was never any shading toward gray. Still, she'd have been open to discussing it further, and had halfway hoped they would. But that discussion had never been revisited. Henceforth, the dogs would reside in the barn.

"You know where the towels are in the tack room? The ones I use on the horses?" Céline said. "Get into some dry clothes and go out and dry them off, if you want. You can hang the towels over the stable to dry."

Edmund frowned glumly. He had removed his other boot and sock and now squished to the back door in his bare feet. The moment he opened the door the dogs began keening, squeezing themselves between his legs and wriggling with delight. He dropped to his knees and flung an arm around each dog's neck, said something in Breeze's ear, then backed away and shut the door.

Céline watched from the kitchen window. When the door closed, Breeze turned and began trotting to the barn. But Cloud continued to stare at the back door, whining under his breath. Finally, he trotted the length of the house and stared up at the bottom of Edmund's bedroom window. Then he turned and reluctantly followed Breeze across the yard. She watched them until they disappeared behind the corral.

* * *

Céline frowned at the lint trap in the dryer, then plucked out the fuzz and held it to the light. Woven into the blue and yellow lint from Edmund's sheets were strands of red and black hair. She would not allow herself to jump to conclusions. Raising a child was not a contest of wills, Céline thought, it was a ping-pong match of managing expectations. Or was that just something she had read in a parenting magazine? She grabbed another tuft of lint, pulled it apart, and studied it under the light. Not Edmund's black hair, which was long and glossy: short, coarse dog hair. It was undeniable.

Céline dropped the lint in the wastebasket, slapped her hands clean and leaned back against the dryer, her arms folded across her chest. How?

Everyone else was gone. Edmund had stuffed a peanut butter sandwich and water bottle into his daypack and had disappeared into the orchard before she was up. He had not left a note. Again. He'd left the open peanut butter jar sitting on the counter. Even though it was Sunday, Gaston had driven to the job site to meet with one of his subcontractors. She'd decided to catch up on some housework, but her routine washing of the family's bedding had turned up … *dog hair*. It's not that she hadn't expected it; it's that it hadn't occurred to her that she'd discover it in such an unexpected way.

Edmund could certainly be willful, but he'd never openly defied her. She and Gaston had laid down the Rules of Conduct for the Vaillancourt household, and one of the rules, explicitly stated, was: *Thy dogs shall reside in thy barn.*

So why was there dog hair all over Edmund's sheets?

Céline frowned. He sure as heck hadn't gathered it up and put it there. He must be sneaking the dogs inside. But when? It couldn't be during the day; he spent most days hiking in the woods or swimming in the reservoir, and when Gaston was home the two of them sometimes patrolled the orchard for bears, Gaston with his grandfather's rifle in the crook of his arm and Edmund with the BB gun Gaston had bought him for his tenth birthday. Gaston called it 'walking the perimeter.'

That night, Céline sat up in bed, reading *Western Horseman* magazine under the lamp on the nightstand. The bathroom door opened and Gaston walked to bed in his boxers and sat on the edge of the bed, running his fingers through his hair. He'd taken off the elastic band that held his long hair back and it fell to his shoulders. He combed it behind his ears and flung open the sheets. She felt the wash of cool air as he slid in beside her, felt the warmth of his rough hand on her belly. She closed the magazine and turned toward him.

Gaston always showered after he finished his workout, and he smelled like a bar of Irish Spring. He was happy to use the expensive emollients she bought him to preserve his skin, but when they ran out he went back to Irish Spring. At least it had a pleasant scent. She set the magazine on the nightstand.

"You ever hear Edmund getting up at night? I mean, like walking around downstairs? We don't really know what he does down there."

Gaston stared up at the ceiling. "I just kinda assumed he went into his bedroom and went to sleep. What do you think he's doing? Raiding the refrigerator or something?"

"I don't know. I was just wondering, is all. He's about that age where kids like to roam around at night. Some of my girlfriends' kids are doing stuff like that. Liz Spence's boy, Robert, he was going into the garage and starting the car because they left the keys in it. He wouldn't open the door to let the exhaust out because he was afraid they'd hear him. He was just sitting there, you know, pretending like he was driving. Luckily, they caught him before he asphyxiated himself."

Gaston scratched the tip of his nose. "You think he's doing that?"

"No. We don't have a garage."

Gaston grinned. "I knew there was something Grand-père forgot. Damn. No wonder I can't keep the truck clean."

Céline punched him under the covers. Hitting Gaston was like hitting a brick wall covered with leather. "I'm serious. I just think we should know, is all. Don't you?"

"Uh-huh." Gaston turned over, facing away from her, his back pressed heavily against her side, warming her bare skin. "Tomorrow I'll nail his door shut," he said. "That'll fix him." He grunted, then rolled onto his back. "No, wait." He held his finger up, as though on the verge of an idea. "I'll tie his little brown ass to the bed. It'll take him until morning to figure out how to get himself untied. Kind of like the Houdini thing. You know, where they tied up that magician guy back in the twenties and threw him into a tank with a bunch of sharks or something? We could do that, except we'll throw him into the lake. I *like* that idea. He already knows how to swim. Plus, it'll give me a chance to practice my knots."

Céline sighed. She switched off the light on the nightstand, and within minutes, as she knew he would, Gaston had fallen asleep. She sensed, as much as heard, the deep, soothing rumble of his breath, which merged with the quick, light cadence of hers; a flowing together of different currents in the same river. But tonight she willed herself to remain awake. She studied the stars outside their bedroom window, pinpricks of light in the black Wisconsin summer sky. Gaston had shown her how to find the North Star, something everyone should know, he told her, because the North Star would take you home. But she'd forgotten where it was.

She sat back up and turned the light on low and picked up her magazine and then she heard him. Quietly—she had to strain to hear, she heard Edmund's bedroom door click open and his bare feet pad down the hallway. She heard the back door open and the nails on the dogs' feet click across the tile floor in the kitchen. She heard his bedroom door close. She studied her magazine for a few more minutes and then put it back on the nightstand and turned off the light.

Chapter Four

"I JUST THINK WE'RE getting overextended, is all." Céline balanced a cup of coffee in her lap. She shivered a little inside her down sweater and wrapped her hands around the cup, enjoying the spot of warmth. It was chilly in the kitchen, a September morning, a hint of the first breath of autumn and the harvest that would follow. Gaston had been stealing time from the construction business to walk the orchard, checking the apple crop and making calls to the pickers who would, in six weeks of frenetic activity, harvest the crop. Céline, with her computer skills and marketing background, was in charge of sales and distribution. She enjoyed the hiatus from her part-time job in town.

Gaston raised his cup to his lips and then put it back down. Even on this cool morning he'd rolled the sleeves of his work shirt to his elbows.

"I don't see it like that," he said. "Right now, real estate is just exploding. It's not gonna go on like this forever. We should get in while we can." He paused with his cup halfway up as tendrils of steam rose and he looked at her as though through smoke.

"But that's exactly what I mean," she said. "Sooner or later it has to crash. It *has* to. I mean, look at history. Nothing goes up forever and ever. I'm just afraid we'll have all these houses and then get stuck with the payments. Then what?"

"Okay, I'll give you that," Gaston said. "I'm not saying it couldn't happen." He tapped his finger on the tabletop, accentuating his points. "But look at the numbers. We're almost making enough on the harvest alone to service the debt, forget about the construction business. With what money's costing, it's cheaper to buy a house as an investment than for me to buy the land and spec one out. We got people lined up to rent the three rentals we already have. That's fourteen hundred dollars apiece every month. We can ride out a pretty significant downturn in the market with that kind of return. We got the business, we got the orchard. And for the last ten years we've had the real estate. I don't know about you, but that sounds pretty diversified to me. Edmund's not going to have to worry about where his next meal is coming from anytime soon."

Céline blew over her cup to cool it and took a tiny sip. The dogs, as they had done every morning since his return to school, had followed Edmund to the end of the driveway, but when the school bus picked him up they trotted back to the yard and spent the day sleeping in the sun and hunting mice. Cloud had flopped into a patch of sunlight and lay dozing, periodically slapping his tail in the dust, moved by his dreams. The cold didn't seem to bother either of them. Céline watched as Breeze paused, bunched her legs together and pounced on a tuft of grass. Even from the kitchen window, the intensity in her brown eyes was startling.

She had known, going into this, how Gaston would react. And in equal measure she had known she wouldn't be able to argue with his logic. Almost no one thought the real estate boom would last forever—no one other than the shills on the radio hawking gold bullion and no-down-payment house mortgages—but Gaston had covered the bases. That was the problem: He always covered the bases.

In Gaston there was not a breath of self-doubt. He analyzed every situation, studied the pros and cons, worked out the numbers on a scrap of paper and then made his decision and ran with it. No second thoughts, no second guessing. So far, he'd been right every time. She had to admit it had been wonderful. She'd never imagined that an orchard and a construction business could rake in so much money. Even from the standpoint of her staunchly Republican parents, they were doing all right.

So why her unease? Why this prevailing sense that they were going too far, too fast? The irrefutable logic of all this (not to mention Gaston waving the numbers under her nose and jabbing them with his index finger) did little to comfort her; instead, it left her with the sense that things were moving in a direction beyond her control and, more unsettling still, beyond her understanding.

Gaston rolled his eyes and gazed over her shoulder in the direction of the living room, his jaw set, not seeing her. "I knew this would happen. You're always like this. Every time."

Céline set her cup on the table, not gently, her nostrils flaring. She *did* always say this. That was beside the point.

"One of us has to ask questions like this," she said. "You never do, Gaston. Never. You never think anything will go wrong. I told you that story Dad told me about investing in that, what, that golf thing? I told you that? I know I did. You remember what happened: He lost his shirt. He always regretted doing that. He said it set him back five years. I don't want to do that. I don't want *us* to do that."

Gaston snorted. "Look, Céline, I always liked your dad. He was cool. I'm not saying that because, you know, he's passed on. But he was a manufacturing rep. He got a nice, fat company pension. He got a salary *and* a pension. I don't have any of that. *We* don't have any of that. We don't take a calculated risk once in a while, we'll be right where we are now in ten years. Okay, that's not bad, I'll give you that, but it could be a lot better, too. Another twenty years we'll both be retired, maybe. I know guys, sixty-five, seventy, they're still out there with their bags on pounding nails because they can't afford not to. I don't want to be like that. Do you?"

"No, of course not." Céline paused, collecting her thoughts. She didn't want to have to work forever. Who wanted to work forever? She hadn't thought much about retirement, that was still a hazy objective on a still more obscure horizon. She'd always had the vague assumption that she and Gaston would spend their golden years traveling, lying in the sun on a beach somewhere warm. That's what her mother was doing. She flew to Hawaii every January.

But ... why couldn't she put her finger on it? She knew he was right. Why, just once, couldn't she accept Gaston's clarity of purpose? Shelve her doubts and without reservation embrace his game plan for the good of the family and their future? What was wrong with her? What was she supposed to say?

"You're not listening to me," she said. It was exactly the wrong thing to say. The words fell from her tongue and left a bitter taste in her mouth.

Gaston slammed his fist into the table. "Oh, bullshit, Céline!" Coffee splashed out of his cup and splattered in an arc across the table. "Every time I try to do what's right for this family, for Edmund and you, I got to fight you for it tooth and nail. You didn't want to buy a single rental property, and now look at them. Look at them, Céline! Have we lost any money yet? A single penny? That first rental we bought is already half paid off. We could pay it off completely if we had to. We could. It's like you think I make this stuff up or something. It's like you think this is some kind of stupid game for me. I'm doing this for *us*."

Céline hid her face in her hands, then put her hands in her lap. How did this always happen?

"I *know*, Gaston," she said. "You *know* how much I appreciate what you do for us." Céline's eyes were burning, and she pinched her lips together to keep from crying. She took a deep breath and began again. "I know you're right. But can we just take a little time to think about this? Just give me a little while, okay? Just a little while."

Gaston pushed himself out of his chair and walked out of the room. After a few tense minutes he walked back into the kitchen and ripped a section of paper towel from its spool on the counter, then slapped it on the table to wipe up the coffee he'd spilled.

"Thank you," Céline said.

Gaston nodded and threw the paper towel in the garbage can under the sink. Then he took the rifle from above the back door and walked into the orchard. Cloud raised his head from his slumber, thumped his tail in anticipation and scampered to his side, bouncing along ahead, growling at imaginary threats and feinting at shadows, checking back to see if Gaston would notice his valor.

* * *

They went to LeMond's for Sunday brunch. A half century prior, LeMond's had been a commercial fishing shack fronting the bay, and the cedar-sided walls adorned with framed photos of wooden boats overflowing with silvery lake trout and whitefish gave it the rustic, north-woods feel that Céline knew her husband loved. Edmund's motivations, on the other hand, were far simpler: He loved LeMond's hand-churned ice cream, the best in Port Landing.

Once upon a time they had reserved Sunday mornings for mass. But Céline's insistence on maintaining some semblance of the Christian ritual she'd been raised with had been met with overwhelming indifference by her husband and son, and so it happened that on Edmund's eleventh birthday, a Sunday, they went to LeMond's. From that day on, church was no longer an option. At least it's family time, Céline thought.

But even family time had been getting harder to come by. Gaston's workload now consumed nearly six days of every week, and in the rare moments of downtime still extant, one of their four rental properties invariably needed upkeep. Gaston believed in preventative maintenance, but even so, there was always something that wasn't closing, wasn't opening, wasn't turning on or wasn't turning off. He used his self-imposed "vacation" time for the apple harvest.

Edmund was perusing the menu, which Céline knew was entirely for show: He would order what he always ordered—chicken marsala with home fries and strawberry ice cream for dessert. Gaston had been able to maneuver their truck into a parking spot directly in front of the restaurant, no easy feat during the height of the fall-colors tourist season in Port Landing, and both dogs were leaning out of the truck bed, begging to be petted by anyone who walked by within arm's reach.

Since Edmund insisted on being accompanied by his dogs everywhere they went, Gaston had leveraged a deal with his son: At least in
the truck, they had to ride in the back. But it was potentially dangerous for them back there. What if they saw a squirrel and jumped out
while the truck was moving? So Céline circumvented Gaston's rules
whenever she and Edmund ran errands in her Subaru. She'd long ago
grown accustomed to the dog hair on the upholstery.

"What do you suppose Edmund will order?" Céline asked, arch-
ing her eyebrows and peering at Gaston over her menu.

"Hmmm. Maybe steak? He's looking a bit puny these days. A big,
thick steak would put some meat on his bones. He's the puniest shortstop I've ever seen."

Céline nodded, frowning. "I was thinking vegetables. Lots and
lots of vegetables. A whole plate full of wonderful vegetables. Broccoli!
Brussels sprouts!"

Edmund made gagging sounds and stuck his finger in his throat.
Céline looked at him. "That's enough," she said. She put her hand on
his arm.

Then Edmund was quiet. He looked furtively toward their truck.
Céline followed his gaze and saw Tony Trumbo and his parents walk by.

"Hey," she said. "There's Tony. Why don't you invite him in?"

"I don't want to," Edmund said. Céline was struck, again, by
Edmund's similarity to his father, even in his childish petulance.
Gaston didn't pout, of course, but there was something about his look
when he was angry, about the lines around his mouth, that were the
same. She wondered sometimes just how much of her genetics had
contributed to the making of this boy who resembled his father in almost every gesture, in almost every mood. Who resembled his father
in this moment.

"But why? He's your friend. Maybe he'd like some ice cream after
dinner."

"I'm not friends with Tony anymore," Edmund said. He blinked
his eyes several times.

"Why, Edmund? Did you have an argument?"

"He pushed me down," Edmund said.

Gaston leaned into the table.

"He pushed you?" Céline said. "Why did he push you? Did you have an argument?"

"He's just mean," Edmund said. "He called me an Indian and then he pushed me down. He made me mad."

Céline sought her husband's eyes, but Gaston's gaze was riveted on his son.

"You've got Ojibway in you, Edmund. That's nothing to be ashamed about. So does your father."

"What did you do?" Gaston's voice was abrupt, hard. *"What did you do?"* His ponytail had come loose and several strands brushed the top of his shoulders.

Edmund frowned.

"What did you do after he pushed you? Tell me what you did."

"I kicked him, but I sort of missed. He made me mad. He laughed at me and that made me madder. But then he left. We were playing catch."

Gaston leaned back in his seat.

"Edmund, fighting doesn't solve anything. Tony wasn't being nice, but the next time that happens ..."

"The next time that happens, punch him," Gaston said. "Punch him right in the nose. That's the only way to shut up bullies."

"Of course he shouldn't punch him, Gaston. What would that solve?"

"It would solve the problem of Tony pushing Edmund, that's what. You've never been punched in the nose, Céline. I have. It works."

"Don't you think they should talk it out and try to keep their friendship? I mean, isn't that important too?"

"It's important." Gaston tucked a loose strand of hair over his ear. The restaurant was filling up—the fall tourist season was a zoo—and Céline hoped fervently that they wouldn't have to have a heated discussion about the ethics of fighting in a restaurant full of people they didn't know.

"But so is standing up for yourself," Gaston said. "I grew up with this … I grew up with this same *crap* from the rednecks around here. It was worse back then. I got called Indian plenty. They made fun of Maman, and Papa being in the bars all the time, so they thought they could get away with it." He pinged his water glass with his fingernail. "But they only tried that once."

Céline shook her head. "Gaston, I just don't agree. I don't. That's not how grown-ups behave." Her father had never been in a fight in his life. And her parents had certainly never gone to bars, not that going to a bar was such a horrible thing. But still.

"He's not a grown-up, Céline! He's eleven! He's got to learn this stuff. Sooner or later, boys are gonna fight. They just do. He might as well come out on top."

Céline violently shook her head. This was wrong, wrong.

Edmund watched them both, wide-eyed. Gaston studied Céline for a moment and then took his son by the arm.

"You did the right thing, Edmund. I'm proud of you. We can talk more about this later. Your mom and I are gonna disagree on this"—he cast a sideways glance at Céline—"but Vaillancourts are never afraid to defend themselves. The thing to do now is to wait a few days and let things cool down some. Then maybe talk with your friend Tony. His dad's a pretty good hand and I'll bet Tony is, too. I'll bet your mom will at least agree with me on that."

Céline picked up her menu. The heat had begun to dissipate and she forced a smile.

"Right?" Gaston said. He grinned at her.

"Yes," she said. "Of course."

* * *

The dogs were gone.

She couldn't believe it. People churned up and down the sidewalks all around them, many with binoculars slung around their necks, smiling and chatting. Two crises in one day, in one afternoon. How bad could their luck get?

Edmund, who had been so stoic during their discussion about fighting (she still didn't agree with Gaston, she would never agree with him on that, but at least they had arrived at a sort of mutual détente), had begun to sob. He clutched her side and when she bent to hug him he threw himself into her arms, still very much a small boy. Gaston awkwardly squeezed his son's shoulder.

"They can't be far, honey," she said. "They were here just a minute ago." She fervently hoped she was right.

Gaston stared above their heads toward their farm, as if he could see it behind the impenetrable curtain of trees on the hills beyond where they stood, as if that was where he would prefer to be, rather than dealing with two lost dogs who weren't really lost at all and would turn up on their own sooner or later. From one end of Port Landing to another, across the breadth of the wooded hills rising above Lake Superior, the forest blazed in a mosaic of orange, red and yellow.

"They've got collars, right? I mean with ID tags and all that stuff."

"Of course, Gaston," Céline said. "We put them on when they were puppies. A red collar for Breeze and a black collar for Cloud, to match their fur."

"Okay," he said, nodding. "So then let's do this. We're gonna do this scientifically. First, we'll walk to the docks. That's probably where they went because there's other dogs and people down there. Lots of stuff like dead fish that dogs like. Then if that doesn't work, which it probably will, but if it doesn't, we'll go to the park. Maybe they remember being there on the Fourth of July. Sound like a plan?"

Edmund nodded and wiped his eyes. Céline put his small, brave hand in hers and they marched off toward the docks.

"Are they going to be okay?" Edmund asked.

"Of course they are." Céline tousled her son's hair with a confidence she didn't feel. "They just got turned around, is all. Why would they run away? I'll bet they both miss you to death."

Edmund sniffed and wiped his nose with his sleeve. "But what if they got lost? What if they don't know how to get home?"

"Those hikes you take in the orchard every day." Gaston stopped and bent over, his hands braced on his knees, facing his son. "They never get lost there, do they? Sometimes they disappear for a while and then they come back, right? Maybe they run off after a deer or something, but then they come back, right?"

Edmund's eyes were still red but his tears had begun to dry. He clutched Céline's hand.

"I remember once Breeze ran off after a deer and I called and called, but she didn't come back," he said. "And then she did, like, an hour later. It was a long time."

"But she came back, right?" Gaston said, studying his son.

"Yeah."

"Well, this is like that. She and Cloud just got sidetracked by something. It wasn't a deer, but maybe it was, who knows, a cat. Or a dog. Could have been anything. They'll come looking for us when they get bored."

Edmund gazed from his father to his mother and let his hand drop from Céline's and began to smile. "She's going to be in the dog-house when we find her!" he said. "Hey, that's a pretty good joke!"

There were people everywhere. Gaston never tired of reminding his wife that Port Landing had once been a sleepy fishing town. Céline had done some research at the town's tiny historical society and discovered that this wasn't altogether true. Tourists had long found Port Landing attractive, with its quaint dockside business district and the cobalt-blue waters of Lake Superior that stretched a hundred and sixty miles to Canada, although in the early years it was indeed the fishing trade and the limestone quarries on the Apostle Islands that established the town's financial underpinnings. But there was no doubt that the tourist trade had grown exponentially since Gaston was in high school in the late seventies.

Like everyone else in Port Landing, Céline resented the tourists' presence, but, also like everyone else in town, the Vaillancourts depended upon tourism in large part for their livelihood. Gaston built outrageously opulent second homes for tourists from downstate and sold bushels of apples to visitors who flocked to town during the height of the apple season, when open-air concerts and festivals were occurring nearly every day.

Somewhere among these milling throngs of tourists were two Border collies, probably having the time of their lives. She wondered if Breeze would even notice they were gone. Cloud, who was timid around nearly everyone, would hang back, waiting for Breeze to make the first move before sidling in and shyly allowing himself to be patted on the head. But Breeze would be all over anyone she saw, especially boys. Boys of Edmund's age seemed to draw the little red dog like an unerring beacon.

Breeze wasn't anything like the image Céline had had in her mind's eye about what a girl dog was supposed to be like. She played rough. Céline had watched Edmund and Breeze wrestle in the front yard, a no-holds-barred, tumbling free-for-all that sometimes made her gasp. But no matter how many times Edmund threw her to the ground, she came back, growling in mock ferociousness, ready for another life-and-death battle. It took no time at all for her to see that Edmund loved these matches. Only later did it occur to her that Breeze did, too.

Gaston stopped and peered ahead and put his hand up to shade his eyes.

"Come over here, son," he said. "Who does that look like over there?"

Céline and Edmund spotted a black dog a hundred yards ahead, its nose to the ground. Gaston clapped his hands and the dog's head shot up.

"Cloud!" Edmund squealed.

Cloud's entire body wriggled with delight. Edmund sprinted toward his dog, who bounded over to him and launched himself into Edmund's arms.

"Where have you been? We've been worried. You've been a bad dog!" Cloud licked Edmund's face, then buried his head under his arm, his tail swishing wildly. "Where's your sister, big guy? Where's Breeze?"

All three of them heard her bark. Just beyond, from under a dock, Céline saw a white muzzle emerge, then the white cravat and red fur of the lost Breeze. She scampered into the sunlight, barked at them once, then disappeared back under the dock and returned with a stick in her mouth. She raced to Edmund and dropped it at his feet. She stared at the stick, then stared at Edmund.

"Jeez," Edmund said. "Couldn't you act like you were happy to see me or something?" He tossed the stick and Breeze caught it on the first bounce and pranced proudly back and forth, clutching the stick like a trophy or a rare prize, her head high, her red fur gleaming.

Céline handed Edmund their leashes. "Put these on, okay? Let's not go through that again."

The dogs rode in the cab during the short drive home. Gaston started to object but Céline wouldn't hear of it. Edmund was asleep in the back seat, exhausted from his worries, the dogs curled up beside him. When they pulled into the drive, the dogs stood and pressed their noses against the window and Edmund stirred but did not awaken.

"I'll put him down," Gaston said. "He's had a long day."

He shook Edmund's shoulder and opened the door and the dogs tumbled outside, happy to be home, happy to be loved, happy to be.

It was almost dark, and rather than take another chance, Céline decided to walk the dogs to the barn. They bounded in front of her, waiting impatiently while she slid the door open and switched on the lights. In the corner, in front of the stalls for Sir Lancelot and Dutch, was the straw bale bed Gaston had stacked together when the dogs were still puppies. Cloud trotted to the bed, turned twice and lay down. Céline saw something peeking out from beneath him and discovered the towel Edmund had used to dry off the dogs on that rainy day the previous summer. She'd forgotten all about it. She tugged it out from under Cloud and held it at arm's length. It was filthy and covered with hair, and she reflexively gave it a shake, snapping it sharply. Behind her, one of the horses snorted in alarm.

"It's okay," she said. "It's just a towel." She folded the towel in quarters and set it behind her, then opened the door to Sir Lancelot's stall. He stood at the far end, his tail swishing nervously. Céline felt her heart go out to him. Such a scaredy cat! Scared of a little towel! She patted the side of the doorway and he saw it was her and pricked his ears happily and walked to her. He nuzzled her hand, neighing softly under his breath. She was seized with the urge to take him in her arms, to tell him what a good boy he was. She threw her arms around his neck and hugged him.

"Do you want a treat?" she said. "I may have something for you." She closed the stable door and found the half-empty bushel of the previous year's apples she'd stored in the tack room. She grabbed two, one for Sir Lancelot and one for Dutch. Each harvest, she hand-picked apples from the orchard as a treat for her horses, selecting the best she could find from each of the varieties they grew. It was silly, of course. She never mentioned it to Gaston. But she told Edmund, and to her immense pleasure, he enjoyed helping her. She gave the first apple to Sir Lancelot and the second to Dutch. Then she felt one of the dogs brush her legs and she turned around.

Breeze stood before her. "C'mon girl, it's time to go to bed," Céline said. Cloud had already begun snoring, a gentle, raspy rumble that matched the rise and fall of his chest. "What's wrong? Aren't you sleepy? I'll bet you'd rather be sleeping in the house, wouldn't you? Bet you didn't think I knew about that, did you? Well listen, kiddo. Houses are for people; barns are for dogs. Tonight you're sleeping out here. Your brother has the right idea." Breeze looked at Cloud and then back at Céline. "Okay, I guess you're not tired, but I am."

Céline rose and walked to the door. As she reached for the light, she felt Breeze's muzzle press against the back of her leg. She turned in surprise and found the little dog looking up, her eyes locked on hers, swishing its tail. Hesitantly, she knelt to stroke her face, and Breeze closed her eyes and pushed her head under Céline's arm. She stayed there until Céline rose and opened the door, then turned and joined Cloud in their bed.

Chapter Five

"Hmmm." Gaston had spread the paper out before him on the kitchen table. Buried at the bottom of the second page was a story about rising house foreclosures. Céline tossed her dish towel on the counter and peered over his shoulder, frowning.

"Where is this they're talking about? Does it say where?"

"Haven't read it all the way through yet, but it's everywhere. Apparently, someone just noticed. Or the bean counters in the government just put the numbers together. Or something. You can't believe anything you read in the paper."

Céline returned to the kitchen and began unloading the dishwasher. A newly minted chip on one of her stoneware dinner plates irritated her. She ran her finger over the gap in the plate and then squinted with faint hope at the bottom of the dishwasher, but the chip was gone, flushed into the plumbing with the detritus from their previous night's supper. The plates were still hot to the touch, so she left the door open to let the steam escape.

"Will that affect us? Here in Port Landing? I mean, we've got four rentals now."

"Pretty unlikely," Gaston said. "That's the whole point, right? We've got four rentals and they all got one-year leases. Even if one of them skips town, we got their deposit. Last time we had a vacancy the phone rang off the hook. Remember? That was what, six months ago? The economy just doesn't turn around that quick, Céline. In a town this small, real estate is always gonna be at a premium. I've been here my whole life and never seen it where rentals were standing vacant. There just aren't that many houses available."

"Okay. But it happened in Minneapolis. Back in the eighties. Mom told me about it. They said the value of their house dropped by a third."

Gaston peered down his nose, and Céline felt her temperature ratchet up. His occasional condescension bothered her, and she knew that he knew. It was like he was trying to figure out how to talk to a child, someone who didn't know anything. But it was she who had graduated from college (*summa cum laude*), and Gaston who, after three years of a largely indifferent academic career, had dropped out.

"That's Minneapolis," he said. "Not Port Landing. Not Washburn, either. Not even Door County. Tourist towns have different economies. I read that Sun Valley—that ski area in Idaho?—has never had a major downturn. It'll slow down some, sure, but even during the Depression it kept growing. Port Landing isn't Sun Valley, but it's *like* Sun Valley. It's a big tourist area like that. I mean, look at all the people downtown. You even said something about that when we had dinner last week. About all the tourists."

He folded the paper, put it aside, and looked at her. Then he nodded curtly, as if it were settled, as if it were settled for *him*. He rose to his feet, grinned at her across the table, and walked out the back door. A moment later she heard him in the driveway, unloading tools from his truck.

Céline pulled a hot spoon from the dishwasher and angrily hurled it into the sink. She remembered, and it was mostly true. She *had* said something about the tourists. They'd taken Edmund to LeMond's on the spur of the moment, not the normal Sunday morning brunch. It was a cool, autumn evening at the height of the foliage season, and there were people everywhere, streaming in and out of every shop along the docks in their plaid shirts and hiking boots and baseball caps. They'd been lucky to get a table at all. The bartender was wearing a stone-washed T-shirt that read: *I (heart) the Apostle Islands.*

Gaston had always overseen their basket of business interests. He'd researched the market—he was nothing if not thorough—and made the decision to buy rental properties ten years before. Each month, she took the accumulated rent and invested it in their SEP IRA. It was not an insubstantial amount of money. They grossed almost six thousand dollars a month between the four houses they owned. Even after servicing the debt, there was a tidy sum. The reservations she'd had about buying the last rental had long since proven groundless.

But bad news about the economy at large, precisely because it was so large, so amorphous, and so removed from their cloistered life in Port Landing, unsettled her, in the same way the distant rumble of thunder on a sunny day heralded the faint but ominous warning of bad weather to come. No one could predict the economy; not Gaston, not their new president, not even Jorgenson at the bank, who managed their investments and had, for a number of years now, extended Gaston one construction loan after another on little more than a signature. But she would adamantly give her husband credit where credit was due. Her girlfriends told horror stories of their husbands' forays into pie-in-the-sky business ventures, but Gaston did his homework and got the numbers right and paid his bills, and their rentals appreciated in value every year.

Céline walked onto the back porch and strode for the corral, whistling to her horses as she approached. Sir Lancelot and Dutch whinnied and stomped their hooves when they saw her coming. She retrieved their curry brushes from the tack room and set to work.

Neither horse needed to be tied; they loved the rough feel of the brush. Céline set to work on Dutch, then had to forcefully slap Sir Lancelot on his rear when he tried to shoulder his sister aside. Céline felt Dutch relax under the curry brush, saw the lazy, sleepy pleasure in the mare's eyes, felt lathered sweat moisten her hands and inhaled the damp warm sweet scent of it. For the hundredth time, she found herself longing for that which she knew would never be: a life of simple pleasures, a life as uncomplex as the brushing of her horses.

Céline knew she was a worrier. But Gaston, who seemed eternally sanguine in the face of any and all potential problems, seemed to her almost unrealistic, as if the very fact of denying that a problem even existed would forestall its happening. Shouldn't they be doing something? She didn't know what that might be, but shouldn't they at least discuss it? Have a backup plan just in case? She gazed across Dutch's broad back toward the house. Edmund had put on his red daypack and called the dogs, waved perfunctorily at her as they scampered past, then disappeared into the orchard in the perennial half-light under the trees. She heard the front door close behind Gaston and when she turned back to Dutch she was alone.

* * *

Edmund clambered into the truck and tossed his glove on the floor boards. They'd gone to the city park to work on his fielding, and the rapid-fire drill of scooping up grounders and whipping them back to his father had left him tired but happy.

Gaston, as always, had plenty of parting advice. He wanted his son to think about what he was telling him before their next practice session.

"Remember," he said. "You don't have to drop down on one knee like you sometimes do. I know the other kids do that. I watch them do it all the time. But what you want to do is crouch, right? Like I showed you. You got to be ready to move. Bend your knees and get down behind the ball. If it gets through your glove, you'll block it with your body. Nobody catches them all. You watch the pros, even they miss short hops sometimes. But the ball doesn't go anywhere because they're behind it. Hell, Edmund, even I used to miss short hops. Everybody does. The point is to make the play."

Gaston never swore around Edmund when Céline was within earshot; the instant grief wasn't worth whatever lame explanation he was able to manufacture. But swearing around your son—within reason—really wasn't such a bad thing. Edmund, he knew, enjoyed the initiation into the rites of manhood. He'd explained to his son that he couldn't talk like that with just anyone, that swearing in the broader public arena was bad form for an eleven-year-old, but he'd cut him some slack when it was just the two of them.

Edmund's eyes had grown wide, and over the course of the next few weeks Gaston listened to his son try on "hell" and "damn" for size, the only words Gaston would allow. The kid mixed up his modifying expletives so often it was hilarious, and it was all Gaston could do to keep a straight face. One of these days, he'd put it all on Céline's video cam. Someday, when Edmund was a young man, they'd watch it over a beer and laugh their asses off.

"Next time we practice? You can hit it harder, okay?" Edmund said. He nodded somberly, wanting to get the thinking part right, wanting to impress his father. Baseball was a serious business and fielding short hops took all his concentration and skill. "I think I'm ready for it, Dad. Hell, I'm pretty sure I am. I was doing good today, right? I hardly missed a single hit. That one time I kind of bobbled it, but that was the only time. We got to keep making it tougher so I get better. That's what you said yourself. You have to keep pushing yourself."

Gaston tried to swallow his grin. He had always loved baseball. He could never remember a time in his life when he hadn't been in love with the sport. He saw in Edmund all the passion for the game he'd had himself at the same age. And now, studying the boy beside him, he saw in his son, as if through a newly cleaned and polished window, the Vaillancourt blood that his wife had been gently insisting had been his since birth. The compact, muscular build. The dark skin and hair. The strength. He was surprised at how strong Edmund had become when they wrestled in the front yard. His own father, and his father's father, had been very much like this boy.

But Céline was in the genetic mix too, and it was that part of Edmund that locker-room tutorials on fielding short hops would never reach. There was a soft side to Edmund that Gaston did not understand, that Vaillancourts did not possess. If, in fact, he could not see its physical manifestation, he could surely sense Céline's Nordic blondness in his son's black hair; his quiet inner reflections when he was lost in his reveries.

Edmund loved to fiddle with his mother's pottery wheel and draw pictures with colored pencils and spend hours playing with his beloved dogs. He loved to sit beside his mother and watch the late sun filter through the trees of the orchard. Edmund's feelings lived just below his skin, waiting for release at slight provocations. The intensity of his son's painful outbursts left Gaston feeling flustered and inadequate, unsure of what to say or do, so he reacted as he'd been raised, with control and discipline. But those same outbursts seemed, in a way that Gaston often felt undercut his authority, to draw Edmund and his mother closer together.

Instead of turning up the road to their farm, Gaston steered the Silverado through town. With Port Landing behind them, the road to Washburn re-emerged, revealing the vast cold blue of Lake Superior to the east, its surface stippled by the breeze. He kicked the truck up to sixty and then almost as quickly decelerated, pulling into a gravel driveway that led to a small lakeshore home with peeling yellow paint and a slat-fenced garden and a pair of abandoned wooden rowboats a few yards above the waterline. A rust-pocked pickup was parked in the front yard. No garage. Edmund searched his father's face.

"Radcliff's house," Gaston said. "Haven't you been here before? I figured you'd recognize it."

Edmund shook his head. "Nope. But I know who he is. He's really tall, right? I see him at practice sometimes. Mom says he's your friend."

"He is. Still is, I guess. Since high school. He kind of went his own way the last twenty years. But he's a pretty good guy. His son's got bad asthma. He's a hard worker, fishing, mostly. We got some business to talk about."

"What kind of business?"

"Business, business. Grown-up stuff. Kind of boring, Edmund. You'll probably want to stay in the truck. You can play on that computer thing you got for your birthday."

"I don't want to stay in the truck, Dad. I could be here, like, hours and hours. Like that time you went into Happy Jacks. I was in the truck for days."

Gaston sighed and gazed out the driver's side window. Radcliff's place would be presentable if he took better care of it. A coat of paint sure wouldn't hurt, but the guy spent every waking moment crewing on fishing boats, so when would he find the time? And why put the money into a rental anyway? You don't own the place you live in, there's zero incentive to take care of it. That was about the first thing he learned when he began buying rental properties. Tenants weren't going to do any more maintenance than they absolutely had to.

Gaston turned toward his son. "Okay, Edmund, listen real careful. You can come in with me. But you got to promise me one thing, okay? Mom doesn't know anything about this. Far as she's concerned, you and I were never here. Got that?"

Edmund frowned. "Okay, sure. But why?"

"You just gotta promise. I mean it."

"We're not gonna do something bad?"

Gaston snorted. "Hell no! We're doing something good. But women ... Someday you'll understand this better than you do now, trust me. Your mom ..."

Gaston couldn't find the words. How could he tell his son that Radcliff, after having worked on someone else's boat since high school, had finally decided to go into business for himself and buy his own fishing boat? That three banks, including Jorgenson's, had turned his request for a loan down flat, and that he'd finally asked Gaston for a personal loan secured by the boat itself. How did he explain to Edmund that his mother's completely irrational fear of financial risk would make her unalterably opposed to what he was about to do? That he'd known Radcliff since high school and knew he could be trusted? And that if everything went to shit and fell apart, they could easily take the hit? That he knew as well as anyone that thirty-five thousand wasn't chump change, but it wasn't gonna kill them, either?

Gaston tried to explain it in a way Edmund would understand. "So, Radcliff, he's my friend—like your friend Tony—and he needs a little help, and we're here to talk about that. About giving him some help. Like you would do with Tony. Helping your friends is good, right? It's the right thing to do. Guys help me, sometimes, even."

"Like for what?"

"You mean, when have guys helped me?" Gaston flicked off the key and wrapped his hand around the door handle, thinking. He'd accepted help, when it was offered, plenty of times. Before he'd got the orchard operational, his friends had helped with the harvest. But he hadn't asked for it. He'd never asked for help from anyone. He swung open the door and stepped outside.

"C'mon. If you're gonna come, then let's go. You just remember what I said."

Edmund shuffled through a soggy carpet of last fall's unraked leaves and followed his father up the concrete steps to Radcliff's front door and before Gaston knocked Edmund caught his eye and ran his thumb and forefinger across his lips as if closing a zipper. They heard Radcliff's heavy footsteps approach across a wooden floor and stop just behind the door and then he was smiling timidly down at them, uncertainly, as if unsure of whether or not they would welcome him into his own home.

* * *

Céline watched it unfold, and had seen her part in it, as if on a slow-motion replay. Edmund's return from the orchard. The dogs bounding ahead of him. The killing of the rabbit. No matter how many times Gaston tried to explain to her the facts of the matter, that all wild animals died violent deaths and there was no use crying about it, the death of any animal upset her, and the rabbit's blood was on her hands.

She had no idea where her son was once he ventured beyond the bounds of the orchard and into the forest. The orchard was bisected with a two-track Jeep trail for the picking crews, and the trail was a comfort to Céline, a lifeline, a long string that wound in a crooked pathway under the trees, but if carefully reeled back in would always lead her home. But the forest was vast and trackless, miles of dark woods so astoundingly fertile that the leaves of one tree were interwoven with the leaves of the next and that one with the next beyond counting, all but obscuring the sun.

That was where her son had been. She watched his return from the back porch, her gardening gloves folded beside her, a cup of hot tea on her lap, while he marched out of the orchard like a small gladiator, a sapling carved into a spear resting casually over one shoulder (didn't he carry himself like his father!), both dogs nosing around the blackberry canes that grew long and untended on the borders of their farm.

She had a vague sense that rabbits lived in the canes. Occasionally one would dart from under the hooves of Sir Lancelot, startling both her and the horse, who would snort and toss his head in alarm, but who was too concerned for her safety to bolt. They were like will-o'-the-wisps, in one place today and gone from that place the next. Now a rabbit appeared directly between her and Edmund.

The dogs found it in short order. Breeze suddenly began casting about in hyperactive circles, snuffling with excitement, her nose plowing furrows in the tall green grass, followed closely by Cloud. Then Breeze paused, pounced, and the rabbit squirted out from under her nose and bolted for the safety of the canes on the edge of the orchard. Céline saw Edmund instinctively turn and spin, the spear in his hand, tracking the path of the rabbit for just an instant, before he loosed it and the shaft flashed across the yard in a hard, flat arc and pierced the hapless creature through its belly.

It was, even for a baseball player with Edmund's precocious arm, a miraculous throw, and for an instant Edmund seemed taken aback, his jaw open in surprise. Then Breeze was on the rabbit, and the rabbit, caught between the jaws of the dog and the shaft piercing its side, began to scream.

Céline stood, sickened by what she'd witnessed, and in the next moment Edmund began to cry, a deep, panicked bawling, and when he spied her watching him he called out to her in panic.

"Mom! Mom! I didn't mean to! Stop them, please stop them!"

Céline bolted from the back porch and raced to her son, who was clutching Breeze's collar and was trying with all his strength to loosen her grip on the wailing rabbit, which had splattered its life and blood all over the dog's white cravat and nose. But the more Edmund tugged, the more Breeze locked her teeth in the animal's side and the louder it screamed. Céline grabbed the dog's collar with both hands and gave it a powerful yank and broke the dog's grip. She dragged her several feet away and forced her to the ground in submission, and Breeze lay on her side and stared up at her in chastened confusion. When she returned to her son Edmund was kneeling, cradling the bloody rabbit to his chest and writhing in misery. The rabbit's screams had been reduced to small, gurgling burbles.

"Can't you do something, Mom? We have to save it!"

"We can't, Edmund. It's dying. There's nothing we can do." Edmund was so miserable, and so sick at what he had done, that she couldn't bear the thought of berating her son for his actions. "We have to put it out of its misery, Edmund. You don't want it to suffer any more, do you?"

Edmund wiped his nose with the back of his arm. "No," he said in a quavering voice.

"Go get me the spade. It's on the porch. Go get it. Go."

Edmund lay the rabbit gently on the ground and went to the porch and got the spade. Céline put the spade against the rabbit's neck and stepped on the spade. The rabbit made several weak kicks then stopped. Céline felt sick to her stomach and looked away.

Breeze approached and timidly pressed her nose against the back of Edmund's leg. Edmund's face changed from grief to rage and he lashed out and punched her as hard as he could in the side of the head. Breeze howled and bolted for the barn, peering at him from behind a corral post. Cloud cowered behind her, his tail between his legs in terror.

"I hate you!" Edmund screamed. "I hate you!"

"Stop that, Edmund! Just stop it! You don't mean that."

"I do too! I hate her! She's not my dog anymore!"

Céline grasped her son's shoulders. Edmund tried to squirm away, tears of rage streaming down his face. She spun him around, forcing him to meet her eyes. "She *is* your dog, Edmund," she said. "She always has been."

Chapter 6

CÉLINE FOUND THE manuscript shortly after Edmund was born, in a shoebox in the attic labeled in crude block lettering with a black Magic Marker: *Gaston Vaillancourt*. Inside, among grade school report cards, stick figures drawn in crayon and letters to his maman, Gaston, in labored cursive, had written, *How the Ojibway Got Dogs*.

The story was nuanced and filled with symbolism, and Céline realized at once that the words and the writing had to have come from his mother. Céline had hardly known the woman before her death at a young age, and the liveliness of the prose surprised her, as she considered herself a good writer and recognized the talent in others.

When she'd shown the manuscript to Gaston, he'd dismissed it out of hand.

"I'm not saying now," she told him, "I'm saying *sometime*. When he's older. It's part of his heritage. I think any boy would like to hear one of his father's stories and I'd like to read it to him."

Gaston was thirty at the time. His T-shirt gathered in thin creases around his muscled waist and the frayed collar was yellowed with sweat and grime. He snorted, then dropped his empty beer can in the garbage.

"What heritage, Céline? Papa was a drunk. Maman had to drag him home from the bar every other week. I don't want to remind the kid he came from all that. It sure as hell didn't do me any good."

"But there's nothing wrong with the *story*. It's a *good* story. I like it a lot. I mean ... I just like it. Maybe Edmund will too, someday."

Gaston slid into a chair at the kitchen table, his elbows propped on the table, his palms steepled in front of his face as if summoning prayer, as if in reflection, as if he were giving weight to what she had said. His gaze rose to her face, then to the ceiling. Then he shook his head and said, didn't they need to be thinking about hiring the picking crews pretty soon?

Céline put the manuscript back in the box and put the box back in the attic and forgot about the story. Ten years later, Gaston hired insulation contractors to install batts between the rafters, and when she cleaned out the attic prior to their arrival, she found the forgotten box. She hid it in the walk-in closet in their bedroom, behind a rack of her summer dresses.

She doubted that Gaston had changed his mind. But she hadn't, either.

* * *

They were sitting on the back porch. Cloud had curled up beside Edmund, content to doze in the sunlight, but Breeze kept dropping her favorite stick in Edmund's lap and Edmund kept throwing it for her. It was a game neither seemed to tire of.

Céline had the manuscript in her lap. Gaston, gone since daylight supervising one of his framing contractors, would not be home before dark.

"Did I ever tell you how the Ojibway got dogs?" she said.

Edmund faked a throw, then flicked the stick to the side. Breeze made a course correction in mid-stride and scooped it up. He shook his head.

"Dad says I'm not really Indian because I'm only one-quarter Ojibway."

Céline thought about that. "Okay, sure. I'm only half Swedish. But that's not what I'm saying, Edmund. What I'm saying is, you know how much you like Breeze and Cloud? Maybe you were born that way. Maybe it's genetic."

Edmund thought about that.

"I think so too," he said. "Some of the other kids think it's funny, you know, but they don't have any dogs, they got brothers and sisters. Like Tony Trumbo. But you and Dad don't have any other kids except for me, so it's kind of like Cloud and Breeze are my brother and sister. You know what I mean?"

Céline wrapped her arms around her knees. "So tell me, Edmund. How are they like your brother and sister?"

Edmund frowned. Breeze dropped the stick in his lap, but he pushed her away. "If I had a brother or sister, I'd love them. Because you can't help it if they're your family. So it's kind of like, Breeze and Cloud are my family, and I can't help it if I love them. It's like that. Except they're dogs, not people."

Céline caught herself nodding a little too vigorously and looked away, blinking. Edmund and Breeze returned to their matter-of-fact game of fetch, as though he'd just walked to the head of the classroom, diagrammed a complex mathematical equation on the chalkboard, and returned to his seat.

"Well," Céline said. "I love the dogs, too."

"I know," Edmund said. "They told me. But I think Cloud likes Dad even more than me."

"You can talk to the dogs?"

"It's not like *talking*, Mom. Not like you and I do. It's sort of like, you just know, right? It's kind of like you can read their minds. There's a word for it but I forgot it."

"Empathy?"

"Yeah, maybe. What does empathy mean?"

Céline rested her chin on her knees. Edmund had hold of one end of the stick and Breeze the other, who growled with mock ferociousness. Even with both hands on the stick, the little dog threatened to drag him from his seat. The collie's strength amazed her. But this was what Edmund had told her many times, that Breeze—thirty-five pounds to Edmund's seventy-five—towed him alongside her, his hands clutching her collar, in the lake beyond the orchard. Céline didn't like to think about her son swimming, unsupervised save for two half-wild Border collies, in the shallow, grown-over, muddy water of the disintegrating irrigation reservoir, and she'd said as much to Gaston, but her concerns had met with little more than an amused snort. Gaston told her that Edmund was just like him, which she interpreted to mean that it was okay if he risked his life doing stupid things.

"Em-pa-thy," Céline said. "It means feeling what other people feel. If somebody said something to Tony and it hurt his feelings, your feelings would be hurt too, wouldn't they? Because it would bother you that his feelings were hurt. That's empathy."

Edmund frowned. He let go of the stick and Breeze dashed away with it in her mouth and turned and wagged her tail. Edmund ignored her and she trotted back and dropped the stick in his lap. He placed it on the deck.

"I want to hear that story you said," he said. "The Indian one about the dogs."

"Well. It just so happens I have it right here." She held up the manuscript. The five pages of closely lined composition paper were yellowed with age and stapled together in the upper left-hand corner. "Your gramma wrote this, Edmund. Did you know that? Before she died."

"Gramma did? She made it up all by herself?"

"It's not made up, Edmund, it's Ojibway legend. It's what the grandparents told their grandchildren, back before they had things like books. It's how those people—your ancestors—learned who they were. That's why I thought you would want to hear."

"So Gramma got it from the Indians?"

"Yes, I think so. She wrote it down for your father. But listen, Edmund, this is a very secret story, and very powerful, so you can't tell anyone about it. Even Dad. When you tell people your secrets, you lose your power. Okay?"

Edmund nodded. "But don't you tell Dad secrets and stuff?"

Céline balanced the manuscript on her knees. "Of course we do," she said. After repeated attempts to get Edmund to throw the stick, Breeze had finally retreated into a patch of sunlight and, propping the stick upright between her paws, gnawed on it contentedly. Cloud had begun snoring.

"Listen to me," Céline said. "This is *our* secret, just you and me." She scooted around to face him, rearranged the yellowed manuscript on her lap, and began:

There were two Ojibway in a canoe, and one day a great storm blew them far from land. They were lost and weak from hunger, and too tired to paddle. They went before the wind like a leaf in a stream, without direction, going only where the wind would go. Finally, after many days on the water, they were blown to shore.

They were hungry so they began looking for the tracks of animals, something they could kill and eat for food. But instead they found the tracks of a giant! They were so afraid of the giant they ran and hid, but the giant found them.

Céline drew herself up and studied her son, who met her gaze with wide, round eyes.

Suddenly, an arrow flew into the ground next to them!

Céline smacked the deck with her hand, startling Edmund and bolting the sleeping Cloud upright.

And there was the giant! He'd been hunting and had a full-grown caribou hanging from his belt, but he was so big the caribou looked like a tiny rabbit. But he told them that he liked little people and wouldn't hurt them, and if they came home with him he would feed them and take care of them.

The two Ojibway had lost their bows in the lake and were terrified and hungry, so they agreed to go with him. But when they got back to the giant's lodge, an evil Windigo spirit blew in and told the two men that the giant had other men hidden in the woods, and that he was going to eat them all. The Windigo spirit pretended to be their friend, but he was very evil and was lying to them, since it was the Windigo, and not the giant, who liked to eat people. But the giant wouldn't give the Windigo the two men, and when they argued he became very angry. He took a big stick—so big it looked like a log—and turned over a bowl with it.

Céline leaned forward and gripped Edmund's shoulder.

Under the bowl was an animal the men had never seen. It looked like a wolf, but the giant called it 'Dog.' The giant told Dog to kill the Windigo, and Dog grew and grew until it was very big, almost as big as the giant, and then Dog killed the Windigo easily. When the Windigo died, Dog became small again and crept back under the bowl and went to sleep.

The Indians were very happy to be alive and very grateful to Dog for having saved them. The giant was pleased and agreed to give them Dog and said that it would take them home. The two men had no idea how this could be, but they had seen that the giant's magic was very powerful, and they agreed to let Dog take them home, which was very far away.

Céline smiled, her eyes twinkling.

The giant took the two men and Dog to the edge of the lake and gave Dog a command. Again, the dog grew and grew until it was almost as big as the giant. The giant told the men to climb onto Dog's back and hold on. But Dog was so big the giant had to pick them up and put them on its back. Then Dog waded into the lake and began swimming away. The men were scared again because they didn't know where Dog was going. But much later, after it had been swimming for days, they recognized the lodges of their people along a distant shore. As Dog swam nearer, it became smaller and smaller, until the two men finally had to put their arms around its neck and swim alongside it. Dog led them to their lodges and then ran away and hid in the woods. When the two men told the tribe what had happened, no one believed them.

Céline grinned. "Would you, Edmund? Who would believe such a story?"

Edmund sprang to his knees. "I do!" he said. "I do! The lake behind the orchard? Breeze pulls me through the water while I hold onto her collar, just like the giant's dog! Just like that!"

"Then it's true!" Céline said. One of her earrings caught the light and sparkled softly beneath her hair. "But wait, I'm not finished yet." She picked up the manuscript.

Many weeks went by and then one morning, while everyone else in the camp was sleeping, Dog came back. The men were very happy to see their friend, and Dog allowed them to pet it and feed it. When the rest of the tribe awoke, they were very surprised to see this new animal, which they hadn't believed was real. But from that day on Dog lived with them. And that is how the Ojibway got dogs.

Breeze rose to her feet and was trying, again, to push her stick into Edmund's hand. He tapped her on the nose with his finger, said "No," and after he ignored her pleading look, she trotted away and resumed her methodical gnawing. "Is that story really true?" Edmund asked.

"What do you think, Edmund?"

"Well, that one part about towing the two Indians on the dog's back might be true, because it's like what Breeze does with me, you know? But I don't know about that Windigo spirit thing. I've never heard of a Windigo."

"I never had either, until I read your gramma's story. Maybe someday you can ask your dad about it. But just not yet, okay?"

Edmund nodded. Cloud stretched and yawned, then lazily extended his paw and rested it on Edmund's foot.

* * *

"The apple harvest is just around the corner, Gaston. You knew that, right?"

Gaston arched his eyebrows in mock surprise. The kitchen table, where it lay exposed to the sun, warmed their hands, but outside, beyond the window that gave onto the orchard and the barn and the corrals, the cool evening air had not yet surrendered to the warmth of morning, and it was clear to them both that in the nights to come the temperatures would drop below freezing. Cool September weather presaged six weeks of a dawn-to-dusk immersion in the business of picking, sorting, packing and distributing apples. It would allow for precious little beyond sleep. They would lay, exhausted, side by side in bed late each night, Gaston's muscular arm draped below Céline's breasts. Now, as if hearing the distant approach of a train and the far-off clack of its wheels against steel rails, both sensed the imminent rhythm of the coming harvest, and both were stirred by the consideration of it.

"Do we have to do this now?" Céline said.

"No," Gaston said. "We don't *have* to do anything. We don't *have* to harvest the apples. We can let them rot. All we *have* to do is make enough money to pay for it all."

"C'mon, Gaston. You know what I mean."

Gaston thrust his chin toward the window, toward the barn. Céline couldn't see the barn from where she was sitting.

"It's time. If we wait much longer it will get too cold, and then you got to wait until spring."

"But right now?"

"It's *time*, Céline. I do this shit for a living. You don't wait for the paint to start peeling before you give it another coat, not if you're smart. And the guys I always use told me they were available. I got them booked solid all summer, and they're pretty fair hands. Half of painting is prep work. I wouldn't hire them if they were hacks."

"It's seventy-five hundred dollars, Gaston. For just the barn. And that rental that just came up, we haven't filled that yet. We're not getting that many calls. Not like we used to."

Gaston shrugged. "That's a fair bid. They aren't going to screw the guy who's been signing their checks for the last seven or eight years. This isn't like it was when we were kids, Céline. *Everything* is expensive. *Everything's* going up. Look at real estate in this town. Grand-père, back in the forties, he built this house right here for something like twenty-eight thousand, or right around that. That's what Papa told me. Back then, it was the nicest house in Port Landing. Now what is it worth? You care to make an educated guess?"

Céline pursed her lips. "I know what it's worth."

"Okay, then."

Céline gazed at the rifle on the pegs above the door, its barrel and receiver worn to a silvery patina. Gaston's weekly patrols for bears had dwindled to perhaps once a month, mostly, she assumed, to get away from it all—from the never-ending crush of work at the job sites, the ongoing maintenance on the rentals, to get away from her. She could rationalize the need, but she did not understand the act. He had never invited her to go along, only Edmund and the dogs.

"Look, Céline, honey. We got plenty in the rental account to cover this. I told Darryl I'd pay him like I always pay him, soon as I cut the rest of the company checks. He didn't have to do that, 'cause this is sort of like a side job to him, not part of his job description for Vaillancourt Builders. You okay with that? It'd be nice if you were on board with this."

Céline rose from her chair and walked into the kitchen, then dumped the rest of her coffee in the sink. She rinsed the cup under the faucet and set it upside down in the dish rack.

"I don't see it like you do, Gaston. The maintenance thing. But if you think the barn needs painting, then let's paint the barn. Consider me officially on board."

"Aha!" Gaston stepped away from the table and pointed at a spot on the ceiling. "Jeez, Céline, don't you ever dust up there?"

Céline's eyes darted up and Gaston reached around behind her, cupped her breasts in his hands and bit her lightly on the neck. The bristly, coarse hair on his chin scratched her neck and she squealed and flung her arm awkwardly behind to smack him, but Gaston stepped lightly out of the way and bit her again, then spun her around and at the same time gently lifted her onto the kitchen table, a hand locking each of her wrists to her sides. He kissed one breast, grinned, and then kissed the other.

"You ain't so tough," he said.

"You wish!"

* * *

The painters arrived the next day. Céline heard the dogs barking and pushed her spade into the black earth of the garden and walked around the house. She saw a white van with the black hand-stenciled lettering *Superior Painting Contractors 719-555-9008* pull into the driveway and two men got out. The driver spied her and immediately extended his hand. He was older than she'd assumed, probably well into his fifties.

"You, of course, would be Mrs. Vaillancourt," he said.

"Yes, yes. Thanks for showing up. Gaston said I should be expecting you."

"Gaston would be correct. This is later in the year than we normally take on projects like this, but we're happy to bend the rules a little for Gaston. Long as it doesn't get too cold, we should be all right."

The other man, Céline noticed with mild distaste, had lit a cigarette, his eyes roaming the property before coming to rest on the barn. He turned up the cuff of his trousers and tapped the ashes inside. Breeze pushed her nose into his leg, snuffling loudly and wagging her tail, but he neither encouraged nor shrank from her nosy affection. He rested one hand on the scaffolding strapped to the top of the van.

"Do you need anything before you get started? Should I show you where the water is? There's a pump beside the corrals, you can see it from here."

The man shaded his eyes, peered, and nodded. A faint blue scar extended from just below his right ear several inches down the side of his neck, like a crude tattoo or a child's cheap earring. Whoever had stitched him up had done a poor job. Céline wondered why he hadn't got it fixed, or re-stitched, or whatever it was plastic surgeons called that kind of repair work. It was very noticeable. Probably didn't have any money. From the looks of their van, he wasn't getting rich.

"Got it," Darryl said. "That's all we need, we got everything else in back. It's just Murray and me, so we're slow, but you don't rush through a project like this, you want it done right. Today, mostly, we're going to set up scaffolding. We work from the shade to the sun, so the paint don't dry out too fast. Oil's worse, but that's what Gaston wants. You do that, and you got to repaint again before you oughta, and then you don't get your money's worth, and then you're unhappy, and so on. I'm telling you this now so you know up front our business practices."

She caught Murray's eye, and he smiled awkwardly and stared at the ground. He was clean shaven and younger than Darryl, closer to Gaston's age. Not a bad-looking man, she supposed.

Darryl nodded at the back of the truck and Murray dropped his cigarette, ground it under his heel and put it in his pocket. He mumbled a few words to Darryl that Céline couldn't hear and then the two of them began the coordinated ritual of flipping open the straps that held the scaffolding to the luggage rack, lifting them off one by one and stacking them beside the van.

Céline waited a few moments, wondering if she was still needed, and then, without further acknowledgement from either man, mumbled, "Okay, if you need anything, just holler," and returned to the garden. Breeze and Cloud happily fell in behind her. She heard the two men working all the rest of the day, grunting to lift the heavy scaffolding onto the pump jacks. Darryl's terse instructions to Murray, the staccato grating of their paint scrapers. She ambled over once in mid-afternoon to offer them lemonade and ice water, and found both men taking a break in the shade of the barn. But Murray's uneasiness in her presence made her reluctant to offer small talk, and after both men drained the glasses she offered them and thanked her, she left and didn't return.

She spoke with Gaston. "I don't know, I never see them much," she said. "They're in the shade. They're scraping and sanding. Darryl says it's prep work."

"Yup, that's right. First they scrape, then they sand. I did a ton of it for Papa in high school. I hated it. It sucks. It's shitty work. But that's what you gotta do or the paint won't stick. That's why I hired him. Darryl's been working for the company for going on eight years, on and off."

"Do you know Murray?"

"Not really. He was behind me in school, kind of ran with a different crowd, I'd see him around. He was kind of quiet. Darryl hired him so that's his business, but he says he's a good hand."

Gaston held a can of beer and peered at the barn and the condensation from the can ran down his hand and his fingers were wet from it. He transferred the can to his other hand and wiped his hand on his pants. Darryl and Murray had left an hour before Gaston returned from work, and the lower half of the barn, which they'd finished prepping the day before, now appeared weathered and gray. Céline was surprised at how much of the old paint had been removed. Gaston had been right—the barn was in worse shape than she supposed. One row of scaffolding was suspended from pump jacks fifteen feet above the ground, and an aluminum ladder was propped against it and tied in place with baling twine. The upper tiers of wooden siding gleamed with a fresh coat of red paint.

In two days, working only with brushes—Gaston had emphatically specified that they brush in the new paint, not spray it on—the top half of the barn was finished. Edmund was still in school, so Céline granted herself the luxury of throwing together a salad she'd picked from the garden, fresh baby greens in a wooden bowl she rubbed with garlic and topped with a sprinkle of balsamic vinegar and olive oil. It was exactly the healthy food neither her husband nor her son would eat, although there might still be hope for Edmund, who devoured the juicy beefsteak tomatoes she grew.

It was quiet outside, and Céline decided to check on the men to see if they needed anything. Darryl's van was missing; perhaps the two had run into town for lunch. All but the bottom half of the front wall of the barn—the side exposed to the afternoon sun—had been slicked over with a gleaming coat of shiny red paint, smooth and flat. Even to Céline's untrained eye, she could see they'd made a first-rate job of it. She wandered slowly around the perimeter of the barn, leaning in to peer at the gaps between the trim and siding, which had been carefully caulked in, smoothed flat and painted over. She stepped back, taking in the whole picture, the prow-like overhang above the open loft with its rusting and long unused block and tackle, juxtaposed against the lustrous red paint below. She was happy she'd allowed herself to go along with Gaston this time, happy with how it was going to look.

She decided to walk around the side of their house she didn't often visit, the lower level facing the lake. Beneath the slatted red-wood decking on the overhanging porch above, striped in zebra-like strips of light and dark from the sun, were the sliding glass doors and the windows opening out from their downstairs bedroom, where they slept when the stifling heat in August drove them from upstairs. Murray stood before the windows, his hands shading his eyes, peering in.

She froze in her tracks, bewildered and embarrassed, as if she'd caught him in a clandestine and erotic act. His hat lay on the ground and a thin, obscene strip of sunlight illuminated the pink skin that shone through the thinning hair on the crown of his head. It repulsed her but she couldn't stop staring at it. It was as though she were looking not at him but through him, as if she were watching an animal casually procreating in a zoo, as if she were party to an intimate violation from which she could not avert her gaze. She saw the back of his white work shirt crease and bunch a little as he turned and then he saw her.

She said nothing. Then she said, "Can I help you?"

Murray mumbled something about water. He wanted a drink of water.

"This is my *house.*" Céline felt her anger rising. There was something wrong about all this. Murray had done nothing more than look through their sliding glass doors. He might have been curious, or looking for something, she didn't know what. But no, it was *wrong.* It was *wrong.* Her heart was pounding.

"I was looking for some water. I'm thirsty, is all. Darryl went to town." His pale face flushed red and he reflexively opened and closed his fists, as if he were kneading clay. He snatched his hat off the ground and put it on his head and pulled it low over his ears. Then he smiled, a thin, nervous smile without emotion. He looked at the lake, still smiling, then made an exaggerated shrug, as if he were surrendering. It struck her that if she made a gun with her hand he would put his arms in the air, like the bad guys in a Western.

Céline pointed at the hose bib jutting from the wall a few feet beyond where he stood.

"Well, I didn't have anything to put it in. But I saw that, I did. I was looking for a cup or something."

"Why didn't you just use the pump?"

"I just wanted some water, is all," Murray said.

"But you could have gotten water at the pump. By the corrals."

Murray shrugged. He stared at the ground at her feet.

They both heard Darryl's van pull into the driveway. As if a spell had been broken or an unspoken truce agreed upon, Murray lowered his head and walked past her, avoiding her gaze, his shoulders hunched around his neck, his hands thrust self-consciously in his pockets. He spied Darryl walking toward the barn with a five-gallon plastic bucket of paint and fell in step behind him, never casting a glance backward, his unacknowledged trespass still hanging in the air.

* * *

Céline watched Gaston's eyes narrow with anger. She knew this look all too well.

"Don't," she said. "He didn't really do anything."

"Fuck him. We're gonna have a little talk."

Céline unfolded her legs from beneath her, then folded them back again. Gaston was staring at her, hard. His untouched beer sat on the end table beside the sofa.

She had known it would come to this. What had Murray really done, anyway? She had caught him looking, maybe the word was *spying*, through their bedroom windows. Now that it was over—she'd waited a couple days to mention the incident to Gaston, no longer sure of what boundaries of privacy, in point of fact, Murray had crossed—her reaction, in hindsight, now seemed a little overblown. Maybe he really had wanted nothing more than a drink of water.

She'd almost decided not to mention it to Gaston at all, knowing he would overreact, knowing how overly protective he could be. But her rationalizations gave her scant comfort. She had *felt* violated, because the house was where the people she cared about, her family, lived; even if Murray had done nothing to harm them. So, after dinner one evening, after Edmund had gone to bed, she mentioned it as casually as she could: "And, oh, maybe it's nothing, but this little thing happened with Murray the other day ..." And Gaston reacted exactly as she knew he would, as she had hoped he wouldn't.

"Gaston, please don't overreact to this. I know how you get. It's not that big of a deal. He just kind of ... startled me, is all. I don't want him to lose his job over this. They've done a good job on the barn, even I can see that."

Gaston nodded, his lips drawn in a thin line.

"That has nothing to do with anything," he said. "They wouldn't be here if they weren't any good." He broke off his gaze and stared out the living room window. Trees obscured the view of Port Landing, a rolling, bucolic blanket of vibrant green splashed here and there with shocking orange and red boughs of newly turned leaves, a portent of what lay ahead, a reweighing of the balance of things.

"What are you going to say?"

"I'm not going to say anything." He was looking at her again. "I don't know what I'm going to say. But I'm gonna talk to him. And I'm gonna talk to Darryl. This shit ain't gonna happen again, not at *my* house."

The next morning, Gaston, who was always gone long before she arose, was lying beside her when she awoke. He'd taken off one of the elastic bands that held his ponytail—she'd given him a package of the multi-colored bands she'd bought at the dollar store in Ashland—and his long black hair draped across his shoulders and nearly obscured his eyes. But she could feel his gaze even if she couldn't see his eyes, knew that they were watching her, knew the anger they still held. She touched his arm and he lifted the covers and rose from the warmth of their bed and dressed.

Darryl and Murray arrived precisely at eight, as they had done every day since beginning the painting job. Gaston was waiting on the back porch. He strode to the van as it was rolling to a stop and waited impatiently as Darryl killed the engine and opened the door.

Darryl sat with one leg dangling outside the open door and the other still inside the van. Céline couldn't hear what they were saying. Darryl was nodding, his arms folded across his chest, then he pulled his leg back inside the van and put his head on the head rest and Gaston walked around to the passenger side where Murray was sitting.

Gaston rapped once, hard, on the window and Murray rolled the window down. He stared at the floorboards, nodding rapidly, while Gaston punctuated his speech by jabbing his finger inches from Murray's face.

Then neither man spoke. Gaston looked back toward the house and saw Céline standing on the back porch and gave no flicker of recognition, seemed not to register her presence any more nor any less than the looming backdrop of the orchard beyond where she stood. He turned back toward Murray, and Céline, almost palpably, could sense the heat dissipating, saw Gaston's bunched shoulders lower and relax. Murray offered a hesitant hand and after a moment Gaston gripped Murray's hand and shook it. Gaston slapped the side of the door and walked to the back porch and saw Céline and smiled, as if he had not known she was there, as if he had not known she was watching him.

Chapter Seven

CÉLINE LOVED THE harvest. She loved the constant stream of picking crews circulating in and out of the orchard, the pungent, cider-y scent of apples in field crates stacked for sorting and shipping, the frenzied rush to get the crop in before the bitter storms of November blew in off the lake and spoiled the crop. Gaston was gone long before daylight, lining out the crew leaders and sending teams to various parts of the orchard where the apples for that day would be harvested.

Gaston let Edmund drive the company truck to and from the crews. Céline made a feeble show of protesting. Edmund was eleven, hardly old enough to be driving a three-quarter-ton truck loaded with field crates, but she was well aware that it was an accepted practice among farm kids elsewhere in the state—Gaston had done the same, a point he repeatedly emphasized—and after what she considered an appropriate show of concern, she had quietly acquiesced. She saw no real harm in it. It thrilled Edmund to be behind the wheel as much as it thrilled his two dogs, Breeze and Cloud, to be riding shotgun beside him. On occasion she'd spy him trundling slowly down the dirt two-track exiting the orchard, sitting on the crate he needed to see over the dash, the two dogs beside him peering through the windshield with equal intensity. A boy with an important job.

Now they were well into the midst of the harvest, into the diurnal rhythm of the work, measuring the day by the stream of trucks laden with field crates that pulled into the loading area below the house, turned around and returned to the orchard. She saw Gaston riding on the step below the driver's side of the company truck, talking to Edmund through the open window, nodding somberly. He hopped off the truck and Edmund continued driving and Gaston strode purposefully into the house where Céline sat at the kitchen table, the day's tally sheets spread before her. He took the rifle from above the door.

"Bear got into it up there last night," he said. "Tore up a whole pile of crates and scattered the apples to hell and Sunday. Then it ate about half of them and ruined the rest. It's almost like they do it just to spite me. Like they haven't been up there all summer already tearing the limbs off of trees. The tracks went right up to one of the trucks and you could see the paw prints on the window. Right up to the truck! Like he owned the place."

"Is it still around?" Céline knew nothing about bears. She'd seen a few in her time in Port Landing: quizzical, shambling creatures that seemed harmless and invariably ran crashing into the forest the moment they saw her. But every harvest she tallied the damage they did and she saw empirically how much a single bear could cost them in ruined apples.

"Hell no," Gaston said. "It's long gone. They run up into the woods where you can't get at them. They always work like that, at night, like thieves. They *are* thieves. I'd shoot every goddamn one if I could. But I can't."

"Department of Natural Resources," Céline said, nodding.

"The hell with the DNR. If you're protecting your livestock, you can kill 'em. That's the way it *used* to work in Wisconsin. Papa used to shoot 'em all the time. Same rifle I got right here. He wasn't much of an orchardist, but he took care of his guns. And he hated bears as much as I do. I see one up there tomorrow, I'm protecting my crop and it's a dead bear."

But the bear was gone the next day, and the day following that, and it did not come back. The bear was apparently satisfied with the mischief it had caused. Gaston repeatedly revisited the pile of splintered crates and rotting apples, hoping pointlessly that the creature would return to the scene of the crime, but its tracks had wandered back into the forest and vanished. He kept his rifle close at hand until his fury began to abate and then he placed it, a shell jacked in the chamber, in the cab rack in the company truck, with stern instructions that Edmund was to call him on the phone if he saw a bear. He was not, under any circumstances, to shoot it himself.

Edmund nodded soberly, but his thoughts that day were only peripherally on bears. He had, in the seclusion of the truck cab, discovered more pressing priorities: practicing his swearing.

"*Damn* that bear," he said, getting a feel for the inflection of the word, of the way it rolled off his tongue, of the salty taste of forbidden language. Driving through the orchard with the windows rolled up was a perfect venue. "Bears can go to *hell*. Those *damn* bears can go *straight* to hell." Breeze stared at him. Edmund slapped his hand on the dash, hard, and the little dog jumped. "*Damn* those *damn* bears!" he shouted. "*Hell*, Breeze, there's *damn* bears everywhere up here, eating up all of our *damn* apples. *Hell!*"

Swearing sent embarrassing, but thrilling, spurts of electricity shooting through Edmund's body, as if he'd suddenly been caught in the rain without his clothes. He wanted to perfect his pitch and delivery, the way his father and his father's friends sounded when he listened to their private conversations, when they thought he couldn't hear them.

But only "hell" and "damn" were permitted. The other words he'd heard his father's friends toss around were not. His mother rarely, if ever, swore, and he knew she'd be horrified to hear him. Yet, some of his friends in school had been swearing for years. And who would hear him here? Not his mother.

"Shit," Edmund said under his breath. He cast an anxious glance at his dogs, who panted happily and thumped their tails against the seat.

"Fuck," he said. "*Fuck!*"

* * *

It was an oversight that Gaston, who was so diligent at parsing all things business related, had somehow never got around to. They didn't own an apple press.

Cider making was a modestly lucrative sideline of the orchard, but in order to produce cider, they used a commercial press at another orchard. Céline had run the numbers, and she pointed out that if they purchased a good press, they'd more than recoup the cost in two or three years. Gaston did not disagree. But somehow there were always other places to put their money.

The apples that were blemished—it always amazed her that people insisted upon perfectly pristine apples, which had no effect whatsoever on their quality or taste—were summarily rejected as suitable only for cider. Céline stored crates of blemished apples in the barn, and then in the basement, but even so, there were vastly more left over than she could store or give away to her friends. So off to the commercial press they went.

She waited until they had several pallets of apples waiting to be processed, then visited the owners of the pressing operation, a friendly, talkative young man and his wife, to go over the details of the mixes she had decided upon for that year. Certain blends rendered certain flavors, and she allowed herself the small pleasure of thinking she had become something of a sommelier of ciders. It was fun, a tiny bit creative, at least compared to the bookwork she'd been doing for years, and it gave her an excuse to get away from her tally sheets and out into the broader parameters of Port Landing, which she rarely got to see when the harvest was in progress.

The pressing operation was in a restored barn, and there were several trucks in the gravel parking lot when she pulled up. Even before she opened the car door Céline could smell the delicious aroma of freshly pressed cider. It was early evening, and lights blazed from the windows, casting a warm glow on the people bustling about inside. She grabbed her purse and walked into the open doorway.

The owner was absent, but his wife greeted her warmly. The woman was enormously pregnant. Céline had uncomfortable memories of her last weeks of carrying Edmund and marveled that she was still able to walk, much less direct a hands-on apple pressing operation. But she was a friendly, efficient girl barely into her twenties, and after she had discussed the pallets of Vaillancourt apples stacked in the lot beside the barn, and written down the mixes Céline had chosen, she left with a cheerful wave and got back to business, leaving Céline to poke around the inside of the barn for a few minutes before heading home.

Crates of apples were stacked to the ceiling along one entire wall; the opposite wall was stacked with cardboard boxes packed with glass jugs of cider. Several men stood in a loose circle in the corner, glasses of cider in their hands, grinning and chuckling under the warmth of a suspended gas shop heater. One of them gave Céline a friendly nod before turning back to the conversation.

She wandered down the row of presses, enjoying the powerful scent of crushed apples, the ancient, hand-pegged oak beams in the barn, the inviting warmth of the place, the peaceful hum of the motors. Then she turned to leave, and at that moment felt someone touch her shoulder.

"Mrs. Vaillancourt?" Céline turned and spied a tall, balding man with a full salt-and-pepper beard. He smiled diffidently, as if her presence made him self-conscious. "You don't remember me, looks like. Bob Radcliff? I'm Gaston's friend. I think the last time I saw you was over the Fourth. Your kid's name is Edward, that right?"

"Edmund. Everyone gets that wrong. But sure, I remember you, Bob. It's been a while. I'm surprised you remember me at all. We've only talked, what would you say, a couple times in the past ten years? How have you been?"

"Well, that's what I was fixin' to talk to you about." Radcliff stopped, as if assembling the words that would deliver his thoughts, his gaze settling on the open door at Céline's back. The sun had just set, leaving the highest leaves of the oaks limned in yellow, as if their edges had been dipped in paint. The cicadas had begun their raspy evening serenade, and inside the barn, under a damp mat of hay and dirt, a cricket chirped.

"What Gaston done, well, no one else would touch me, I guess he told you about that, what he done made all the difference," Radcliff said. He frowned deeply and thrust his hands deep into the pockets of his overalls. "I bought the boat, like I said. That was with the loan money. Took me a couple months to get her seaworthy, but that was all money I saved up myself. I'd been saving it up for a long time, trying to get a loan from a bank, you know, but no one would even talk to me, like I said. You could see what they was thinking. But Gaston, he came through for me, and I bought myself a nice little boat I had my eye on for years. I put her in the water a month ago and she's already made me enough to pay part of it back. I ain't never been self-employed in my life, always had to crew for someone else or do this and that, and that's okay, I ain't never been afraid to work, but I always figured a man oughta pay himself first. I just never could see myself working for someone else the rest of my life. Kind of like you and Gaston. You know, self-employed. It's growing on me." He grinned shyly.

Céline nodded, trying to remember. Had Gaston ever mentioned making a loan to Radcliff? Maybe he had broached the subject; she seemed to recall they had talked and decided against it. She wasn't sure if she should be upset with Gaston for making a financial decision without her or happy that it was so obviously the right move for his friend Radcliff. But buying another rental, she thought with a touch of rectitude, had also been his idea, and that particular rental was still vacant.

"Well," she said. She badly wanted to know how much the loan had been for, but felt it was impolite to ask. "I'm happy to know it's worked out so well for you. We were happy to do it."

Radcliff blinked several times and looked away. "I just wanted to tell you that, is all," he said. "Would you express my appreciation to Gaston? I ain't seen him much lately. I been working on the boat pretty much every spare minute, like I was married to it. Used to be, you know, I was down at Happy Jacks a couple nights a week, spending my pay, but this is better. It's *lots* better. Give me some responsibility, I guess. But I just wanted to say thank you."

He stopped, looked at her, and then, impulsively, gave her a rough, embarrassed hug. It happened so suddenly, and was so unexpected, that she hadn't time to return the embrace, and her purse was crushed awkwardly between their bodies. Then, as if he'd gone beyond the bounds of personal propriety, he stepped quickly away and lumbered out the door.

* * *

Breeze galloped through the men in the orchard with her stick in her mouth, shamelessly begging anyone who cast her a sideways glance to throw it for her. Some, resting momentarily from the labor of climbing ladders and hauling heavy crates of apples, made the strategic error of complying, and these were rewarded with the endless devotion of a small red dog repeatedly pushing a disgusting, gooey stick into their hands. They eventually had to be rescued by either Gaston or Edmund, who would show up, smile apologetically, and drag her away, allowing them to return to their jobs.

Cloud had little interest in the sport of stick-fetching, and preferred to remain close by Gaston's side or in the truck with Edmund. That the two dogs were so dissimilar was a puzzle. Breeze, the perpetually upbeat, everlastingly happy companion to Edmund; and Cloud, nearly a third larger, yet far less outgoing, far less sure of himself, wanting nothing so much as to remain quietly in Gaston's shadow. At night, both stole from the barn and crept into Edmund's bed; making four, Céline, Edmund, Breeze and Cloud, who now were in on the well-known secret. Edmund said nothing, Céline looked the other way, and eventually their indulgence became habit.

It had become Gaston's custom to arise before dawn, but Céline had long ago given up rising with him to prepare his breakfast. She preferred to sleep in, for she knew how important her rest was, but with the harvest nearly complete, the two of them had time on this morning to catch a few minutes of conversation over coffee. Céline had her tally sheets stacked neatly on one side of the table, a sharpened pencil before her.

"I'm a little worried," she said.

Gaston peered over his cup.

"About the rental. We've never had to wait this long before. We usually rent them out in two or three days. I think it's the recession."

"It *is* the recession," Gaston said. He sipped his coffee and stared out the window. Céline's worries did not seem to concern him. Several trucks had parked in the turn-out below the house, and men were walking into the trees carrying fruit-picking baskets and stepladders. They really didn't need his supervision—he'd hand-picked good crews who knew what they were doing—but as a matter of principle he needed to be out there soon.

"Well?"

"Well, nothing. We're in a recession, Céline. You just said so. It might be slow for a while."

"But doesn't that worry you? Even a little?"

Gaston thought about that. He had not yet pulled his hair back in a ponytail, and it fell in long, glossy hanks across his shoulders. Céline had the notion, at times, that with his olive skin and fierce jaw, he looked a little like an Apache, those old pictures of Geronimo.

"Some," Gaston said. "It worries me *some*. But I watched Papa and Grand-père go through recessions when I was a kid. Okay? I didn't pay any attention then, but they told me about it later. They had rentals too. Sometimes they had tenants and sometimes they didn't. It comes back around sooner or later, like a big circle. Eventually we'll get it rented."

"But what if we don't?"

Gaston snorted with exasperation. "I don't *know*, Céline. What if our apples rot? What if people stop buying these crazy mansions they're putting up all over the damn place? What if Obama decides to tax the shit out of all the rich people? What then? I don't *know* what then. You just gotta deal with it. We got enough income from the other three to support the empty one, right? At least for now we do."

Céline sighed and touched her lips to her cup. It was still too hot, and she blew across the surface to cool it, which didn't help.

"I don't like this … this not knowing," she said. "Every month we have a mortgage payment to meet, and for the last three months we haven't been getting any income to offset it. It worries me. If we lose any of the others, we might have to sell them."

"No, no, no!" Gaston set his cup down, hard. "That would be a huge mistake! Those rentals are appreciating. Look, that first one we bought is worth twice what we paid for it. There's no way we're going to lose by holding on to them. And sooner or later it'll get rented. Like I said. It has to. You only got so much land left in Port Landing, all the rest is national forest. Once everything is built up, and we're already pretty close to that, once everything is built up, there's always gonna be more renters than available places to rent. Every now and then the market is going to go south. I'm not saying that's never gonna happen; I'm *predicting* it's gonna happen. What I'm saying is, selling out just because we've got a vacancy or two is a mistake. If it gets like that, we got to cut back some. Matter of fact, I been thinking about that lately."

"Really?" Céline hadn't heard about this.

"Yes." Gaston nodded, took a sip of coffee, set his cup back down. Céline's haughty tone irritated him. "Business is slowing down. I've got half the jobs lined up this winter I had same time a year ago." He looked at Céline, then let his gaze wander out the kitchen window. Men were still walking into the orchard, baskets in hand. It was cool, and most were dressed in sweatshirts and Carhartt jackets. "It's like, I was expecting this, right? It's been balls to the wall for almost ten years now. You had to know it was gonna end sooner or later. Jorgenson's been predicting it for years. But it ain't gonna kill us, Céline. We just buckle down and keep going. Recessions last a couple years, and then you come out of them. That's what Jorgenson says, and he oughta know. Grand-père's papa made it through the Depression. But for the time being, we may have to cut back some."

"And how will we do that? We have payments on all four rentals. And remember, one of them isn't rented. And we've got payroll to meet." Céline tapped the stack of tally sheets at her side. "And just in case you've forgotten, we've got an expensive kid to feed."

Gaston's eyes snapped into narrow slits. He shook his head slowly from side to side, the muscles in his neck taut. "You didn't hear a thing

I just said, did you? We have to look down the road and make some plans. You even interested in what I been thinking about?"

Céline turned away, her lips drawn in a line. Her cup of coffee sat cooling before her.

Gaston stared at her, his jaw set, but Céline said nothing. "Okay, I'm gonna tell you anyway," he said. "We got to let some people go. The rest of the guys will have to pick up the slack, which shouldn't be too difficult because we don't have that much work right now anyway. The hard part is it's gotta be in management. The carpenters aren't getting enough to make a difference."

Céline turned back. "Who?"

"I don't know. I don't know. It's hard. They're all good hands. But Lloyd Trumbo keeps floating into my head. Tony's dad? You like his wife, Gail. I do too. I mean, I like *Lloyd*. He's just damn good at what I hired him to do. But we don't need a half dozen overseers with nothing to oversee. So him and maybe someone else."

"Lloyd's got kids, Gaston. Tony is Edmund's best friend."

"I know that. I know. But Lloyd doesn't have nine hundred thousand in short-term construction loans hanging over his head like we do. And Gail's got a good job at the high school." He shook his head again, this time in exasperation. "I don't know! I just can't figure it all out. It's not like I won't hire him back the second the economy turns around. I'm gonna do just that. But what am I supposed to do until then, Céline? I've got to look ahead at what might be coming. And no matter how I look at it, no matter how many times I turn it around every which way in my head, all I see is we got to cut back. We're paying Lloyd sixty-five thousand a year. I eliminate two jobs like that and I'm taking a big chunk out of our overhead."

Céline exhaled and reached for her coffee. The hard lines in her face began to soften and she stood and walked to the microwave. She put her cup inside and punched the button.

"I've got to get out there," Gaston said. "You turn some of these guys loose without supervision and they'll be cutting down our apple trees for firewood." He grinned.

"I'm in agreement," Céline said.

Gaston reached for his coat. "I don't see we have any other choice."

"No, you're right," Céline said. "I see what you're saying. I just wish there were some other way."

Gaston threw his hair back, a gesture Céline always thought of as different, somehow, from the way she did it, and tied it back with an elastic band. He frowned and looked at his wife and then looked out the window, as if the clarity he sought was beyond the confines of their home. Then he nodded, once, as if it were decided between them, as if it were settled within.

Chapter Eight

EDMUND AND BREEZE played while Céline watched. Cloud had followed Gaston and his rifle into the orchard on patrol, so after her request for help, the two of them, her son and Breeze, had reluctantly gone with her to the garden to apply a final coat of compost, but as she'd known would happen, Edmund had quickly tired of turning over the flinty Wisconsin soil and turned instead to his dog.

Céline didn't altogether mind. She was tempted to remind Edmund that her toil in the garden provided them with half the food they ate, but knew how pointless it was to impress gratitude on an eleven-year-old mind. Besides, gardening was peaceful and a kind of meditation, a gentle way of putting a period at the end of the sentence that had been the frantic last few weeks of harvest. Breeze and Edmund started a game of fetch, which eventually spilled out of the fenced confines of the garden plot and into the yard. Céline thrust her spade into the earth and sat cross-legged beside it to watch.

Edmund had added a new wrinkle to their favorite game. After taking the stick Breeze pushed into his hand, he threw it as far as he could, then hid behind the house or one of the trees in the yard. Watching Breeze puzzle out his hiding place was at once hilarious and endearing. After nabbing the stick, which she could catch within a couple bounces no matter how hard or far Edmund threw it, she would pause, look around, and then, aware that the rules of the game had just changed, wag her tail slowly and begin her search. Was he hiding in the corral? No. Behind the barn? Not there, either. Sooner or later she'd find him, prance and wag her tail in ecstatic self-congrat-ulation and the game would begin anew.

Céline couldn't fathom the endless pleasure Edmund took in the company of his dogs. Discounting the only dog she'd had growing up, her mother's churlish Cavalier King Charles spaniel, she'd never spent much time around them. Most dogs, she found, were like the boyfriends she'd had in college: overly attentive but not particularly interesting.

But Breeze was nothing like that, and from the moment Gaston brought home the mewling puppies, one or both of them had been Edmund's constant companions, fellow adventurers during his long hikes in the forest and co-conspirators who shared his bed. That she'd seen nothing like this didn't fully describe it. Having never owned a dog, she hadn't known what to expect, and so found her son's bond with the two Border collies as unexpected as it was fascinating.

She'd observed the dogs' behavior when Edmund was at school. Both would wander the yard, and occasionally the two would trot into the orchard by themselves on some private mission, Breeze for-ever in the lead. The rest of the time they seemed content to lie in the sun or chase the rabbits that tried to sneak into the garden. But pre-cisely at 4:30 every afternoon, as if notified by some internal alarm, they'd arise from their slumber and trot to the bottom of the driveway to greet the arrival of the school bus. How could they be so unerringly punctual? In the two years they'd owned them, Breeze and Cloud were never more than a few minutes late for Edmund's return.

She watched her son again hurl a stick and then immediately scamper away. But this time, rather than hide behind a tree or the house, where Breeze had learned to look, Edmund dropped into the ditch bordering the road. Breeze dashed back with the stick in her mouth, paused, and then ran behind the house. When her lost boy wasn't there, she made a quick, anxious circle around the barn, the stick still in her mouth. She stopped, looked around, and whined softly. And then she did a curious thing.

Carefully, as if placing a teacup just so, she put the stick on the ground between her paws and sat on her haunches and looked all around, as if pondering what to do. Her gaze fell on Céline and their eyes met. Breeze rose to her feet, walked to where Céline sat in the moist, freshly turned soil, and gently, her tail wagging in entreaty, rested her head on Céline's knee.

* * *

"Can I invite Tony?" Edmund asked, beaming with pleasure. His hair, as black and lustrous as a pony's mane, cut short on the sides and long on top, brushed his eyes. Gaston glanced at his wife then scratched his nose.

"Well, it's kind of a party for grown-ups," Céline said. "I'm not sure Tony would have any fun."

"But I'm going to be there, and I'm not a grown-up."

"You have to," Céline said. "You live here." Why did boys ask such impossible questions? Why couldn't he just go along with the game plan? How did she explain to her son that his father had just laid off Tony's father, Lloyd? And that having him there might be awkward, not just for Tony, but for everyone? Notice had been given the previous afternoon in Gaston's downtown office and it had left Lloyd Trumbo in shock and Gaston in a rare mood of introspection. That evening, hoping to mollify his pain, she reminded him that he had had no other choice in the firing, but he had grown angry and had snapped at her and his shortness had stung. Still she sought to protect him, to nurture, and Gaston listened and his pain began to subside.

"No, Céline. Let the kid come," he finally said. "I don't have a problem with Tony being there." He tried to feign nonchalance. "Might as well."

Edmund yipped with delight and leapt from the table and ran out the back door with his schoolbooks under his arm. Céline caught a glimpse of Breeze and Cloud galloping from the barn to greet him. Breeze sprang at him and Edmund ducked and the little red dog sailed neatly over his back. She turned toward her husband.

"I know what you're thinking," Gaston said, "but I been thinking too. I think we should invite Lloyd and Gail."

"Gaston."

"No, listen. We run this business like a family, right? I always said that, just like you. Lloyd's been with us a long time. It killed me to let him go yesterday. He didn't do anything wrong! He's a good hand! I told him it was temporary, soon as the market turned around he'd be the first guy I hired back. I explained all that. He said he understood. I'm not saying he was happy about it, but he got it. I mean, we shook hands on it. So it doesn't seem right to leave him out. All his friends will be here. They'll at least get a good meal out of it. We're gonna cater this thing like we always do, right? I feel like I owe it to the guy."

"Gaston, I just don't know. I don't think he'll be happy. I wouldn't be. Seeing all the other people he works with at the company party, but not being part of the company anymore? It's like attending your own funeral or something."

Gaston drummed his fingers on the tabletop, frowning deeply. Several strands of hair had draped across his cheeks like thin, black scars. He brushed them away. Céline heard the school bus chug up the road and knew that within minutes, Breeze and Cloud, having delivered Edmund safely to the bus stop, would return and begin their morning schedule of napping and circumnavigating the yard.

"I mean, don't you think?" she said.

Gaston rubbed his face between his hands. "How the hell did this happen? That's what I want to know. We were doing great and then, all of a sudden, things just hit the wall, just like that." He snapped his fingers, and the sound, like the distant crack of a rifle, gave Céline a start. "I feel like I got to. I feel like I owe it to the guy."

Céline nodded. "Okay. I'll send out the invitations. Maybe it will be okay. I know it will make Edmund happy. You saw how he got this morning. Maybe you're right. Maybe he'll enjoy himself. It won't hurt to try."

* * *

Cloud had become such a familiar adjunct to Gaston's rituals—weight lifting in the basement, bear patrols in the orchard—that Gaston paid no more attention to the stout little dog than he paid to the wind off the lake or the rasping crickets in the barn. Cloud hovered in his periphery like a shadow, padding silently behind him wherever he went, happiest when Gaston was in sight.

For the umpteenth time, Céline marveled at the difference between the two dogs. From an early age, Cloud had stationed himself at Gaston's side, accepting the petting he received from guests but doing little to encourage them. Breeze, on the other hand, was working the room, trotting from one person to the next with her stick in her mouth, begging all she encountered to throw it for her. This invariably delighted the guests and embarrassed Céline. It didn't matter that Breeze had stolen in from outdoors and crashed the party, or that the stick was so thoroughly masticated no one would touch it, or even that a game of fetch wasn't appropriate within the confines of the Vaillancourts' living room.

Céline tried to hide the stick, standing on the back porch and throwing it as far away as she could, a pointless exercise that served only to give the dog more incentive to find it and bring it back. When Céline finally tired of the game and dropped the stick in the trashcan under the sink, Breeze simply scouted the back yard until she found another. Her guests found this uproariously funny.

There wasn't much Céline could do about it now, anyway. The house was packed. Following her lead, most of the women had arrived wearing skirts and heels, but the men, perhaps following Gaston's example, were dressed in jeans and boots, barely one sartorial notch above what they wore at work. Some of the older men, either harangued or persuaded by their wives, had donned ill-fitting blazers in which they fidgeted uncomfortably, the fronts unbuttoned around their protruding bellies.

Céline had suggested to Gaston that they produce the party on their own, which would have involved days of preparation but would have saved them hundreds of dollars. Ultimately, they decided to opt for the caterer they'd always used, although with construction projects falling away like leaves from the trees, neither knew how much longer they'd be able to afford it. But for the time being they wanted to bolster the illusion of the Port Landing economy's imperviousness to the world at large, a display of continuity that in their unspoken fears both knew they would not be able to maintain much longer.

Céline had turned on the CD player when guests began to arrive (Willie Nelson made everybody happy, although she preferred classic rock), but within a half hour the general din had all but drowned it out. She didn't care. She loved the exhilarating bustle of the company party. She spent most of her days in the cathedral silence of their home, which was nearly two hundred yards from the next residence and buffered by a half mile of dense woods from the traffic in Port Landing. Having so many guests was exciting and reassuring at the same time. It pleased her that both her husband and son seemed to feel the same way.

She walked into the kitchen for a tray of cheese and crackers and saw Breeze scamper to the front door. A second later she heard the doorbell ring and saw Gaston push his way, grinning, through the guests to the front door. She offered the tray to a circle of women who politely demurred, then turned again to see who had arrived, and saw Gaston talking to Lloyd and Gail Trumbo. He nodded, vigorously shook Lloyd's hand, then stepped back and elaborately welcomed them inside, as if presenting them to the rest of the guests.

Céline heard him say, "You should of brought Tony. That would have been okay. He's a pretty good kid."

Lloyd nodded and smiled and glanced around the room. He looked at his wife and then back at Gaston. "Tony didn't want to come," he said. "Baseball practice today. The kid loves baseball, you know how he is." Gaston nodded in hearty agreement. He knew how Tony was. Lloyd looked at Gaston and punched him lightly in the arm and then turned away, as if looking for someone else, as if finding someone else were important. A guest caught his eye and he smiled broadly and walked over and slapped him on the shoulder and pumped his hand.

Gail smiled and folded her hands before her, as if clasping them in a handshake. She was heavily made up, her eyes lined with thick black mascara. "Nothing but baseball for Tony," she said, beaming. "It's all he ever thinks about."

"Well, Edmund was asking about him, is all," Gaston said. "But that's alright. You want anything, just ask Céline, okay? She's in charge of all that stuff. She's in charge of everything."

"I'll bet I can find my way to the bar!" Gail said.

As if suddenly remembering he was holding it, Gaston took a sip from the can of beer in his hand. He dabbed his mouth on his sleeve.

"Really great to see you here," he said. "I mean, it's really great to see both of you. Lloyd."

"Oh ..." Gail waved him off. She was still beaming.

"Okay. Well, I got to get back to the party," Gaston said. "Céline says I gotta spread myself around. Like people ain't had enough of me already."

Gaston took a step back, then turned on his heel and made his way to a group of men on the opposite side of the room. Céline watched Cloud, a step behind her husband, disappear behind a sea of legs. Gail walked to the hallway and examined a quilt tacked to the wall. She leaned forward and touched the fabric and frowned.

It was a cool evening, perfect weather for a party. Gaston started a fire in a metal fire ring outside, and several men were now warming themselves around it, drinking and talking. One smoked a cigarette, flicking the ashes pensively into the flames. Céline saw Sir Lancelot and Dutch press against the rails of the corral, their ears swiveling eagerly toward the voices and flames, as wide-eyed as colts. Sir Lancelot nickered, tossing his head and shaking out his mane.

Sir Lancelot. Céline couldn't remember why she had chosen the name, only that it seemed to fit. Until Gaston had offered to buy the horses for her, she had forgotten how much she'd loved them as a child in Minneapolis, forgotten she still wanted horses at all. They'd been colts, spindly-legged siblings, and they stopped her heart the first time she saw them. Gaston paid the owner on the spot, but they'd had to wait nearly a year before the two were old enough to leave their mother.

Céline had spent the ensuing months immersed in everything equine: books, magazine articles, videos she watched online or checked out from the library. How to feed horses, how to train horses, how to build a stall your horse will love, how to make your horse your best friend. Saddles and bridles and blankets and Ariat riding boots and hand-woven, horsehair reins. She'd asked for a tack room and Gaston had built one for her opposite the stalls in the barn.

Céline found a riding instructor in Ashland—she had no idea they had a riding instructor in Ashland—and booked twice-weekly lessons for six months. They had money then.

She'd taken riding lessons as a teenager, and the muscle memory was still there. There was never a moment's reassessment when she felt out of place, never a time when she couldn't find her balance on the horses her instructor supplied. She'd been an athlete for too much of her life not to rise to this new challenge. She graduated early, and her instructor gave her a certificate. It was a silly thing, really, just an embroidered slip of paper with lettering in faux gold leaf, but Céline had it framed and proudly hung it in the upstairs den, beside the photos of Gaston's hunting and fishing trophies.

Riding Sir Lancelot and Dutch, but particularly Sir Lancelot, bolstered her courage. With Sir Lancelot's broad back beneath her, she was no longer quite so hesitant to venture into the woods beyond the orchard, no longer fearful of the unknown and unseen beasts within its emerald, shaded depths, no longer afraid that she wouldn't be able to find her way home again. But, like a kettle brought back to a boil when replaced on the burner, her fears began to simmer the moment she dismounted. So she rarely left the safety of her saddle. She refused to drink coffee or tea before riding, so she wouldn't have to dismount and pee. She knew she was being silly, and Gaston loved to tease her about it. But her overactive mind, nurtured on Victorian Gothic literature in the private schools she'd attended, would have none of it. She remained topside.

Lately, though, she hadn't ridden much, not nearly as much as she would have liked. Edmund's upkeep was becoming increasingly expensive, and because of the recession, their income was dropping. They'd put a healthy chunk of it away—Céline had insisted that they open an IRA, and had breathed a sigh of relief more than once that she, at least, had had the foresight to insist upon doing so—but the way IRAs were set up, you couldn't touch them until you retired. Not that she resented the cost of her child; she *loved* her son. Not that she would have chosen any other life than to be a mother to Edmund.

And now he was standing before her. "Mom," he said. "I think Mr. Trumbo is crying."

Céline blinked. "Where?"

Edmund pointed toward the barn. Breeze made a little yip and dropped her stick at his feet, intently watching his face.

"No," Edmund said. He kicked the stick away and Breeze pounced on it and brought it back. "No!" he said again.

"Outside? Where?"

"Out behind the barn. Mrs. Trumbo's there, too, I think it's her, anyway. I was outside and I heard something, this noise. So I went to investigate and I saw them. They're by the corrals. I figured I better get you and tell you. Maybe something's wrong, maybe he's sick or something. But why would he come to the party if he was sick?"

"Show me, Edmund. Let's go." Céline offered her hand and Edmund took it.

"If we go into the stable we can, like, spy on them," Edmund whispered. He had begun to crouch as they approached the barn, as if he were stalking a wild animal. Edmund opened the barn door and Céline closed it quietly behind them. Then, with exaggerated care, Edmund crept into Dutch's stall and peered out the half-open door. In the corral, the horses swung their heads around and cupped their ears. Edmund motioned Céline to come see.

Lloyd Trumbo stood at the opposite end of the corral, leaning against the rails, his back to them, his shoulders heaving. Gail stood beside him with her arm around his waist, saying something under her breath. He might have been crying, Céline couldn't tell. She heard sounds. Lloyd rubbed his face with his hands and looked at the sky and looked at the ground. Céline wanted to back away, to walk Edmund out of the barn and make him promise not to tell. She felt she'd crossed an unmarked boundary, like an intruder. Here she was: spying on this private act between lovers, imposing her unwelcome presence upon their grief.

Céline led Edmund out of the stable and out of the barn.

"Are you sure? I didn't hear anything," she said. But she knew.

"Mom." Edmund looked at her sternly. "I *heard* them. I know what crying people sound like. I've been around the block a few times, okay? Give me a little credit."

"Okay, Edmund. I believe you," Céline said. "Let's go back to the party, okay? I don't want you to talk to anyone about this, okay? You have to promise. I'm going to speak to your father."

Edmund nodded and frowned. "I can keep a secret, Mom. They can even torture me or something." Edmund's chest swelled with self-importance. So much like his father, she thought. The way his body told her what he was going to say before the words came out. After fifteen years of marriage, Gaston's body language was as clear to Céline as the pages of a book. Her son was part of the same story, the same script, with a different font. His story would be told differently, in a different sequence, but it would be told with the same words. Soon—too soon—he would be grown. She gave him a gentle push and the dog Breeze pranced at his heels and Edmund ran to the crowd of people on the back porch, a boy in her eyes once again.

She found Gaston tending the grill, talking to his friends. Everywhere there were empty bottles of beer: on the porch railing, on the floor beside his feet, on the lawn; the detritus of a party. She stood close beside her husband and told him what she'd seen at the barn. Gaston's grin dissolved and he handed his spatula to one of the men he'd been talking to and took his wife's arm, leading her into the yard.

"Where?"

"In the corral with the horses. Edmund found them. They've been out there awhile, I think. Maybe you should go talk to them. Maybe you should say something."

"What's he crying about?"

Céline looked at him.

Gaston stared into the orchard. The pickers had left their debris behind, though they'd been asked to pick up after themselves. Broken field crates lay where they'd been strewn, and the apples unfit for the cider press had been scattered in rotting lumps under the trees. As they did every year, it would be up to Céline and Gaston and Edmund to gather the crates and broken branches and burn them when there was a safe covering of snow of the ground. Gaston cursed and kicked the toe of his boot into the earth. He shook his head.

"Why?" Céline said. "He used to work for you. You said he was a good hand."

"That has nothing to do with it," he said. "I can't just … Nothing's gonna change. I'm not giving him his old job back. I can't. What am I going to tell him?"

"Maybe that you're sorry."

Gaston spun on his heel. "I *am* sorry, goddamnit! I told him that! There wasn't anything else I could do! We already talked about this!"

Céline had known, somehow, that he would react this way, with anger before sympathy. He and Lloyd had known each other since high school. Why couldn't he just say something? This was so stupid.

"How about if we both go talk to them? Would you feel better about it then?"

Gaston glared at her but the anger began to leave his face and he looked past her at the party. Someone had turned up the CD player, which was still blasting out Willie Nelson. Somebody was singing.

"I can't," he said. "I just can't. I'm sorry. Maybe you can. I don't know how. It was hard enough when Gail and him arrived."

"They don't hate you, Gaston. They'll understand. I talked to Gail and she's nice. There wasn't anything else you could do. You told them that."

Gaston shook his head. "I can't."

Chapter Nine

GASTON, SHE COULD tell, was trying not to act smug. He stood with his back to the sink, his arms folded loosely across his chest, talking evenly. Céline was loading the dishwasher. She listened. She wiped her hands on the towel and hooked the towel through the handle of the dishwasher.

"So he called at the end of the day," he said. "He said he saw the ad we put on Craigslist. Said he didn't even need to see the place. Said it sounded perfect. He said he'd take it on the spot but I told him he had to do a walk through so at least I would know that he knew what he was getting into. I had to at least do that, right? I met him down there about an hour ago and he signed the lease." Gaston held his arm straight out and dropped the lease on the counter.

"Who is this person?"

Gaston shrugged. "Not from around here. Some techie from the east coast. Seems like an okay guy. He said he'd always wanted to live in the north woods, likes to hunt and fish, yadda yadda. Go figure. Young guy, maybe late twenties. I asked him if he had a job lined up, and he said he's some kind of consultant. He gave me first and last month's rent and the deposit right on the spot."

Gaston fished a crisp, folded wad of hundred dollar bills from his shirt pocket and dropped it on top of the lease. Céline wondered how someone so young could come up with over three thousand dollars in cash with the economy like it was, with everybody out of work except this whiz kid from the east coast, but the money was right there on the kitchen counter.

"So there it is," Gaston said, as if underscoring what she had just been thinking. "We now have full occupancy in all four rentals. I told you we'd rent that unit, didn't I?"

Céline pursed her lips and nodded. "He's not doing drugs, is he? Dealing drugs or something like that?"

Gaston snorted. "No. He's a consultant. But you know what? I don't care if he is. We've been funding that damn place for six months. He can be running a meth lab far as I'm concerned. Money's money. That was a joke."

Céline thought, Gaston *had* predicted this would happen. He had been right. It was a relief to have the unit rented. He might have missed the point of the discussion they'd had—that she'd been worried about the economy, not that she doubted his prescience—but it was a moot point now. She'd deposit the money in their IRA tomorrow and it would be another step toward their distant retirement.

She smiled and gave Gaston a kiss on his cheek. "My hero," she said. Gaston pulled her to him and ran his hands across her bottom and gave it a hard squeeze. Céline pushed him away. "Stop! What if Edmund walks in? He'll be home from school at any moment."

"You don't think he wants to see his mom bent over the sink with her panties around her ankles?"

Céline slugged him in the chest. As always, it was like bouncing her hand off the side of the barn. She had figured out early in their marriage that he *liked* it when she hit him, it was the stupid macho thing. Gaston grinned and squeezed her breasts but she pushed him away and nimbly skated out of reach.

"So why don't we take a hundred bucks and go to LeMond's?" he said. "Round up that kid who lives here and have dinner? We can afford to celebrate for one night. It's been a long time."

"Hmmm," Céline said, teasing. "I might be expensive. Do you think a hundred dollars is enough?"

"You *are* expensive," he said. "Most expensive hobby I ever had. We'll make it a hundred and a quarter. All Edmund's gonna want is ice cream. How's that sound?"

"It sounds like a date," Céline said. She leaned in close, pulled him to her, and ground her hips into his pelvis. Then, while Gaston gaped with surprise, she darted away.

* * *

They hadn't been to LeMond's in ages, Céline thought. Their Sunday morning brunches had been short-circuited by the summer tourist season, when there had been a forty-five-minute wait just to get in the door. Now the place was deserted. There was just one other couple in the far corner of the dining room. They would have the restaurant to themselves.

Gaston feigned surprise. He arched his eyes and slowly turned his head in a half circle.

"Nobody's here," he said. "Wonder if that will improve the service?"

Céline grinned. Edmund had dashed ahead to the bank of windows overlooking the docks, scanning the bay for, well, she never knew what Edmund was looking for. He just *looked*. He scampered back and danced around his seat until Gaston tapped it sternly and he sat down.

"There's a guy out there with a salmon," Edmund said. "A *big* salmon. I mean, it's the biggest salmon I've ever seen. You should go look."

"Bigger than that salmon you caught that day you and I went out a couple years ago?" Gaston said. "Do you remember that day? I caught a pretty big salmon myself, but yours was bigger. Remember that?"

Edmund jumped up.

"Sit down, Edmund," Céline said. "It's not polite to stand up at the dinner table. I've told you that before."

Edmund sat down, squirming. "Are you kidding, Dad? That was the biggest damn salmon I ever caught!"

Céline's eyes opened in surprise. She glared.

"I mean darn," Edmund said. His cheeks flushed crimson and he sank into the rungs of his chair.

"Where did you learn to talk like that, with swear words like that?" Céline said.

Edmund's gaze darted toward his father, but Gaston frowned and looked away.

He turned back toward his mother. "I don't know," he mumbled.

"Did you learn that in school? Do you think it's polite for little boys to cuss like, like …" Céline didn't know what little boys cussed like. She had no idea. But it didn't matter.

"I'm not that little, Mom," Edmund said. "I'm almost twelve." He stared at his hands.

Céline slapped her fingers on the tabletop. "Don't you talk to me like that! Do the other eleven-year-olds in school swear like … Do you think their parents approve of that kind of language?" Céline knew she was overreacting, but she didn't care. This was an issue she meant to resolve immediately.

"No," Edmund said.

"No what, mister?"

"No, they don't. But some of them *do*, Mom, really." Edmund was near tears, and he began sniffling in quiet, guttural spasms. He wiped his nose.

"Your father and I do not approve of this, young man. I don't want to hear that word out of your mouth ever again. Is that understood?"

A final time, Edmund sought his father's defense, but Gaston said nothing. He stared at the ceiling, his chin resting on his clasped hands, frowning, as if deep in thought. As if he'd heard nothing.

Edmund dropped his head and began crying quietly and rubbing his eyes. "I'm sorry," he said.

Céline took a breath. "That's better, then," she said. "We all make mistakes." She patted Edmund's hand. Edmund sniffed and raised his head. Tears coursed down his cheeks, gathering in tiny pools at the corners of his mouth. He gazed at his mother and squeezed his eyes shut.

Céline's heart went out to her son. He was still so young, still just a baby. Maybe she'd been too hard on him. She turned toward Gaston, but Gaston, oddly, seemed ill at ease, as if she'd been admonishing him, not their son. He opened his menu and then, without looking at it, closed it and slapped it down on the table.

"I'm going for the rib eye," he said, loudly. "How about you? Edmund? Rib eye's the smart choice! You with me?"

Edmund nodded and wiped his eyes. He stared at his hands.

"Don't you want a salad, Edmund? Something healthy?" Céline asked.

"Yes," Edmund said.

"What kind of dressing? You like the Thousand Island they have here, don't you?"

Edmund nodded. "Can I have strawberry ice cream too? For dessert?"

"Of course, you can have ice cream!" Gaston boomed. "I'm going to have ice cream! What do you think about that? *Everybody's* going to have ice cream!"

Céline stared at her husband, but he seemed not to notice.

Gaston waved down the waiter, who had been sitting at the bar, waiting. He slid from his stool and jogged across the room to their table.

"We're ready," Gaston said. "This is gonna be simple. Rib eyes all around, medium, salads, all that stuff. And a Coors Lite for me. What do you want, Edmund? A soda? And bring him a soda, okay? You want a Coke?"

Edmund said he wanted a Coke. And strawberry ice cream for dessert.

"Yeah," Gaston said. "Me too. And strawberry ice cream for dessert for everybody."

Gaston's outburst left Céline subdued, as if the two of them, she and Edmund, had been left standing in the wash of a passing train. Céline hadn't planned to order the rib eye—she was trying to cut down on her consumption of red meat—but correcting her husband after his enthusiastic display of bonhomie seemed pointless now. Steak would be fine.

The waiter nodded and disappeared into the kitchen, and a moment later a short, portly man with a handlebar mustache strode toward their table.

Gaston rose and stuck out his hand. "Terry!" he said. "You remember Terry, don't you Céline? He owns this hamburger joint. And this guy here, that's my boy, Edmund."

Terry grinned, flashing two rows of even white teeth. A fringe of gray hair encircled his shiny bald pate, but his eyebrows and mustache were still dark.

"Of course, I do," Céline said. "We just haven't been here in a while. You're the only real Italian in Port Landing. How could I forget?"

Terry grinned and tousled Edmund's hair. He hooked his thumb over the top of his apron, which was flecked with spots of dried brown blood.

"You folks, this meal is on me. Carl gave me your order but I wanted to see if there was anything else you wanted. Whatever, it's on the house. You've been good customers for a long time. It's the least I can do."

Céline smiled with pleasure. Gaston had always paid for their meals at LeMond's—it was a treat she'd grown accustomed to—but it was not an inexpensive restaurant, and even if the tab seemed to make little difference to her husband, cost mattered.

"Double ice cream!" Edmund chirped. The tears had dried on his olive cheeks and he was a happy little kid again.

Céline patted his thigh. "Okay, kiddo, but let's see you finish dinner, first," she said.

"Terry," Gaston said. "This ain't like you. You're usually such a tight old coot. Word on the street is you shot a guy once when you found him stuffing spaghetti in his pockets."

Terry flashed a toothy grin. "I remember that guy," he said. "He was cutting into my overhead."

"So how, pray tell, do we account for this generosity?" He cocked an eyebrow at Céline.

Terry snorted. Across the room, the only other patrons were settling up with Carl, who took their charge card and ran it through the card reader beside an ancient brass cash register. They were quite young, and Céline wondered how anyone so young could afford dinner at LeMond's.

"I'm done," Terry said. "I'm closing. I can't keep my doors open in this kind of economic climate anymore. It's eating me alive. It's been like this since last year. I thought it would be like the other recessions

I've been through, but this one's worse. I've got perfectly good food I already paid for that's going to waste. You might as well have it."

Gaston's smile dissolved. Céline studied Terry's round, thoughtful face. They'd been eating at LeMond's practically forever. Gaston had taken her here several times while they were still dating, long before they got engaged. Nothing had changed. Terry was as bald and mustachioed then as he was today. The ice cream was still churned by hand in the kitchen. It had been then, and remained today, the best restaurant on the south shore of Lake Superior.

Gaston tilted forward, resting his elbows on the table, his tanned arms loosely crossed. "I just got a lease on our last rental," he said. "It was empty for six months. I have to look at that as a positive sign. You know, maybe things are turning around, right? We've been in the middle of this thing for a couple years. Maybe I'm full of—" he cast a furtive glance at Edmund, "But I'm thinking it's over."

Terry shrugged. "Maybe it is, maybe it isn't. I don't know. But for sure it's too late for me. This was always a shoestring operation. Putting out good food costs money. I don't want to do it anymore. It's time for me to retire, anyway. The wife wants to spend the winters someplace south where it's warm."

"Like Washburn?" Gaston said, grinning.

Terry laughed. "Like Florida. I don't know, Florida's starting to sound better all the time, you know what I mean? Thirty-seven years is a long time to be stuck at one job. That's how long I've been here; I figured it up. I used to serve your folks, back in the day. They used to bring you in after baseball practice. You were a cocky little snot."

Edmund giggled.

"He's still a cocky little snot," Céline said. Gaston rolled his eyes.

"No, look," Gaston said. "Business is picking up. I got a new job I'm bidding on this week; I'm gonna make him a bid he can't refuse. I know what the other guys around here are charging and what you get for your money. He's gonna go with me."

Céline swung around in her chair. "You didn't tell me that," she said.

"Because it wasn't a done deal," Gaston said. "I didn't want you to get your hopes up. But yeah. It came in on Tuesday. I've already been out there and looked it over. And if he goes for it, and he probably will, I'm going to be real busy this winter. We've got to put the foundation in the next couple of weeks and that's what I told him. Otherwise, you know, it'll freeze. But I told him that. He didn't seem to have a problem with the ballpark price per square foot I quoted. He's a doctor. All I'm working up now is the details which includes all the custom stuff he wants." Gaston slowly drummed his fingertips on the tabletop and frowned. "It's a good job. Of course, nothing's guaranteed, but …"

Céline leaned back a little. Edmund had been following his parents' conversation with rapt attention, his gaze shifting from one to the other. They'd almost forgotten about Terry.

"Congratulations," Terry said.

Gaston nodded somberly. "Well, it ain't a done deal, but yeah, it looks pretty good."

"Maybe I'm going to have to charge you for this meal after all," Terry said. Gaston jumped a little, prompting an explosion of laughter from Terry. "Man, you're easy, Gaston. I was just yanking your chain. This one's on me. And the kid here"—he gave Edmund a light punch in his shoulder—"he can have all the strawberry ice cream he wants."

* * *

Céline hadn't seen him this energized in months. Gaston left the house before first light, long before she and Edmund awoke, folding back the thick flannel sheets and woolen blankets and expensive quilts and swinging his legs into the cool of the bedroom, her reluctant arms sliding across his broad back and seeking warmth around herself, the covers pulled over her eyes, listening to him move around from within her warm cocoon. Gaston dressed in the dark, silently, so as not to awaken her, renewed in his sense of purpose and the work that engaged his mind and body.

The bid sailed through. Now, with the mornings laced with frost, the concrete subcontractors were working twelve-hour days to get the concrete poured before the first hard freeze of the season. At night, they draped the forms with sheets of Visqueen and poured heat into them with propane salamanders, but still Gaston worried, even getting up once at three in the morning to check on a section that might have been left exposed to the cold night air. It had not.

With the harvest over and the crop sold, the discarded apples in the orchard were left for the deer and bears. One day, as she drove to town, Céline saw one of the bears, a large brown-tinged boar that squinted indifferently at her car. When she stopped it snorted and loped reluctantly into the trees. It looked like a fuzzy, over-fed dog.

"There's probably ten of them up there," Gaston said later. "Well, maybe not that many, but more than one for sure. They're filling their bellies before they hibernate. That's when Papa used to hunt, this time of year when the bears are out stuffing themselves before winter. They gave him all kinds of depredation permits back in the eighties."

"I'm worried about Edmund," Céline said. "You know how much he loves going up there with the dogs."

Gaston scratched the bristle on his chin. "Well," he said.

Edmund had already left the dinner table, dashing Céline's hopes that she'd be able to keep all three of them together for an entire meal. She understood the business of pouring concrete. But she had hoped. She had cornered Gaston that evening and pushed him into his seat, but the three had dined together for only as long as it took Edmund to bolt his dinner and dash out the back door and into the orchard. He and the dogs rarely returned from their hikes before dark, and the chilly air seemed to prolong his desire to spend time outside, as if the coming of winter lent an urgency to the decreasing hours of the day. Céline preferred to remain in her rocker wrapped snugly in a quilt, but it was not in her son or her husband to linger long in the warmth of their home.

Yet with the nights threatening snow, the strain of racing the weather was beginning to show on Gaston's face. He spoke, but his thoughts were elsewhere.

"He'll be all right," he said, drumming his fingers impatiently on the tabletop. "Like that one you saw the other day? Bears'll always run away if you let them. He knows he's supposed to leave them alone if he sees one. He knows what to do." He rose from his chair.

"What about the dogs? Aren't they going to chase them?"

"I'm gonna assume they're not stupid enough to do that."

"But what if they do?"

Gaston shook his head. "They won't. Not with a human around. I've seen this a million times, Céline. The bear'll run away. They're scared of people and dogs. Edmund knows he's supposed to leave them alone. What are we going to do, tie him up? You know how much he loves hiking around up there."

They had had this conversation before. It always left her unsatisfied, with no assurance of her son's safety, although he'd never been in danger before; and unconvinced that Gaston was right, although she had yet to find him wrong. Even though he'd grown up in these very woods and knew of the animals that lived there and how they behaved. Even with that. She wondered if it was her own uneasiness about the forest beyond their farm that caused her to worry, a reasonable reaction to her unreasonable fears.

None of the other mothers in town seemed worried about bears, now that she thought about it. But still, it would be nice to have her fears validated by her husband once in a while. She folded her napkin and turned toward him, but Gaston was already striding toward the back door. He had equipment to unload from the truck. He shrugged apologetically and she smiled and sent him on his way.

* * *

Two days later, Gaston's concrete crew finished the pour and then a week went by and there was a hard freeze. They had known it was coming. The discarded apples in the orchard withered and turned brown and the stock tank in the corral froze a quarter inch down, the bubbles below the clear ice shiny, transparent and still. Gaston looked out the window and glared at the lake, as if that cold, blue and silent expanse were to blame. It was cold in the house.

Céline clicked the thermostat all the way up. She threw a quilt around her shoulders and still she shivered. Her husband's anger and worry were palpable, like a wall she could touch but not see: an angular, sharp-edged part of him she felt even from across the living room.

She waited but Gaston said nothing so she said, "Do you think they froze?"

Gaston banged his coffee cup down on the windowsill. The coffee slurped over the side and onto his fingers and he slapped his hand angrily on his pants. "Fuck! *No.* It couldn't have. We finished the pour a week ago. I mean, that's why I was running around like a goddamn idiot all last week, so this wouldn't happen, right? I've done this before, never had any problems. You get a little flaking, maybe, but it's all cosmetic, not structural. I made 'em put heat on it all week. It'll be fine." He looked at her, his lips pursed, the lines on his face drawn taut as violin strings.

She folded back her quilt and squeezed his arm.

"He's gonna call," he said. "You just wait and see."

"Let's have breakfast, okay?" Céline said. She tugged him away from the window and Gaston picked up his cup and walked to the table. Edmund was still in bed. She'd have to wake him soon or he'd be late for school. She heard toenails scrabbling impatiently on the back porch and wondered how the dogs had vacated Edmund's bed that morning without her having heard them, how her son, who was nearly impossible to wake on the mornings he was to go to school, could manage to haul himself out of bed to let the dogs out long before she awoke.

There was no point in trying to talk Gaston out of his anger; fifteen years of marriage had taught her the futility of that. Gaston lived in a world defined by work, no less so than by the apples he raised in his beloved orchard. Acts of nature he could not change were nonetheless acts he bore full responsibility for.

When she was in school, his pride and arrogance set him apart from the other young men who orbited around her. He monopolized her attention (and her lust, although she would hardly admit to it), but those traits of his were also invisible shackles that bound him for days as he railed at constraints he could do nothing about. There was no reaching him then, no talking or reasoning with him. She had learned to ride out his moods as she had learned, under his amused tutelage, to endure the terrifying waters they sometimes encountered on their power boating excursions across the bay.

Eventually, as if he had finally found the door in a dark room, he would emerge into the light of the larger world and pick up where he had left off, no more concerned than as if he had, without a backward look, stepped over a mud puddle. Though she'd lived through it many times, she had no understanding of these transformations.

Gaston stared into his coffee cup while Céline set bowls and a box of cereal on the table. There was no point taking the time to cook something hot when he was running full bore on a project. Gaston tipped the sugar bowl into his cereal and reached for the milk.

"We pulled the forms off three days ago," he said. "I personally inspected every inch of that foundation and it looks just fine. Grey and cured, just like it's supposed to be. Problem is, with frost like this, you know, with a hard frost it can get frozen underneath and that'll cause a little flaking in spots. But like I said, it's all cosmetic. It's gonna get back-filled, anyway. But before that we got the inspection."

"Did you explain all this to him, the doctor?" Céline took a seat and peered at him over her coffee. She poured a few spoonfuls of cereal into her bowl and splashed it with milk.

Gaston snorted. "No. But contingencies and stuff like that, it's all written into the contract. He told me he worked construction in college before medical school, like that makes you an expert on concrete or something. He said he's already got a licensed inspector lined up he wants to use. He's coming out tomorrow and told me I don't need to be there. I guess I'll just head on down to Happy Jacks and sit on my thumb, like all the other professional contractors down there who got people telling them how to do their jobs. I should of waited for something else."

"There wasn't anything else, Gaston."

Gaston finished his cereal and dropped his spoon in the empty bowl with a ping. "So tell me something I don't already know. I

111

thought getting a project like this meant business was picking up. But I might of been jumping the gun on that. I don't know. Guys I'm talking to are still laying off their crews. But then, you know, it's almost winter and work always slows down in winter. You gotta factor that in. So, bottom line is, I don't know nothing about anything. I'm just glad I got any work at all."

"Me too," Céline said. Gaston hooked his hair behind his ears, but several strands came loose and hung limply across his cheeks. She wanted to brush them away, to pull his hair back into the clean and simple ponytail she loved.

"Yeah. Well, me three," Gaston said.

Chapter Ten

THE INSPECTION WAS delayed. Over the phone, the doctor informed Gaston his inspector had suffered a family emergency and had been called out of town for a week and insisted that they were not to begin building until his inspector got back and had a chance to look at the foundation. Gaston's protests that the foundation was fine, that he'd personally inspected it, that they were running out of time, went nowhere. Gaston, his agitation growing but with little else to occupy the day, resumed his bear patrols. In the morning he went to his office in Port Landing and made phone calls and leafed through a stack of trade magazines, but he was home by noon, wearing his impatience like an ill-fitting work coat.

After wolfing down lunch, he took the rifle from the pegs above the back door and disappeared into the orchard, Cloud scampering happily at his heels: the tail to Gaston's sturdy kite. Breeze, more interested in rabbits than bears, was content to remain on the back porch awaiting the school bus that deposited Edmund at the end of the driveway. Gaston returned shortly before dinner, having not seen a bear, having not seen bear tracks or bear scat or sign of any denomination, yet certain nonetheless that he would see a bear soon because the nights were cold and experience told him they would come. But they did not.

"At least Cloud's getting some exercise," Céline said.

Gaston had to agree. The black Border collie was a wonder. "That Cloud dog never stops moving," he said. "It's like that Energizer Bunny thing on TV. Like he's hunting for something. Every now and then he'll stop and growl and run off into the trees, like there's something there that he can smell but I can't see. I keep thinking he's gonna flush something out, but he never does. Maybe a bear. A bear would pay for all that dog food I've been buying for him." Gaston had finished his sandwich in three bites and now was rifling through the coats hanging in the hallway. He found his heavy work coat under several summer-weight windbreakers and put it on.

"Have you ever noticed how much that dog loves you?" Céline said.

Gaston stopped, then turned and grinned. "Everybody loves me," he said. He zipped his coat and smirked.

"No, I mean, Breeze is Edmund's dog. Edmund is who she's chosen. Cloud has chosen you. It's his gift, Gaston."

Gaston thought about that. Then he said, "I had a dog when I was a little kid, just for a while. Did I ever tell you that?"

"I don't remember," Céline said. This was true.

"Well, I did. It was a pretty good dog, a Border collie just like the two we got now. It was black. I wanted a dog like every other kid does but Papa was always … Papa was running around, so Grand-père bought it for me. Kind of pissed off Maman. She was like you, didn't like the hair all over the house, so I had to keep it in the barn, just like you again. I had it three months and it got hit by a car, right down there on the road in front of the house."

Gaston thrust his chin toward Port Landing, toward the memory.

"This was back in the late seventies, back when there was *no* traffic on that road. There's not much now, but back then it would be days before we saw another car. And this guy was coming up to see Papa for something or other and he ran over my dog. He wrapped his coat around it and threw it in the trunk and brought it up to us. He felt real bad, but not as bad as I felt. I kept looking at the blood all over the coat, I remember doing that. Like maybe if I wiped it off I could put it back in my dog. I was maybe what, five or six? I can still remember that, for some reason. I still think it's weird that the only car on that road all day was the one that killed my dog."

Céline clutched her bare arms across her chest. She'd nudged up the thermostat a week ago—she knew exactly how far she could go before Gaston complained about the heating cost running up their utility bill—but it was still chilly, and she was not yet ready to surrender the brief Wisconsin summer by retreating into one of her hand-woven sweaters. She sidled over to a floor vent and felt the delicious flow of warm air around her legs.

She couldn't remember if Gaston had told her about his dog. *His* dog. That pronoun was hard to reconcile within the emotional parameters of Gaston's life, a life she had probed, analyzed, dissected and acquiesced to for nearly eighteen years. Gaston seemed to have minimal interest in animals other than the deer he shot on his occasional hunting trips. Even her horses, which he had bought for her and willingly helped care for on her biannual trips to visit her mother, were fed and watered reliably and efficiently but with no more emotional attachment than if he were changing the oil on the company truck.

Early in their marriage, it had bothered her that he didn't love her horses the way she did, that he couldn't see how special and unique they were, but she had learned that he could not, and so was reconciled. She understood this not as a failing in her husband, but as something he could not access, in the same way those who are colorblind are unable to see red or green. But now there was a long-ago puppy that her husband, in his childhood, had loved in the same way Edmund loved Cloud and Breeze, in the same way she loved Sir Lancelot and Dutch. She wanted to know more about the love he had felt, the color and the shape of it, whether it was playful like Edmund's love for Breeze or shy like Cloud's devotion to her husband, whether the taste of it could be shared and the light of it seen by anyone other than Gaston. But Gaston was gone, the rifle above the back door gone, and without looking she knew Cloud had fallen in step behind him and would accompany him into the orchard.

* * *

"Do we know a Dr. Gregory Goetting?" Céline asked.

Gaston snatched the envelope from her hands, startling her. She blinked and dropped the rest of the mail on the kitchen table. Then it dawned on her.

"Oh," she said.

Gaston sliced open the flap with his pocket knife and began reading, his lips moving and his brows knitted in a deep, unhappy furrow. He kicked a chair out from under the kitchen table, slapping the letter down hard enough to rattle the salt and pepper shakers. "I *knew* this was going to happen," he said. "I *knew* it."

"Am I privy to any of this?" Céline asked. Dr. Gregory Goetting was the doctor who had hired Gaston to build a summer home.

"He says he wants to put things on hold. Says they found some problems with the foundation he wants to have remedied. I tried to explain to the guy that you can't just throw up a house overnight, especially this late in the year, especially in Wisconsin. He wants it by spring, but if he keeps putting it off it won't get done at all. You can't hang rock or paint or run copper pipe when it's fifteen degrees out. PEX maybe, but not copper, which is what he wants because that's what he used to use when he was supposedly in construction."

Gaston pushed the letter toward her. She picked it up.

"There's nothing wrong with that foundation," Gaston said. "It's just as good as every other foundation I ever poured. What's wrong is our friend the doctor is an idiot."

"But he just wants to put things on hold, right?" Céline knew she was sticking her neck out, knew that Gaston wasn't interested in a positive spin when he got like this. She did the books, but she'd never completely understood the hands-on side of the construction business, although Gaston had built two dozen houses in the last fifteen years. "I mean, maybe that's really all it is. He just needs some more time to figure out it's okay. Don't you think?"

Gaston said nothing.

She'd read somewhere that men retreat into their caves when they're upset, in some book she'd seen about the differences between men and women. But it was true. Gaston's moods had always been

116

unfathomable—when she longed to comfort him was invariably when he pushed her away. He wanted solitude then, time to deal with the impediments to his headlong progress that infuriated him. She thought then, as she had always thought, that it upset him more *not* being able to do something than to do anything else at all, even if it was clearly wrong. Movement informed him, focusing his vigor on a narrow but powerful track, restoring his sense of purpose, easing him out of his black moods and back into the family orbit of her life, where she had learned to bide her time. Yet still she struggled to understand, for rejecting the people who most wanted to help made no sense to her at all. She had even suggested counseling once, but he had laughed at the idea.

She saw none of this in her son. No retreating, no walling himself off from the solace she offered. He certainly had his father's quick temper—it seemed to her a Vaillancourt trait, passed down on the male side of the family—but when Edmund was hurting, he still ran to her. She wondered if he would always be this way, if his future girlfriends, and a future wife, would be able to look into each other's eyes and talk, which was the way it was supposed to be and the very thing she and Gaston were so often unable to do. But nothing was the way it was supposed to be anymore. Until her father died, her parents had still held hands. How many married couples still did that? Did anyone?

She watched Gaston stare out the window, his fingers drumming angrily on the tabletop. How often had they had found themselves right here, within the territorial boundaries of this same familiar table? Its worn mahogany boards delineated their lives. It was here they had discussed the business of building homes and raising apples. It was here they had discussed the death of her father, and in turn, those of both of his parents. It was here he had seduced her in the passionate early years of their marriage; here where Gaston had so often pounded his fists in anger and frustration; here where they had delighted in each other's company; and here where, side by side, they had sat in unyielding silence, too angry to speak. And it was here they had first talked of having a son.

Gaston pushed himself away from the table, rose to his feet and took the rifle from above the door and walked outside. Céline heard Cloud scramble across the back porch. Somehow the dog always knew, always seemed to be there when Gaston was about to embark on a patrol. Gaston put the rifle under his arm and closed the door behind him, quietly, as if to soften the edge of his wrath.

* * *

Edmund patted Breeze on the head and accepted the stick she presented him. The doors on the school bus closed with a sigh, and Edmund began the short walk to the back porch. Just before he hopped on the porch, he heaved the stick into the yard and then dashed inside the house. Breeze trotted to the porch with the stick in her mouth and gazed at the door in resignation. Then, sighing, she let it slip from her mouth and lay down beside it, her chin resting on her paws.

Edmund giggled and tapped the window. Breeze's head shot up and he pulled the curtain across his face.

"You shouldn't do that, you know," Céline said. "Tease her like that. What if she did that to you?"

Edmund rolled his eyes. "Mom," he said, "get a life."

"No, really. It's not very nice."

Edmund nodded and dumped his books on the table. She'd been after him for years to put them on the antique roll top desk they'd bought for him in his bedroom. Instead, he preferred to study at the kitchen table, his colored Hi-Liters and textbooks and iPad strewn from one end to the other. At least she'd finally got him to leave his hiking boots by the back door. She'd had enough of picking up the dried clots of mud that fell from the cleats.

Despite his sloppy workspace, Edmund was a good student, which delighted Céline and mystified Gaston, who professed to not having any idea where *that* particular trait had come from. She'd heard enough of her husband's stories about his less-than-stellar academic career to know it was true. Edmund was good in all his subjects, but he seemed to enjoy art classes the most, at least when there wasn't a baseball game he could play. But Little League had been over for two months, and winter would not be long in coming. Céline glanced at the ominous bank of clouds looming over the far end of the orchard like the distant prow of a ship. Low-slung clouds meant snow. She could feel the change coming, the hard and sharp-edged feel of the air, the faint metallic taste of it on her tongue.

Edmund pulled out a chair and slumped into it, his toes just touching the floor, watching her.

"What?" Céline said.

"There's this girl in school I kind of like," he said. His dark complexion flushed with embarrassment.

Céline clapped her hands. "No! Really? What's her name?"

"Melanie."

"Melanie who?"

"Melanie Aldrich. She sits next to me sometimes, like when we're doing writing stuff. So I think she likes me, too."

"Have you talked to her?"

Edmund frowned. "Sort of. I don't know what to talk about. She kind of just sits there and doesn't say anything."

"Girls can be like that, sometimes," Céline said, nodding.

Edmund studied the top of one of his textbooks, opened it, absently flipped through the pages and then closed it again. He lined it up with the textbook resting beneath it, so that the edges aligned. Céline's eyes were drawn to her son's hands. They were small and strong and darkly tanned. The mornings were cold enough now that he wore gloves to the bus stop, and school kept him indoors most of the day. But, like his father, the tan persisted. She wondered if, like his son, Gaston had ever been awkward with girls, if he'd ever had moments of being less than sure of who he was. She doubted it.

"Maybe you can offer to buy her an ice cream cone," Céline said. "That would be nice. I'll give you the money if you want to do that. It would be like a date."

Edmund flopped a Hi-Liter on the table in disgust. "A date? Mom, you're old. People don't do *dates* anymore. That's, like, from the olden days."

This was news to Céline. Edmund's words stung a little. She was thirty-seven and he might as well have called her a crone.

"So what, then?" she said. "You have to go someplace or do *something*, Edmund. I mean, what do you call it when boys and girls do things together?"

Edmund shrugged. "I don't know. But it's not a *date*, that's for sure. I already asked some people."

"What people? What did they say?"

Edmund shrugged again. "I don't know. Not much. That's why I'm asking you. You and Dad did stuff together back in the olden days, right?"

Céline blinked. Maddeningly, now that her son had put her on the spot, she couldn't think of anything she and Gaston had done back in the "olden days" that would qualify as "stuff." She decided to take a different tack.

"Where does this Melanie live? Have you asked her? Maybe we could pick her up sometime. Is she cute?"

Edmund frowned. "Uh-huh."

"She is?"

"Uh-huh. She's pretty. Tony thinks so too. But Tony already has a girlfriend. At least, that's what he *says*. He says he's going out with Emma Griffith. He says he got to first base."

"*What?*"

"Chill, Mom. That's just what he said. Tony always talks big. You know how he is."

Céline sputtered. "What is this ... this, *first base* business, mister? Could you please explain that to me? Do you even know what you're saying?" Céline felt her temperature skyrocket, as if little streams of lava were surging through her veins and about to explode from the top of her head. She forced herself to take a measured breath, then another, counting to three on the exhalation. All this was happening a little more quickly than she'd anticipated. Too quickly, as far as she was concerned. She glared, her mouth drawn in a thin, unhappy frown.

To her relief, though, Edmund blushed. "I think it means he kissed her or something," he said. "I don't know." He stared at his textbooks.

Céline took another breath and walked to the window. Breeze was lying on the back porch. When the little dog saw her she bolted upright, her tail thumping furiously against the wooden deck. Céline's cellphone rang and she reflexively reached into her pants pocket, then remembered she'd left it on the counter. She walked the long away around the kitchen table, her eyes fixed on her son. The call was from Gaston.

"Don't bring him up here," he said.

* * *

Céline would recall the orchard, the leaves just beginning to turn, and the sky still and blue and cold, the way it was in the waning days of fall before the arctic storms began roaring in off Superior. The silence. That was how it had been. The silence stuck in her head. She had not heard the shots.

"I just killed a bear," Gaston told her. "Cloud is dead. Don't tell Edmund. I don't want him up here. I don't want him to see this." Gaston's voice was urgent, strained.

Céline pressed the phone to her ear, trying to calm herself, trying to make sense of what she'd just heard. Two hours earlier, she'd watched the stout black Border collie happily scamper behind her husband into the orchard. How could he be dead? What had gone wrong? She glanced at her son, then turned away from him and cupped her hand over the phone.

"What happened?" she whispered.

Edmund sensed her panic and rose partway out of his chair, his eyes widening in alarm. Céline snapped her fingers and violently motioned him to sit, then snapped them again, hard enough to hurt, and jammed her finger into the tabletop, but Edmund paid no attention.

"What?" he said.

"Sit down!"

Gaston's strained voice: "What did you say?"

"Edmund's here," she said.

"God, don't tell him," Gaston said. "Don't bring him up here. It's a fucking mess. Don't bring him up here, Céline! Send him to his room or something. I need you up here."

Céline spun away from Edmund and strode into the living room, out of her son's earshot. He tried to follow and again she jabbed her finger at him, but this time, mercifully, he remained. She nodded tersely into the phone, her hand still cupped around the mouthpiece. She would leave immediately. No, Edmund didn't know; she hadn't told him anything. She would leave right now. She slipped the phone in her pocket.

"Edmund," she said, "you have homework to do, right? I want you to finish your homework. Your dad needs help with something and I'll be back in a little while. Can you please do that for me? I bought some cookies; they're in the refrigerator, the oatmeal ones you like, okay?" She stared at him, willing him to agree.

"What's wrong, Mom?" he said.

"Nothing's wrong. Your dad just needs some help with something. I have to go right now so I want you to agree to do your homework while I'm gone. Can you do that for me? Please?"

Edmund made a barely perceptible nod.

"Okay, good," she said. "That's good. I'll be back soon. You know where the cookies are."

* * *

Gaston was waiting for her where he said he'd be: on their property line at the end of the access road, just where it disappeared into the woods. He'd crept along the road and caught the bear raking the rotting fruit off limbs left behind by the pickers because the apples were too difficult to reach or too small to pick or too deformed to sell. The bear lay partially sprawled across the road, its legs extending fore and aft as if death had arrested it in mid-bound, the dog Cloud between its legs, his head matted sticky and black and glistening with blood, his teeth bared in a fierce dying grimace. Gaston was standing in the mud of the road and the mud stuck to his boots. He gripped the rifle in one hand, the hammer back.

Céline stared at the rifle and Gaston released the hammer and then looked at the bear and laid the gun on the ground. He was white.

"He was right there, right in that tree," he said. "I was over here, but I couldn't see him. And then all of a sudden there he was! You see those limbs he tore up—those limbs on that tree right there—he was tearing the hell out of them. I don't know where my first shot went, I know I hit him pretty good but it didn't kill him and he bawled and jumped out and came out after me on a dead run. I never heard a bear sound like that. It was like someone screaming. Like something from hell."

The bear lay with one leg over the dog, blood trickling from its broad snout. Céline wanted to drag Cloud out from under it, to remove him from further harm.

Gaston shook his head. He spoke in a rush, burning off the adrenaline. "You can't believe how fast everything happened," he said. "I jacked in another shell but by then he was about on top of me." Gaston wiped his nose with his sleeve, leaving a red streak across his face like war paint. There was a deep, freely bleeding gash on his chin.

"And then Cloud was there. He came out of nowhere, behind me, maybe. He went straight for the bear's face, he was screaming, that's what it sounded like, I never heard him like that. He hit it and knocked it back some but the bear got his head in its mouth and that's when I shot it again."

Céline listened. She watched the blood from Gaston's chin drip in small, bright spatters on his work coat. She watched the silent blue sky. It was cold, and she'd forgotten her fleece jacket, the one she'd had stenciled with *Vaillancourt Apples* on the back. She began to shiver.

"It might of been me," Gaston said. He wasn't looking at her now. "I might of hit him instead. I shot and they both fell away, you know, but I heard Cloud, I heard him make a little yip like I might of accidentally hit him … it might of been me. I don't know. I shot again and that time I know I hit the bear in the head because it dropped right there where you see him."

"You were defending yourself," Céline said. "Anybody would. It was an accident. No one's going to blame you."

Gaston said something and picked up his rifle and began unloading it and the shells slid from the magazine into his hand and he put them in his coat pocket.

Céline felt the rising heat of anger. Angry at her husband's pointless crusade against bears, angry that he'd allowed the dog to go with him. What harm had the bear done? Scavenging apples they couldn't sell? And now Cloud was dead. How could he not have been aware of the risks? But Gaston was so obviously distraught, so shaken in a way she'd never seen him, that she said nothing. If a discussion were necessary, and she wasn't sure it ever would be, it could wait. Everything could wait.

Gaston put the empty rifle in the crook of his arm. He said he would bring the backhoe up in the morning and bury them. So. That was what they would do. They'd bury the bear and the dog. He began walking back down the access road, Céline falling in beside him. They didn't speak again until they were a hundred yards above the house. Gaston had built a log bench here and she loved to visit the spot to watch the sailboats on the lake and listen to the faint thrum of traffic from town.

"What are we gonna tell Edmund?" Gaston said.

"We could tell him the truth," Céline said.

"That I shot his dog?"

"You don't know that for sure."

Gaston gazed at the lake. He never came here, not in the way she came here, to sit and look at the sailboats. Instead, he was always on his way *to* someplace: the orchard, the forest, a patrol; relentlessly brisk, working things out on his feet, movement burning off his impatience to get on with things. Céline hurried to keep up with her husband as they crossed the property in the growing darkness. Ahead she saw the light from the kitchen. Edmund, she imagined, would be studying at the kitchen table where she'd left him, his legs dangling from his chair, his feet not quite touching the floor.

* * *

It surprised her, in the same unwelcome way her husband sometimes surprised her, that Edmund said so little. He sat between Céline and Gaston on the living room sofa. He asked, quietly, where Cloud's body was. It's almost like he's trying to be polite, Céline thought, not wanting him to be polite for just this once, wanting him to cry out in anguish, wanting to comfort him, to explain Gaston's actions as an impossible situation he had tried to avoid. But Edmund did not ask for explanations. He listened. She'd been prepared for a heartbroken, sobbing boy. Instead, his somber questions left her conflicted and un-settled, uncertain of her role as mother.

Gaston, as if following the example of his son, also said little. Exasperated, Céline finally implored him to speak, wanting him at the least to tell Edmund how sorry he was, wanting resolution. Gaston nodded and looked at his son and then looked off somewhere else. And said nothing.

"Do you want to talk about any of this?" Céline asked, turning again to her son.

Edmund stared at his hands. He'd painted one of his thumbnails with a green Hi-Liter. She hadn't noticed before now.

"You already told me."

"Yes, but, we can still talk, if you want. It's okay if you want to talk about it. We all loved Cloud. We're all going to miss him. Maybe you're sort of in shock right now. Do you want to say something?"

Edmund put up his feet and pushed off the coffee table, wedg-ing himself awkwardly against the back of the sofa, his hands clasped tightly together on his lap.

"Do you think he's cold? I mean, I know it's sort of stupid, but is he cold up there in the orchard all by himself? He's used to sleeping inside." He caught his mother's worried eyes. "In the barn."

Céline didn't know what to say. Was Cloud cold? Cloud was dead. How do you say that to an eleven-year-old? How do you answer such a question?

"I think he's in heaven now, Edmund," she said. "Where all good dogs go. It's always warm in heaven."

"But I don't want him to be cold, is all."

"No, no."

"I just don't want him to be cold, is all," he said again. "I know it's kind of dumb. But he doesn't like being cold. He doesn't have his winter coat grown in yet."

"No, dear, no." Céline squeezed Edmund's hand. Gaston cleared his throat as if to speak but did not speak. He patted Edmund's leg. "Maybe you need to sleep a little," she said. "You'll feel better if you sleep. And you've got school in the morning."

Edmund rose from the sofa and Céline rose too and hugged him. He held her passively, without strength. Then he turned toward his father. Gaston hugged him and thumped him self-consciously on the back.

That night, Céline lay in bed, listening. She heard Edmund's bedroom door open and his footsteps crossing the kitchen and then the door to the back porch open and close behind him. She lay beside her sleeping husband a long time listening in that dark void and when she heard Edmund return it was several hours later and his footsteps were slow and labored.

That morning, he ate his oatmeal and said little and put his textbooks and iPad in his daypack and went to the bus stop. She walked with him. Upon her return, she saw the trail of dried blood across the back porch and the faint streaks of brown blood on the kitchen floor he'd missed with the sponge she kept in the plastic bucket under the sink. She opened the door to Edmund's bedroom and looked inside. She closed the door and called her husband. Gaston answered the phone. Behind him the backhoe rumbled like distant traffic.

"Cloud's not here," he said. "The dog's gone."

"I know," Céline said.

Chapter Eleven

"YOU COULD INVITE Melanie, maybe," Céline said. "Would you like to do that? I can drive her home after the funeral."

Edmund rolled a colored pencil under his fingers. He was drawing a picture of Cloud, which he wanted to bury with his dog in the grave. Céline had encouraged him, hoping it would act as a catharsis. Gaston had taken Cloud's bloodied body from Edmund's room, wrapped it in a sheet and temporarily stored it in the chest freezer in the basement.

"I mean, what if she thinks it's weird, going to a dog funeral? She might think it's funny or something."

Céline supposed it *was* a little weird, but she hadn't really thought about that. She'd been thinking about the party afterward. She'd bought carrot cake and strawberry ice cream. Edmund was going to make a little speech and then they'd eat the cake and ice cream. It would be nice. She'd made Gaston promise he'd be there.

"I think she'd be honored," Céline said. "Lots of people have dog funerals. I'm surprised she hasn't already been to one." She had no idea if any of this was true.

Edmund nodded, unconvinced.

"Do you want me to call Madeline?" Madeline was Melanie's mother, whom Céline had met once during her brief stint as a volunteer at the Port Landing thrift store, which donated its proceeds to a hotline for battered women.

"That would be okay," Edmund said. "But I'm like, what if she doesn't want to go? What if she thinks it's stupid or something?"

"Woulda, coulda, shoulda," Céline said. It was a phrase her mother had used, endlessly, when she was growing up. It didn't really fit but she liked the cadence of it. "You'll never know unless you ask."

"Unless *you* ask," Edmund said.

"Okay, kiddo. You got me on that one."

Edmund had been slow to come around. It had been a week since Cloud's death, and she wasn't prepared for the depth of his grief. Each day after school, he'd go directly to his room, emerging only to eat, saying little, when she called him for dinner. It was only this afternoon that he'd finally taken Breeze and gone for a brief hike in the orchard, which Céline seized upon as a long-awaited sign that he was on the mend. Maybe having Melanie for company would take his mind off his loss. Even the perennially cheerful Breeze seemed pensive and subdued. In the mornings, after she'd walked Edmund to the bus stop, Breeze would disappear into the woods. Exactly ten minutes before the afternoon school bus dropped Edmund at the end of the driveway, she'd reappear again and escort him home. Neither boy nor dog seemed interested in a game of fetch the stick.

Gaston wasn't enthusiastic about the funeral.

"I still haven't told him what happened," he said. "But what would it accomplish? I mean, it was self-defense. The bear was." There was an eight-foot by four-foot patch of freshly turned earth in the orchard where he'd excavated a trench for the bear's rigid body. He made Céline promise not to tell anyone. "Especially the game warden," he said.

Céline had no intention of telling the game warden. She didn't even know who the game warden was. She had no intention of telling anyone anything. She'd found Cloud on the floor beside Edmund's bed after he'd left for school. The braided throw rug Edmund had laid him upon was stiff with the dog's dried blood, and the matted brush he'd used to comb out the dog's matted fur was on the dresser. It scared her. She'd called her husband and then put Edmund's bloody pajamas and sheets in the washer and scrubbed the brown streaks of blood from the wood floor with Pine-Sol and a wet sponge.

But over the next few days, Edmund seemed to come around. He said nothing further about Cloud until Céline suggested the funeral.

It worried Céline that her son wouldn't speak, and out of her torment the thought had come, suddenly and viscerally, that her Edmund had never had to deal with the death of anyone he loved before now. He was in pain, as was his father. Pain manifest in the boy and the man. Gaston's guilt pushed him out of the house to his office in town with his blueprints and trade magazines and his cracked leather tool belt on the hook behind the door. Edmund had withdrawn within, no less removed, as if all that he had been—the happy, talkative boy, the lover of baseball and the drawer of pictures—had been wrapped in his grief and put in a box. Both had abandoned her. But she understood. She would wait.

* * *

It was odd, she thought, that this tree alone should still have leaves. In the forties, Gaston's Grand-père had planted the ancient apple tree of a Wisconsin Department of Agriculture cultivar that had all but vanished. The rest of the trees in the orchard lost their foliage two weeks earlier. Here and there, like flames from a match, yellow leaves still clung tenaciously to the uppermost branches, but most had fallen in a mosaic of translucent color, as if yellow paint had been flung from a giant brush and spattered against the still-green grass below. A solitary sentinel, this tree was protected from the wind by the house and watered by the lawn sprinklers, so the branches had spread unencumbered to take in the light and the moisture and perhaps, she thought, that was why it was able to hold fast to the autumn rapidly passing.

The sun warmed the simple print dress she was wearing, but she sensed the relentless push of winter, the cold patiently awaiting its turn, inexorable.

Gaston stood behind her. Céline saw Melanie shyly take Edmund's hand.

Edmund blurted out the few words she'd encouraged him to write and then he laid the picture he'd drawn on the sheet that wrapped Cloud's body. It was a quiet and thoughtful ceremony, nice, exactly as Céline had hoped it would be. She'd already put the bowls and plates for the cake and ice cream on the kitchen table. They shuffled inside while Gaston backfilled the grave and tamped the mounded soil with his boot. Then he followed them inside, knocking the dirt off his boots with the back of the shovel.

"Thank you for inviting me, Mrs. Vaillancourt," Melanie said. She was wearing braces, the new kind, the ones you can see through.

"Edmund invited you," Céline said. "I was just the one who called your mother. Edmund is a little shy." Edmund's face immediately turned crimson and he cast a furtive glance at Melanie. Good, Céline thought. I can tease him a little.

But he *did* seem better, almost happy. Happy to have said goodbye to his dog in his thoughtful, self-conscious way; secretly happy that Melanie was here, even though she'd yet to see him look at her or hear him utter more than two complete sentences to her; happy to be eating cake and ice cream in the middle of the afternoon, a treat Céline usually limited to a single serving after dinner.

Gaston was sitting quietly at the end of the table, a half-finished bowl of ice cream before him. He'd removed his work jacket to dig the grave, and his shoulders bulged beneath his T-shirt. At least on this day, Céline had hoped he'd find some small thing to be happy about, despite his remorse at having killed Cloud, despite the economy. Gaston had found no further work, leaving him no choice but to rebuild a foundation that would, in a matter of a week or two, have to be postponed until spring, frustrating him beyond anything she'd seen him endure in their fifteen-year marriage.

With no income other than their rentals, Céline had been forced to prioritize their needs: food, clothing, supplements for her horses. They had nearly twenty thousand dollars in their IRA, but she had not insisted on saving more because she had never really believed it would become necessary. There had always been enough money. Nothing in the progression of her life, from being the only child of comfortably well-off parents through schooling at an expensive private college to her marriage into the third generation of an established Port Landing construction firm, had given her any reason to think there would not be enough money forever.

Gaston's killing of the dog, as much as the precipitous collapse of the economy, had skewed the arc of their future. Her assumptions on how things were because that was how they had always been had died with the death of her son's dog, and she had no way of knowing what was to come, only that it would not be what it had always been. Cloud's violent death had redirected her forward momentum, as if she'd been brought up short at the washed-out remains of a bridge. In the past week, they'd buried a bear in the orchard and a timid black Border collie whose courage not one of them had understood. Céline could find no respite from her thoughts: Hundreds of bears were shot each year in Wisconsin, and she knew of no one who hadn't suffered the loss of a dog. Yet she had not foreseen this.

She heard a car pull into their graveled driveway. Madeline had told her she'd pick up Melanie at five o'clock, and she was right on time. She saw Melanie look toward the windows in the living room, her dark ponytail flipped over one shoulder.

"I'll bet that's your mom," Céline said.

Melanie grinned through her braces. "Can I come back again sometime, Mrs. Vaillancourt?" she said. "This was fun. Especially the cake. It was kind of like a birthday party. Edmund said he'd take me on a hike."

She saw her son nod self-importantly. The top of his head barely reached Melanie's chin.

"Maybe you can go hiking in the orchard," Céline said. "Edmund knows it like the back of his hand. It scares me a little, because it's kind of dark and spooky up there. But Edmund will take care of you."

Edmund flushed with pride. "I know how to survive and stuff," he told Melanie. "Dad showed me how. I can build a fire with just one match and I know how to make an emergency shelter, too. You cut down a tree and then you sort of cut the limbs off and make a burrow underneath. He and I did that once when it rained but we were really warm, right Dad?"

Gaston blinked and nodded. "I remember that," he said.

"It's like, you gotta know what you're doing or you can *die* out there," Edmund said. He was very serious. He was directing his

131

speech in the general direction of Melanie, not looking at her directly but rather, talking *at* her, as if he were speaking to the air around her body. "That's what Dad says. It's kind of dangerous for city people. But I've been going out there on my own, for, like, at least seven or eight years? I've had some close calls, too. You probably don't know about those. I mean, I got my dogs with me, but you know."

This was news to Céline. She had no idea her son had such a swashbuckling view of himself. Girls will do it every time, she mused. Gaston had made the same kind of rambling boasts to her when he was twenty.

Madeline knocked on the door and Melanie took her coat from Céline. There were polite hugs all around. Finally, Melanie hugged Edmund, who turned bright crimson once again. He patted her woodenly on the back.

"I'm really sorry about your dog," Melanie said.

Edmund frowned. "It's okay," he said. "I mean, I missed him a lot at first but now I don't very much. He was just a dog. And he chewed on stuff and ate a lot more dog food than the one I still got."

"Well, I'll bet he was a nice dog, anyway. We have a dog and he's a nice dog, too."

"Yeah," Edmund said. "He was. He was a pretty nice dog."

* * *

Céline had never timed it but she didn't need to: She'd winterized their house and yard so many times she knew to the minute how long each chore would take.

She insisted on washing all the exterior windows before installing the storm windows, knowing that she wouldn't have another chance to do so until the following spring. Window washing always took longer than anticipated. No matter how many ways she tried to improve her efficiency, it was still a half-day job. She had once watched a professional window washer effortlessly clean a display window in Port Landing and had asked him about his method, which he had been more than happy to explain. Her technique improved, her windows got cleaner faster, and she cut her ladder time by a third. But it still took time.

Then she'd segue into the job she disliked most: installing the storm windows. What was the old saying about the mechanic's wife never having a car that ran? Gaston had promised for years that he'd replace the windows in their old house, but somehow, the houses he was building for other people always got in the way. Instead, they'd been stuck with the drafty single-pane windows that Gaston's Grand-père had installed in the place, and Céline, tired of freezing during the everlasting Wisconsin winters, had finally shouldered the chore of installing the storm windows herself.

A ladder and raw muscle were requisite. She couldn't budge the huge storm windows that covered the bay windows facing Lake Superior—even Gaston had a hard time lifting them—but she could do the rest of the windows by herself.

The wild card was second-guessing the bitter November storms that blew in off the lake. The weather app on her phone was never right, and being on a ladder in freezing rain was both miserable and dangerous. She'd fallen once already and twisted her ankle, which had kept her off Port Landing's only tennis court for the remainder of that season, and she had no intention of falling off again anytime soon. When it rained, she sat by the fireplace and drank green tea, waiting for the rain to stop. Barring bad weather, however, installing the storm windows was a two-day job.

Rototilling the garden took three hours tops, including breaks for drinks from the ice water she kept in a blue plastic Thermos. Some of her friends were using mulch and forgoing rototilling altogether, but she considered herself a traditionalist and enjoyed working the bare soil with her fingers. She liked the musty, peaty scent of it and the way it clumped in loose balls in her fist and the way it drank in the water from the hose, as if the roots of the tiny plants she'd planted were drawing it into their tiny green veins. Over the years, she'd composted so many kitchen scraps into the loam that her garden now had the loose, arable texture of the rich farmland she'd seen on her high school volleyball tournaments across southern Minnesota.

She would order half a flatbed of alfalfa for Sir Lancelot and Dutch, running the numbers in her head since they could no longer afford the extra cost for bales unused by spring. Edmund was finally big enough to help drag them off the truck and into Gaston's front loader, and she thought it would be fun to watch her son show off the muscles Gaston was teaching him to develop in the basement weight room.

There were bushels of apples to sort and store, which she would make into pies and applesauce and (since there would be far more than her small family could ever use) give away. That people refused to buy apples with the slightest blemish amazed her. The blemished produce from their orchard, even the wormy fruit, was vastly better-tasting than the picture-perfect and stunningly insipid apples they sold at the CostLess grocery store in Duluth. On this, she and Gaston were on the same page. Gaston had said, jokingly, that they should take some of Edmund's paintbrushes and paint over the blemishes and no one would ever notice the difference. The idea had merit.

The storm windows were stacked behind the hay, protecting them from breakage. Edmund followed her into the barn, Breeze prancing at his heels. She'd asked for his help.

Edmund fidgeted, twisting impatiently. He'd been in school and wanted to go for a hike before dark. Couldn't he help tomorrow? He'd be free all day, a Saturday, since it wasn't a school day. She *had* to know how busy he was on school days.

Céline grunted and pulled the heavy single-axle cart she used for garden work out from an empty stall and paused to catch her breath. She'd hitch it to her riding mower, which she'd parked outside. Breeze affectionately pushed her cold snout into Céline's leg, then began exploring the crevices between hay bales, snuffling loudly, hoping to ambush a careless mouse. She paused and stuck her head into the space between two bales and wagged her tail.

"I was kind of thinking *today*," Céline said.

"Yeah, but, Mom, today's Friday. Tomorrow is Saturday. I can help you all day tomorrow."

"Can't you take a hike tomorrow, too? Can't Breeze wait one more day?"

Edmund frowned and squirmed uncomfortably. He was still wearing his daypack. Breeze had returned to his side and was watching Céline's face. It was something she'd always done, this little dog: watching her. As if she were expecting permission, as if she understood what Edmund had asked and was throwing all thirty-five pounds of her weight behind his request. As if she would do anything *but* take a hike in the orchard with the boy she belonged to.

Céline pulled the cart outside and slid the tongue over the mower hitch and dropped it in place, then pushed the latch closed and threaded the locking pin through and yanked on the tongue to make sure it was locked and it was. She thought, I can make him do this. Was he still mourning the loss of Cloud? She didn't know, but you couldn't grieve a dead dog forever.

Tomorrow. Tomorrow she'd make him live up to his promise.

Céline tossed her gloves on the seat of the mower.

"Do you have your raincoat and vest? It says it might rain."

Edmund grinned. "Yes!" he said.

"Then get going before I change my mind." Breeze yipped and bolted toward the orchard, Edmund happily following. She watched them disappear into the trees until boy and dog were lost from sight, until she could no longer hear them.

Chapter Twelve

T HE BOY TALKED to Breeze. He would say things she understood. If he were poking a stick into a muskrat run he would tell her that they needed to trap the muskrat before it squirted past his legs and escaped into the depths of the irrigation lake. The words meant nothing to her, but the sound did. The sound was the sound of the boy making trapping-the-muskrat noises, and she understood then that she was to watch the run for the muskrat.

He was ahead of her. She couldn't see him, but she could hear him and she could scent him. The boy's scent was the air she breathed. Sometimes, when he was out of sight, his scent was gone too, and then she would cast back and forth until her nose found his scent again.

The other two were different. The man's scent was like the boy's, but heavier and richer, almost like the horses in the barn where she sometimes slept. The woman's scent was not like the boy's or the man's. Beneath the floral bouquet that irritated her sensitive nose was a delicateness, a sensitivity and lightness she could feel. She understood people in this way, through the feel of their scent. There was no separation between scent and feel, in the same way there was no separation between sunshine and warmth.

She knew where they were going. She loved these long hikes with the boy, and on the days when he disappeared, after he had stepped through the wheezing doors of the yellow school bus, she would sometimes wander through the orchard on her own, although less so now that her brother was gone. She understood that her brother was gone but she no longer missed him; she still had the boy.

They were going to the irrigation lake. She liked the lake because it was wet and boggy and redolent with the scent of animals: deer, rabbits, squirrels, grouse. Sometimes there were bears, which involuntarily made the hair on the back of her neck bristle. Scent told her what kind of animals they were and when they'd passed and if they were still close enough to chase. She liked chasing the rabbits and deer past the boy so he could throw his spear at them, but sometimes she'd get so caught up in the pursuit that she'd run out of earshot and then, when she had lost what she was chasing, as she invariably did, she would stop and listen and then anxiously circle downwind until she found the boy's scent again.

She watched him take off his daypack. They were not yet at the lake. She pricked her ears forward and trotted to him, her tail flicking back and forth. The boy usually had something in his daypack for her to eat. He grinned and took a swig from his water bottle, enjoying her impatience. Then he shoved his hand into his daypack and rustled it around and withdrew it. She thrust her nose into his hand but there was nothing there and the boy laughed. He thrust his hand into his daypack again and once more she found nothing in his hand. She barked impatiently and pinned her ears back, growling in mock ferociousness. The boy howled with delight.

Finally, he unzipped a side pocket and pulled out a Ziploc bag bulging with crackers and smoked salmon, then carefully placed a square of salmon on the cracker before making her take it gently from his fingers. She loved his teasing but the anticipation was more than she could bear and when her nose was within two inches of the prize she lunged for it. The boy tried to yank his hand away, but the food fell into the grass and she gobbled it down, then searched his face for more, her tail wagging with excitement. The two of them had been playing this game since she was a puppy.

The boy was talking to her again.

"This is a pretty cool place," he said. He sat cross-legged in the dappled sun beneath a maple tree, a few hundred yards into the forest above the orchard. "We could camp here overnight if we had to. We could have a fire and everything. But Mom would worry. Mom doesn't like camping

very much. Dad says he thinks she doesn't like sleeping in the dirt." He had propped his daypack between his knees and loosened the toggle that cinched the top closed. His pants were flecked with bits of grass and dirt. In reluctant deference to his mother's concern that it was getting colder, he'd stopped wearing his shorts the week before.

The dog studied his face, her head cocked to one side, her ears pricking forward with each inflection in his voice. He was making contented sounds and because of that, she was content, too. Now he was pulling things out of his daypack. A baseball glove. A raincoat. A wool stocking cap.

"It's kind of chilly up here, don't you think?" the boy said. "Goddamn straight it is." He put the stocking cap on and put the glove beside him and lay on his side, his head on the glove and the raincoat thrown over him like a shawl. When he lifted up a corner and called to her, she darted underneath, curling up against his chest in a cozy, warm ball. The boy threw his arms around her and slept.

* * *

With a final tap, Céline wedged the storm window in place and laid her work gloves palm to palm, as if in prayer, on the paint tray of the stepladder. She met Gaston in the driveway dragging a pair of plastic buckets filled with concrete tools out of his truck. His Carhartt jacket was unzipped and beneath it his T-shirt was clean and unwrinkled. He was frowning and he set the buckets under the deck and kicked them against the wall.

"I'll get to these later," he said. "I sure as shit don't need them now."

Céline felt her insides draw closed, as if they were pulling away from her chest.

"What, Gaston? What happened?"

Gaston walked into the front yard, toward Lake Superior quiescent and gray beyond the Apostles and Chequamegon Bay and Port Landing in the near distance. Hardwoods shone yellow and maroon and orange and shed their leaves in sedimentary color beneath partially barren limbs. But across the lake the horizon was shrouded in clouds; the forecast called for rain.

Gaston, swearing, kicked at a stone. The stone skipped a few times toward the road and rolled to a stop.

"It's Murray!" he said. "The son of a bitch can't even paint a straight line and now he's a foundation inspector?" He walked to the truck and yanked his ball cap off and threw it in the bed in disgust. The elastic band holding his hair back snapped and his hair fell across his eyes and shoulders. He shoved it violently out of his face.

Céline didn't understand. "I thought Murray was a painter," she said. "The guy that was looking in our window? That Murray?"

Gaston snorted. "Apparently there's not enough painting work going around," he said. "He got himself hired as a private inspector out of Ashland. I wouldn't hire that idiot to inspect a doghouse. But guess what, Céline? Oh, you're gonna love this. Goetting hired him to inspect the foundation. And guess what again? He says it's flawed. Says it was too cold when we poured it and it's flaking off. Goetting wants me to pay for it."

Céline slowly lowered herself to the ground and hugged her knees to her chest. She stared at Gaston's legs, at the threadbare spots across the creases of his work pants that had nearly worn through two layers of reinforced fabric and the patches she'd stitched on top of the creases. She put her head to her hands and closed her eyes, then gazed up at him.

"We already took out a loan on that. We can't."

"I know."

"Did you tell him? Dr. Goetting? I mean, it's in the contract, what happens in case they change their mind like that."

Gaston stared over her head. He closed his hands into fists and then snapped them open, his fingers spread wide, as if reaching for something. "He took it to his lawyer. I didn't have any choice. He put in these bullshit contingencies. I didn't like them but I figured, you know, nothing like this was ever gonna happen. It never has before. We needed the money."

"What were the contingencies?"

"Does it matter?"

Céline lay back, the gravel beneath her back sharp and uncomfortable through her heavy canvas coat. It struck her, incongruously, that she'd never seen the sky in exactly this way before, from her back in the middle of the driveway. She'd lived in this home with Gaston for fifteen years and never once lain on her back in the driveway in exactly this position. One side of her view was framed by the house, the other by the spruces lining the road below the house. She rolled upright and saw a spark of lightning dart from beneath the clouds creeping over the top of Basswood Island, but there was no sound, no distant report of thunder.

"I'd pound the shit out of him if I could get my hands on him," Gaston said. He had begun pacing. "Really, I would. There's nothing wrong with that foundation and you and I both know it. Foundations flake all the time in freezing weather. Doesn't hurt a goddamn thing. But Goetting's a fool. He believes everything Murray tells him. Murray, the peeping Tom." His face was dark with rage.

"Gaston, if he stiffs us on that foundation we won't have enough to finish the house. We're maxed out at the bank. You know what Jorgenson said."

Gaston glared, his lips set in a thin, angry line. He thrust his hands in his jacket pockets. Céline saw the folds in his jacket crease as he clenched his fists. Rage worked through him like sediment rising to the top of a boiling pot of water. Woe to those nearby when it boiled over.

"We have just enough for Edmund's school supplies," Céline said. "If it weren't for the rentals we'd have to sell out. We've used up just about everything in our IRA. We missed last month's mortgage payment."

"I know all that."

"But Gaston, it's …"

"I know all that! Goddamn it, Céline, I know all that!" He spun around to face her. "What happened to all the money we used to have, would you just tell me that? We're spending a hundred and fifty dollars a month on hay and grain for your horses. The dog and the chickens are another fifty. That much didn't used to matter, remember? I mean, it was chump change. Now we aren't gonna get paid what we got coming for work I already did in good faith. I barely got enough to meet payroll this month, and then what? What happened to the money from the harvest? I don't get this. I don't get any of it. I'm gonna have to shut it all down if we don't get paid for that foundation. The business, the rentals, the orchard, everything. We'll have to do a Chapter 11 or something. I don't know what else to do." It had begun raining over the Apostles. From their farm it looked like a gray curtain drawn over the backdrop of the world.

"I can get a job in town. A full-time job. That would help."

Gaston was silent.

"I will, Gaston. I don't want to leave. We can't leave."

Gaston walked to the truck and leaned over the hood and buried his face in his arms. He wiped his eyes and heard his son's voice and gazed at the orchard. Edmund emerged from the trees wearing his raincoat, Breeze prancing beside him with a stick in her mouth. She spit the stick at his feet and without breaking stride he bent over and hurled it away. The game she loved. Breeze was on it in an instant. Edmund waved at them and disappeared behind the house. They heard the porch door close and then Breeze was bouncing toward them, her tail wagging. She spied Céline sitting in the driveway and thrust a wet nose into her shoulder. Céline pushed her away and Breeze playfully slapped her arm with her paw.

"No," Céline said.

Breeze whined and thumped her tail.

"No."

Chapter Thirteen

I T WAS IMPORTANT for Edmund to understand why she was asking. "You're old enough to start paying for some of your own stuff," Céline said, irritated at her own nervousness at broaching the subject. "So, it's like, this is one way you can do that. You have those old baseball gloves and bats, from when you were little. You can sell those. And those old fishing poles in the basement? You haven't been fishing in years. They're taking up room and you can make a little money from them, maybe."

Edmund appeared unconvinced. "I was planning to get back into fishing," he said. "Like, next summer. I was really thinking about doing that."

"Okay, kiddo." Céline sighed. She had anticipated this. "But I'm going to be selling all of my old stuff, too. We just can't afford to keep it around. Mom doesn't have a job in town anymore."

"What happened to that marketing thing you were doing?"

"If people aren't making widgets, there's nothing to market, Edmund. That's the way the business world works." Céline had been given a month's severance pay and she supposed she was grateful for her former employer's thoughtfulness, who had been under no obligation to give her anything. But now, even the loss of her small salary was eroding their finances.

"What's a widget?" Edmund asked.

"Forget widgets," Céline said. "We have to simplify. That's going to be the new Vaillancourt motto: *Simplify*."

"I like the old Vaillancourt motto better: *Buy lots of cool stuff*."

Céline grinned and tried to poke him in the ribs, but he grabbed her fingers and twisted them gently. She had no idea if he'd round up all the childhood toys he had long ago abandoned, the clothing he'd grown out of that was taking up space in several closets, the forgotten spin-casting rods and BB guns Gaston had bought him, and all the other things he'd accumulated in eleven years of being a boy, but maybe that was asking too much. She herself would not have done so at his age. She'd have to collect it herself.

"You do it or I do it," she said. "I'm serious about this. If you do it, you can figure out what you still want that's important. If I do it, I'm going to sell everything I get my hands on." She sighted down her finger like a rifle and pointed it at his nose.

Edmund frowned. "I want a trial by a jury of my peers," he said.

Céline's eyes opened wide. "Where did you learn that?"

"In Mr. Duchateau's civics class. You made me take it, remember?"

She recalled that she *had* made him take it. But a jury had nothing to do with having a garage sale; garage sales were decided by executive fiat. There was simply no need to accumulate a house full of junk they would never use. But she was just as bad as any of them when it came to hoarding junk. She had closets full of cocktail dresses she hadn't worn in years. Where would she wear a cocktail dress in Port Landing? And that was assuming she could get Gaston to attend an event that *required* a cocktail dress. The last time she remembered him putting on a tie was for their wedding reception. Well, at least she wouldn't have to worry about getting rid of a closet full of suits he didn't own.

"But Mom, what if it turns out I need that stuff later on? Why do we have to simplify? I don't even know what that's supposed to mean. I mean, I know what the *word* means, I just don't know why we have to."

Céline tapped her fingers on her knee. Breeze was on the back porch, pawing impatiently at the door, and Edmund was anxious to begin another hike. With winter moving in and nights dropping below freezing, his yearning to spend the last few hours of daylight in the woods seemed to her to border on obsession. She didn't understand either of these men, the big one she'd married and the little one she'd given birth to, who both seemed to get inordinate joy from mucking around in cold, dirty places surrounded by potentially dangerous animals. Gaston insisted that black bears rarely attacked humans, but what about the one he'd just shot? And what about skunks and coons? Skunks and coons got rabies, she knew that much. She'd finally arrived at an uneasy stasis: She would allow herself to trust her husband's assurances that Edmund would be fine, or that, in any event, he could take care of himself, because Gaston told her he had done exactly the same things at exactly the same age.

He was so much his father's son. She gazed at him. Already his shoulders were broadening, and with the dark eyelashes and square chin—so like Gaston's, that strong chin—was she wrong to believe he would become a handsome young man? Edmund would never be tall, but then, neither was Gaston, and that had never bothered her.

Even the way her son argued, the clumsily pedantic way he tried to explain to her that he couldn't possibly be wrong, reminded her of Gaston. There was a time when Edmund had done everything she'd asked of him, but that was before he'd begun growing ... *shoulders*. It occurred to her that she could just skip it all and have the garage sale without his help. Any upward tick in their finances would be small, no matter how much they netted. Things had gone from bad to worse. After a tense exchange with Dr. Goetting (she'd begged Gaston to let her act as an intermediary, knowing how quick he was to anger), he was now threatening to sue. But the truth was that even if they lost, they were in no danger of living on the street. They could stretch the income from their rentals to cover the mortgage and there would still be enough to keep food on the table.

She pushed herself out of her chair.

"Some things you just have to do, Edmund. It's called being a grown-up."

Edmund rolled his eyes.

Céline wanted to shake him. "You look at me when I talk to you, mister!" she said. "We've got rules around this place that everybody has to follow, including you. Got that?"

Edmund frowned. "Whatever."

She glared at him, but Edmund refused to meet her gaze. He stared over her head, bored, his lower lip jutting out in defiance.

"Did you hear what I said?"

"Yes."

"Is that clear, then?"

"Yes."

He was infuriating. She wanted to slap his smart-aleck mouth, but he had, ostensibly, agreed to her terms.

"Okay," she said, dismissing him with a curt wave. "Be back by dark, understand? It's supposed to snow and I don't want you out there in a blizzard. No later than dark."

Céline caught his eyes as he slung his daypack over his shoulder. They were resentful and angry. She thought: so much like his father.

* * *

There were so many tools here: shovels, leaf rakes, hoes, garden rakes, dandelion prongs, pruning shears, axes, grain shovels, mauls. She examined them one by one, unsure which to sell. Two ancient come-alongs and a tamping bar she could barely lift. A huge anvil, three Disston hand saws (rusting and dull) and a blue coil of PEX. How had they accumulated all this stuff? She examined them one by one and decided that she'd sell the rusted ones, since the unblemished ones would theoretically still be in use. That would leave at least two of everything else, certainly more than enough. She wouldn't ask for Gaston's input. He kept his job-related construction tools locked in the back of his truck and visited the tack room only sporadically.

She heard one of her horses nicker and put the shovel she had been examining against the wall and walked out of the tack room and over to the stall. The open end of the stalls faced the interior of the barn, and the horses were craning their necks over the top rail of the fence watching her, their ears pricked forward in happy anticipation. The moment he saw her, Sir Lancelot nickered again.

Céline loved the sound of her horses, loved their sensitivity and strength, loved the warm sweet sweat on their backs after a ride. In the gated subdivision in which she'd grown up, her family had not been able to own livestock, but she'd begged her mother to take her to the stable across town, and when her parents bought her a car on her sixteenth birthday, she spent her free time after volleyball practice encamped at the stable, happily lunging horses and cleaning stalls in exchange for riding lessons.

Now she barely rode at all. She didn't know why. She thought maybe she had become too busy but she knew that wasn't true. She still loved the thought of it, the view from the back of a horse that was so markedly different from the view on the ground; the thrill of letting Sir Lancelot run on the gravel road below the house; her control over a gentle beast so infinitely more powerful than she. She hadn't ridden in months, maybe longer. Sir Lancelot nipped her sleeve, gently, the way he did when he wanted attention. He pinned his ears back when Dutch tried to shoulder him aside, wanting attention, too.

She didn't know when she'd ride again. As a newlywed, before Edmund was born, she'd ridden almost every day. Gaston had been building the business and was rarely home before dark so she rode, often in the orchard, and, when she was feeling confident, would sometimes make brief forays into the dense woods beyond. She had a poor sense of direction, unlike Gaston, who could find his way home blindfolded, but she trusted her horse if she became lost. She'd read that a good horse could do that, that in the west the pioneers who had been caught in blizzards had turned loose the reins and their horse had found the way home. But she'd never been caught in a blizzard and had never ventured into the woods far enough to become lost.

But mostly she had ridden in the orchard. Before the storms knocked them to the ground earlier in the month, she could, from the back of her horse, reach the apples the pickers had left at the top of the trees, and it seemed to her that those apples tasted especially good, stolen from the sun in which they'd been left to sweeten. She always put two or three in her coat pockets as a treat for both horses at the end of the ride.

She didn't know when she would do that again.

The horses had never been at the forefront of Gaston's thoughts the way they were in hers. She had always supposed he liked them well enough, in the same way he liked Cloud well enough or the way some people liked their tractors well enough, useful adjuncts to a rural life that merited the cost of ongoing maintenance.

But the price of hay and grain was going up. Vet bills were infrequent—thank god for her horses' good pedigrees—but the last trip to the veterinary clinic for an inflamed tendon in Dutch's leg had required overnight boarding and had left her with a bottle of expensive anti-inflammatories and a bill of nearly nine hundred dollars. Once, nine hundred dollars would not have been much money, but now it was. When the housing market was booming, when they'd been too busy to accept all the jobs they'd been offered, nine hundred dollars was nothing. But now it was.

Sir Lancelot nuzzled her pocket, begging for a treat. She stroked his face and gently pushed him away. The horses' bridles hung on brass pegs beside the stall; Dutch's tan bridle on the left and Sir Lancelot's black bridle on the right. They'd been handmade for her by a saddle maker in Montana with carved latigo browbands and braided elk-leather reins that were very elegant and expensive. Maybe she could sell those.

Céline walked to the window. It was still nice out, a November afternoon, clear and warm like cider, with no sign yet of the snow that had been forecast for later that evening. How long had it been since her last ride? She put her hands on her hips and turned toward Sir Lancelot and Dutch, a teacher addressing her class.

"Well," she said. "Should we go for a ride? Would you like that? Which one of you wants to go for a ride?"

The horses stared at her happily; their ears pricked forward, their eyes open and wide and happy. Dutch nickered under her breath and Sir Lancelot pinned his ears back and nipped her neck. Dutch swung her head away from him.

"Okay, big boy, I guess we're going to have it your way," Céline said. She took his bridle from the wall and opened the door to the stable and stepped inside.

* * *

Maybe it was too late for a yard sale. Summer was the season for yard sales, but she'd set the wheels in motion with her conversation with Edmund, although Edmund had really never come around. After an indifferent effort to round up his abandoned childhood toys, he'd dumped the few he'd gathered in the cardboard box she'd supplied and disappeared out the back door, his daypack over his shoulder and Breeze at his heels.

Well, then. He'd been warned. And if he didn't like the fact that she planned to sell the things he no longer used? Maybe he'd be a bit more proactive next time around. Tough love.

She did feel obligated to give Gaston an accounting of the garden tools she planned to sell, but his anger at the rejection of the foundation had finally given way to a dispirited resignation, and he merely shrugged and waved her away. Even suggesting that they sell the anvil—a prize he'd found at an auction, years earlier, but never used—merited no objections. The anvil didn't matter. The garden tools didn't matter. The garage sale would be up to her.

She set the date for the upcoming weekend and went to work. She wheeled out the clothing racks she'd stored in the basement and began methodically sorting and hanging clothing she'd collected from the two walk-in closets upstairs. It didn't strike her until she was nearly finished that she'd arranged a kind of sartorial history of her marriage. On one rack, she'd hung her dresses from her early twenties, when she and Gaston had been newly married, before the arrival of Edmund. Here were cocktail dresses, evening gowns and the occasional business suit, many in black or red, which showed off her olive skin and blond hair. On another she'd hung clothing from her early-childcare years, when Edmund had been a toddler: maternity dresses as well as the Carhartt work clothes she used for gardening and harvest. A final rack held the clothing she'd bought in the hectic years prior to the recession, when Edmund's upkeep had no longer been a daily ritual: designer jeans and the simple, elegant tops she favored for the rare but relaxed Port Landing social functions she and Gaston had once attended. In a separate cardboard box, filled to the brim below a sign that read *$15.00 Per Pair*, were her old shoes, each secured to its mate with a wire tie, from the thin stiletto heels she'd worn in her twenties to the shorter, more sensible pumps she would favor a decade later. There was enough clothing here, Céline thought, to supply an army. Until she'd been forced to sort through it all, she'd had no idea she had so much.

She carefully arranged Gaston's tools in a circle around the apple tree in the back yard, ringing the trunk in a garland of wood and painted steel and shovel blades speckled with orange rust, then stepped back to study the overall presentation, which she decided looked good, certainly as good as the display in the hardware store downtown, although such artistry would of course be entirely lost on the men who were in the market for tools like these.

She put the horses' saddles on racks under the porch overhang in case it rained and hung their bridles from the corresponding saddle horns. These she couldn't bear to sell at giveaway prices, so she marked them at what her research on the internet told her they were worth.

There were many more things she found to sell: cooking utensils and paintbrushes and a badminton set (in an unopened box) and the anniversary gifts that she no longer wanted or had never used. She sold what she could of Gaston's and Edmund's forgotten possessions, giving consideration to each, wanting to be fair.

She had no real idea how much she would net, but it appeared that it would be several thousand dollars if even half the stuff artfully displayed on racks and stacked in neatly arranged cardboard boxes went to new homes, enough to pay the bills for at least the next two months. At the end of the day, she put an ad on Craigslist and took out a brief ad in the *Port Landing Dispatch* just in case, and among the items to be sold she listed: "Fashionable women's dresses—nice! Garden and shop tools, boy's toys, furniture, custom tack, livestock."

* * *

On Saturday morning there was a stream of cars and trucks driving up the road below the house. Gaston stood on the porch and drank from a cup of coffee as he watched them, then walked back inside.

"I see at least six," he said. "That's six already and we're not even supposed to start until eight. You lucked out on the weather."

The forecast called for clear skies with highs in the low sixties. Céline had checked it a half dozen times, nervous that all her work would be for naught if it rained, but it was, by any reckoning, a perfect morning for a garage sale.

"Are you coming out? They may have questions about your tools and stuff."

Gaston sipped his coffee and shrugged. "Yeah."

Céline felt a jolt of irritation at his offhand response, but decided to let it pass. There would be people in their yard all day long. She told Edmund to put a leash on his dog. Breeze was so friendly she would be in everyone's way and Céline didn't want anyone to be distracted from their shopping experience, which is how she'd jokingly begun to refer to the garage sale: the Vaillancourt Shopping Experience.

By ten o'clock the driveway was packed with cars. Breeze was running amuck; after keeping her on a leash barely an hour, Edmund had turned her loose and she'd spent the morning scampering from one person to the next, pushing her wet nose into the backs of knees, presenting herself for a scratch behind the ears, her eyes wide with excitement. To her relief, Céline saw that nearly everyone enjoyed the attention of the little dog. She was too busy to do anything about her anyway.

She'd taken a thousand-dollar advance from her Mastercard; there hadn't been enough money in their checking account to cover the change they'd need for the stream of transactions she anticipated. Now she wondered if she'd have enough money as float to get her through the entire day.

Gaston wandered among the racks of clothing and other paraphernalia Céline had assembled, talking to the men he knew, occasionally picking up an item to look at the price before putting it back again. A man in grease-blackened overalls swung out of his pickup and walked directly to him and Céline heard the man ask about the anvil. Gaston led him to her.

"He wants to know how much the anvil is," he said. "There's no price tag."

"I'm thinking eighty bucks," Céline said. "I looked it up and that's about a third of what they go for new."

"Eighty bucks," Gaston said, facing the man. The man hooked his thumbs under his suspenders and stared at the lake. Then he reached into his back pocket for his money clip and unfolded four twenties. Céline took the money and thanked him. She glanced at Gaston's face but his countenance revealed nothing, as if the anvil were no more nor less than the inanimate tool it was, of no more significance than the shovels ringing the apple tree in the back yard, no more precious for having been forged in the last century. He offered to help and the two of them carried the anvil to the man's waiting truck.

By late afternoon the stream of people had dwindled to a handful of women picking through the few items that remained. Céline's dresses had been snatched up in the first hour. All of Gaston's tools had sold as well. There were still a few pairs of shoes in the cardboard box; to her surprise the stilettos had been the first to go. Alone among the racks of clothing and tools and tack that Céline had carefully arranged, Edmund's toys remained largely untouched. Toys were subject to the whims of childhood fantasies that rarely endured from one generation to the next.

Céline heard the rumble of a truck on the road below the house. Her heart leaped in her chest remembering the call she'd got the evening before. The truck was towing an old horse trailer. She knew who it was and she sat in a lawn chair and waited. When the truck pulled into the driveway she took a breath and remembered to smile as she walked out to greet them.

The man and his wife were about her age and the woman's eyes shone with excitement. The man put his hand on his wife's arm and said, "Wait just a minute, okay? We need to talk first."

"No, it's okay," Céline said. "She can see them if she wants, they're in the barn." The woman squeezed her husband's hand and dashed away.

The man grinned.

"She's never had a horse," he said. "She's a little bit excited, I guess. I wasn't really planning on two."

"They've been together since they were born," Céline said. "They're like people, they form a bond. They look for each other when they're apart. It would be hard on them to be separated."

"Well, I talked it over with Lauren and we've got room so I came around. We've got about thirty-five acres a hundred miles downstate. I saw your ad yesterday morning and I called and here we are."

"Here you are," Céline said. "You've got a good barn? They need someplace to get out of the snow."

"Yeah. Guy that had our place before us built it. He did a pretty nice job; it's insulated and has gas heat. Prince Valiant and Dutch will like it there."

"Sir Lancelot. Her name is Duchess; Dutch for short." Céline glanced over the man's shoulder, her eyes shining. The trailer was old but well-kept. She had hoped to see something like this; a trailer that was well cared for.

"My mistake," the man said. "Well, listen. Will you take a check? It's good, I haven't bounced one in a week." He grinned. He seemed kind, the kind of person she could feel good about selling her horses to.

Céline nodded. A check was okay, a check would be fine. "I'll help you load up," she said. "They're easy loaders, but they don't know you yet."

"Would you? I'd really appreciate it. I'm kind of new to all this horse business. Lauren, she grew up riding but never lived anywhere she could have horses of her own until we got married and bought our place last year. God, it's all she ever talks about. Sometimes I think she married me because I bought her a horse property."

Céline nodded and thought about making a joke about men buying the women in their lives horses but didn't and made a little smile and then nodded again. The man lowered his eyes.

"Well," Céline said. "I guess I'll go get them." She walked to the barn and led out Sir Lancelot and Dutch on separate leads and loaded them one by one into the back of the old trailer. The inside had been hosed out and swept clean and fitted with trailer mats, which were good. Good quality mats weren't cheap but they were easy on the horse's legs. Lauren would know this. She backed away from the tailgate and swung it closed and threw the latch.

She saw the top half of Sir Lancelot's face in the open window, his eyes wide with anticipation, happy as he always was to be embarking on another road trip. Her big boy. Céline stood on the wheel housing and tried to reach through the window to stroke his nose, but the window was partially closed and she couldn't reach him.

"You be good," she whispered, pressing her face as close to the open half of the window as she could, so close that the man and woman couldn't hear. "Be a good boy for these nice people. I'll come and visit, I promise." But Céline knew it wasn't true, she would never see Sir Lancelot and Duchess again, and when the trailer pulled away she turned toward the house and found Gaston awaiting her in the yard, uncertain as to what had transpired, uncertain as to what he could offer in comfort.

Chapter Fourteen

THE MONEY FROM the garage sale alone would provide, at best, a respite from their rapidly dwindling income, covering their expenses for perhaps another two months. She wished now she had asked more for almost everything. Gaston's tools had sold so quickly that she realized she'd underpriced them, but by then it was too late and he hadn't seemed to care one way or another. There were still a few tools left in the barn, and it occurred to her she could have put those up for sale, too. Now, with her saddles and bridles and halters and blankets gone, all that she'd owned and loved in the service of horses, the tack room seemed sterile and without purpose or support, as if, in the absence of Sir Lancelot and Dutch, it had exhaled a final breath and then collapsed in upon itself.

For a week, she could not bear to go near the barn and when she finally did, it was only to see and to remember. For over a decade she had lived in the periphery of her horses, their great, warm presence in the corral and stalls, their puppyish delight whenever she entered the barn. She had lived within their happy anticipation of her visits and their gentle devotion, but now they were gone. When she had been offered thirty-five hundred for both animals she'd accepted without argument. They were worth far more. But the thought of negotiating the price seemed almost profane, as if she were bidding on the value of love.

They needed the money. Edmund was back in school and school cost money and thirty-five hundred would see them past the first of the year, less than two months away, and then the garage sale money would kick in. By then Gaston would certainly have the foundation problem solved and perhaps even another project lined up for spring. So maybe it was not such a big thing to sell a horse; no more than selling the tack that was part and parcel of the animal. But she had never thought that, having owned horses, she would ever again be without them, or how empty the stables felt without horses to lend them warmth. She sat on a bale of straw in the corner and buried the toe of her running shoe in the duff.

This unused corner of dusty straw was supposed to be Breeze's and Cloud's bed, but it hadn't been slept in for weeks. She had intended to say something about the dogs sleeping with Edmund, but after Cloud died she hadn't had the heart. She still had no idea how he got her in and out of his room each night without waking her, but the back door was far enough away from their upstairs bedroom that she might not have heard him creep across the kitchen to let her in.

She wished, abruptly, that she had spent a night in the stable with Sir Lancelot and Dutch, the way Edmund did with Breeze, lying beside them, lulled to sleep by the cadence of the great, deep bellows of their breathing; safe and warm in the comfort of their bodies. The thought was soothing, even if it was too late. She had never before considered any such behavior and hadn't known she'd felt this way until now.

Edmund had told her he talked to Breeze when they were alone and she wondered if it was the way she had talked to Sir Lancelot. Baby talk. *You're a good boy, aren't you? Do you want a treat? I have an apple for you, but you have to share it with Dutch. Can you be a good boy and share?* But that was silly. It didn't matter anymore.

And maybe it didn't matter anymore that she had abandoned two simple, loving beasts whose happiness depended upon her alone.

Céline's eyes stung, and she angrily wiped away her tears on the sleeve of her work jacket. Hadn't their companionship been worth more than thirty-five hundred dollars? Wasn't the warm vapor from Dutch's breath on a winter morning an even trade? Hadn't the safety she felt in the forest, a place she rarely ventured on foot, been worth the protection she felt from her perch on Sir Lancelot's broad back?

Hadn't her horses spoken to her?

Edmund had told her that Breeze spoke to him. She understood that he was speaking metaphorically, though he'd been too young at the time to understand the word. But he had insisted.

Now she wondered. She had often spoken to her horses and she was as certain as Edmund that they had understood her in their own way. Speaking didn't always require words or a linear progression of thought; speaking was the same as knowing; speaking *was* knowing and knowing required only understanding. Knowing did not require words at all.

She had sold them both without speaking to them, without their understanding. Now, too late, she wished for that above all else: for them to have understood.

* * *

Gaston had been lifting for so many years he no longer had to concentrate on proper form, but he took pleasure in routine, charting his weekly progress and adding or subtracting plates accordingly. When he'd married Céline, he sold the budget-priced, hardware-store set of barbells he'd owned since college and bought Olympic bars and nine hundred pounds of cast iron plates, more than he would need in a lifetime of weight lifting. He bought a powder-coated steel squat rack and a massive adjustable bench; kettlebells from twenty to eighty-five pounds; a stiff bullhide lifting belt, and a cake of powdery white chalk to improve his grip.

It took him nearly an hour to drill into the ancient concrete floor of the basement to anchor the squat rack with expansion bolts, but he didn't want it skating around beneath him when he had 280 pounds of iron across his shoulders. He thumb-tacked a poster of human anatomy to the wall next to the rack, and beneath it, on a stout shelf he built from laminated two-by-fours, were his progression charts and several books on muscle development and lifting technique. Opposite the squat rack he lag-bolted a pull-up bar into the wall studs, far enough up that he could hang freely an inch above the ground. Céline, who could reach the bar without jumping, had to fold her legs in order to do a single pull-up, all she could muster. Gaston could do eighteen pull-ups with twenty-five pounds of iron hanging from a strap around his neck.

It was important to maintain the same cadence on successive lifts, so Céline had loaned him one of her aerobic dance CDs and it had worked so perfectly he never gave it back. Different lifts had different cadences: Deadlifts were explosive and quick, but he liked to perform curls slowly, two counts on the concentric and eight on the eccentric, squeezing his biceps at the top of the arc, lowering the weight incre- mentally until his arm trembled and burned with the effort, hungry for the exquisite pain of tearing muscle and lactic acid buildup.

He loved curls and deadlifts and bench presses and even the bru- tally efficient bent-over rows, but he hated squats. Everyone hated squats, precisely the reason they worked so well: They hurt like no other lift but were incomparable for building total body strength.

Squatting under a fully loaded, 280-pound barbell was skating perilously close to serious injury. Each squat was a searing, grimacing exercise in tunnel vision: Focus had to be absolute. Shift your body too far forward or round your back a scant two degrees and you could blow a disc and be done with weight lifting forever. Gaston concen- trated on driving through his heels, feeling the tension shift from the gastrocnemius in his calves through the biceps femoris at the back of his thighs, slam into his glutes and finally scream through the entire chain of muscles in his lower and upper back. It was *supposed* to feel like you were dying, it was *supposed* to hurt.

Now he began: standing under the bar, adjusting it across his shoulders until it was exactly centered, thumbs on top of the bar; then rolling it down an inch so it rested squarely on his trapezius muscles; the easy part. Now. Breathe. Concentrate. Inhale and lift the bar off the pins. Exhale and bend the knees until the bar just touches the safety stop—pausing is resting, and resting is cheating—then explode through the heels to raise it back up again.

The first two or three reps were bad, but by the fifth his legs were trembling so badly he wondered, for the thousandth time, if they would support him. By the sixth rep his mind screamed at him to quit, but he wouldn't quit until he'd reached failure, until his body could no longer muster the strength to achieve what his mind had commanded it to do.

He failed on the seventh rep. That was the point of certainty, the crux of pain, beyond which his will could no longer bear the weight.

Gaston crawled from beneath the bar, huffing in great, heaving gasps, and peered out the sliding glass doors that gave on the front yard. Edmund was playing a game of fetch with Breeze, his baseball glove on, whipping out one of the three dozen baseballs he must have bought the kid in the last five years. Edmund had a good arm, a very good arm, actually. But that dog. The little red Border collie was a pretty fair retriever, but every now and then she'd run off with one of his son's baseballs and stash it somewhere behind the barn, never again to see the light of day. He could no longer afford to buy Edmund an endless supply of Rawlings Official R100 League baseballs at $8.95 a pop, and he planned to tell him that one of these days. Edmund was old enough to buy his own goddamned baseballs.

Gaston felt his strength returning, so he put his shoulders under the bar and, teeth clenched, was just able to hoist it back up to the pins at the top of the rack. He collapsed on the bench and recorded the day's weight on his progression chart, then set it back on the shelf and picked up the opened envelope lying beside it. He pulled out the letter and read it again, as if somehow the words might have changed since that morning when he'd first read it, as if perhaps he had not understood what he understood perfectly well. It was from Dr. Goetting's lawyer. "The inspection by an independent and experienced contractor indicates a dangerously weakened foundation. In the event that a satisfactory solution cannot be reached, we reserve the right to seek all available legal and equitable remedies."

* * *

The apple trees' leaves had fallen, and Céline and Gaston's feet left furrows in the fallen leaves, a hyphenated trail that wound through the orchard along the access road buried beneath. Wizened brown apples clung to the uppermost branches, unwilling to let go and too high for the bears and deer. Céline wondered, again, how many imperfect apples they'd chosen to leave behind.

"I can get another line of credit," Gaston said with little conviction. "They better let me do that." He was still angry. Céline watched his canvas jacket bunch across his shoulders as he pulled down a branch, yanked off the apple at the end of it and flung it into the trunk. It exploded with a wet plop.

Céline said nothing. They had both talked to Jorgenson. They had used up their line of credit building the foundation. What little there was from the rentals was servicing the second mortgage on their home. There was no credit to be had.

She couldn't understand how this had changed and how quickly the change had come. There had been no time in her marriage to Gaston when bank loans hadn't been theirs for the perfunctory price of a signature. She'd been frugal nonetheless—she would credit her Scandinavian heritage for that—but it had been a self-imposed discipline, a way of properly aligning herself with the world she was trying to create for her family, not an imposition. None of that mattered now. Their savings had vanished. They'd tapped all but a couple thousand dollars in their IRA. With Dr. Goetting's foundation stalled, only the income from their rentals was putting food on the table.

"He won't give us any credit." She looked at him.

"Jorgenson."

"Yes. He already said so. He said they won't let him. He said we're already over-leveraged. You remember."

Gaston folded his arms across his chest and glared at the ground. He began walking.

They were into the orchard a good long ways, near the edge of the forest, where the access road diminished and then was absorbed into a bog of white spruce and tamarack and alders growing. Gaston stopped and peered into the trees, the tamaracks yellow and dormant and shedding their needles against the cold. Then he turned and began walking back downhill. Céline followed, shortening her stride to stay in the narrow furrow he left in the brown leaves.

"I might have to talk to Radcliff," he said. Céline stopped but Gaston kept walking. Céline skipped once to get back up with him.

"What about?" She knew what about.

"Things. Business."

"It's about his boat, isn't it?"

"I never said that."

"I know about the boat, Gaston. About the loan. I ran into him that day I took the apples in to get them pressed. He told me. He actually thanked me. I felt like an idiot because I didn't know what he was talking about." She tried to level an accusing glare, but it felt wrong, as if she'd tried to smile at an accident.

Gaston stopped. "You'd had a fit if I told you, right? Go on. Admit it."

"I would have liked to have discussed it with you first."

"Uh-huh. Well, it's for sure done and over with now. For what it's worth, I was trying to help the guy out. But he's supposed to pay me cash at the beginning of every month and then he goes and misses the last three payments. So I might have to repossess it. That's what's in my head right now."

"Gaston, he's got his whole life wrapped up in that boat. You *know* that. How do you know he hasn't got financial problems or something? How do you know he won't pay us what he owes?"

"Because he hasn't," Gaston said.

"No, but ..." Céline stared at the back of her husband's head, at the black hair jutting from beneath his baseball cap. Even in cold weather, Gaston wouldn't wear the thick woolen stocking caps she bought him. He told her they were too hot. He told her his hair kept his ears warm. She'd finally donated them to Goodwill.

Gaston suddenly spun to face her. "Look, Céline," he said. "That was part of the deal. I got it all down in writing. You miss two payments and you pay a penalty and we're even-steven, okay? You miss three payments and you lose your collateral. He knows the rules. He signed the contract. It's all perfectly legal. I'm within my rights."

"But, I mean, did you ask him why? I know that his wife isn't well. Maybe that has something to do with it."

Gaston shook his head, agitated. "That's irrelevant. Listen, Céline, you think I *want* to take his stupid boat away? I've known Radcliff since high school. We played on the same team."

His voice was pitching upwards, the words tumbling into each other. He got this way when he was angry. Loud. Excited. It was like a wall came down, not so much to shut others out, but to shut himself out from the others he didn't want to hear.

Céline squeezed her eyes shut and then opened them. "What are we going to do with his boat?"

"Sell the goddamn thing. I've already thought about that. We oughta get at least eleven, twelve thousand for it. We can put it on Craigslist for fourteen or fifteen, see what the market will bear. There's plenty of guys out there looking for a fishing boat, even in a recession."

Céline didn't like any of this. She gazed downhill, toward their house and barn. The nights had been much colder and any morning now she expected to awaken to snow. But Port Landing and the Apostle Islands beyond were still a patchwork of drab, leafless oaks and dark green pines. Low clouds roiled daily in a silent procession across the becalmed bay, threatening snow that never came. Through the trees, she watched the distant, rapidly dispersing wake of a boat inch silently across the bay.

"I don't think we should," she said.

Gaston exhaled twin plumes of condensation, which curled and dissipated in the cold air.

"I'm not asking."

Céline felt like she'd been punched. "Oh, I see," she said. "So that's how it's going to be."

Gaston came apart. "What the fuck am I supposed to do, Céline? We got just enough to get us through the first of the year and then what? You tell me! Where's the money coming from for Edmund's school supplies? Shit, where's the money coming from for his stupid dog? Rebuilding that foundation will take everything we've got and then some but I got no choice! It's either that or get sued! You tell me! Tell me what to do!"

Céline had begun crying. "I don't know what," she said.

"We have to! It's like there's this gun pointed at my head. We don't have any other choice."

Céline wiped her eyes on the back of her mitten. She nodded.

"Okay then," Gaston said. "Okay."

Chapter Fifteen

EDMUND FANCIED THE boat a ship on the high seas. Since he was too short to haul himself over the side, he took a stepladder from the barn and propped it against the gunwale. To Céline's surprise, Breeze clambered up the ladder behind him, climbing the short vertical pitch as if she were strolling up the stairs in their home, which, it occurred to her, she might well be doing when Edmund was in the house alone and left to amuse himself. Edmund's amusement usually involved his dog.

Radcliff had nearly completed the restoration. The boat's hull had been carefully scraped, sanded and primed, then top-coated with a color known locally as "Superior Blue." The mahogany gunwales and decking had been meticulously sanded, then patched and coated with several gleaming coats of shiny new spar varnish. As a precaution, Gaston had crawled into the engine compartment with a flashlight, but he had found the motor clean and apparently sound.

All this served to further Edmund's fantasies. He stood at the wheel, Breeze perched proudly on the seat behind him, pretending he was a captain on the high seas, blasting the air horn and jolting Céline out of her reveries. She finally had to ask him to stop. The horn seemed almost vulgar to her, as if they were rubbing Radcliff's nose in it.

Radcliff had not spoken to either of them. They had sent him a certified letter and then they had repossessed his boat. Gaston drove the company truck to Radcliff's rented shack and backed up to his boat and towed it back to their farm and parked it on a level spot beside the barn. Radcliff did not come out of his house.

The boat, in full view from the kitchen window above the sink, engendered in Céline a disquieting sense of failure, as if the vessel were a diminished substitute for all they now stood to lose. She had been tempted several times over the past week to drag Edmund from the cockpit and remind him that the boat wasn't really theirs, but she hadn't because that wasn't exactly true either; the boat *was* theirs, in every legal sense. Gaston made a show of putting the contract on the kitchen table for her to read—tapping it with his finger, *here*—but she hadn't read it. She knew him well enough to know that he would have dotted his i's and crossed his t's.

A week later, he had not put an ad on Craigslist and so the boat did not sell. Nor did he seem to care. Céline finally put an ad in herself, taking it upon herself to lower the price a thousand dollars below what Gaston had estimated the boat was worth, but the only calls she received were from tire kickers, old men with raspy, cigarette voices who coughed and offered five thousand below her asking price hoping she was desperate enough to bite. She wasn't, not yet.

Gaston had kept on the only man from his crew who would agree to work on spec, delaying his payment until the rebuild of the foundation was complete and Gaston had been paid by Dr. Goetting. The two spoke little. His crew's absence left him uncommunicative and lost in bitter thoughts, alone even in the company of others. At home, he did not reject his wife's companionship, but neither did he seem to desire it. He would speak if spoken to. He had turned down the thermostat to save on utilities and so rarely took off his work jacket before going to bed. Céline bundled up in the only hand-knit sweater left from the garage sale, snugging the collar under her chin and pulling her hands into the sleeves. It had never dawned on her before this how big their house was. There were at least four rooms that were never used, rooms she had once thrown open to the precious heat she had taken for granted, rooms she now shuttered tightly and never entered. Why would she? There was nothing much in them anyway. There never had been.

Removing the foundation was back-breaking work. When Gaston couldn't knock the wall over with the bucket of his backhoe—as the project stretched into the first of December, the harder the concrete set and the more difficult it became to do so—he and his lone helper were forced to pound it to pieces with sledge hammers, then cut away the reinforcing rebar with a Sawzall. This was brutally slow, exhausting work for both of them. The first few days left him nearly too muscle-weary to get out of bed the following morning, but eventually his body adjusted to the strain. He told Céline that, if there were good to any of this, it was that they were taking the walls down to the footer now, before the concrete had completely hardened with the onset of winter, when removing them would have been next to impossible. In a terse meeting with Dr. Goetting, he warned him that once they'd removed the walls, they wouldn't be able to re-pour them until spring. Dr. Goetting reluctantly agreed. He was, he said, a reasonable man.

"So he says he's gonna pay me half when I got the foundation out, half when it's rebuilt," he told Céline. Despite the chill in the house, he'd fished a cold beer from the refrigerator. "That's what he said; that's what we agreed on. It'll be enough I can cut Dick a check for what he's got coming and you and me and Edmund, we'll be okay for a few months. Things will pick up when the weather warms, right? Like always. The worst of this recession is over."

Gaston took a sip from his beer and set it beside the recliner in the living room and forgot about it. Céline would empty it in the sink and toss it in the recycle bin before they went to bed. It began to rain, wind-driven drops spattering like icy buckshot off the tall east-facing windows overlooking the bay. Edmund had returned from school just long enough to grab his daypack, Breeze dancing with joy on the back porch, and dart outside for a quick hike, ignoring Céline's concern about the rain, promising to be back in an hour for supper. Like his father, he seemed to enjoy bad weather, even the bitter rains of late fall. He told her he could always bivouac under a pine tree if it got bad. She said, couldn't he bivouac inside the house, where it was warm? He gave her that look.

"So, couple days ago, I was talking to Edmund," Gaston said, as if running with Céline's thoughts. They heard Breeze's happy bark fade as boy and dog were absorbed by the orchard. "He's picking up chunks of concrete like I told him and throwing them in a pile and that stupid dog of his is constantly getting under the bucket which pissed me off and I keep telling him to keep her under control, you know? Like he knows how."

"But he's working out okay. I mean, that was the idea, wasn't it, to give him a part-time job helping you out on weekends?" Céline folded her arms. She had shoved her hands into the sleeves of her sweater, but her fingers were still freezing.

"Yeah. Yeah. But I mean, he's just a kid. He gets in the way more than he helps, but he's learning. He ends up playing with Breeze after an hour or so and I have to remind him to get back after it. But Dick and him get along pretty well because Dick likes dogs too, he's got one of his own. And I think Edmund likes thinking he's part of the crew. He reminds me of me sometimes."

Céline nodded absentmindedly and excused herself and walked into the kitchen to check the thermostat. Unbelievably, it was still pegged at sixty-seven degrees, exactly where Gaston had set it. She had hoped it had dropped below that, giving her a valid excuse to turn it up. She couldn't believe she could be so cold in a sixty-seven-degree house. She wore a halter top and shorts in sixty-seven-degree weather in the summer, but then, as Gaston always reminded her, the humidity that kept her warm then was what made the air feel so cold now. She glanced over her shoulder at Gaston before nudging the thermostat up two degrees.

"So I didn't tell you what Edmund said," Gaston said. "We were loading up, Dick had already left. He was fussing with his dog and for some reason, I guess I was kind of curious, I asked him what he wanted to be when he grew up. I said, 'So what do you think you're gonna do when you grow up and get out of college?' Like that. Never asked him that before, you know? Never have, I don't know why. It just never came up. And I just assumed he wants to go to college, like you and I talked about. But I thought we could talk about that some, what he wants to do with his life. It's not like it's all that far away." He remembered his beer and reached for it.

"So, yeah, I know he's only eleven," Gaston said. "But he didn't even have to think about it. Baseball or construction, just like that. Like it's already preordained." Gaston cocked an eyebrow.

"Well, his father's in construction. Why wouldn't he want to do that too? Don't boys always want to be like their fathers?" Céline had taken a seat on the sofa, folded her legs beneath her, wrapping herself in the wool throw she kept draped over the back. Gaston unzipped his work jacket, as if the sudden two-degree rise in temperature were unbearably hot.

"Yeah, but … maybe that's not such a great thing in this day and age, you know? I mean, look at us."

"I don't think we're doing all that bad." Céline heard the defensiveness in her voice but couldn't stop herself. "What do you mean, 'look at us?' 'Look at us,' what? I don't get that."

"No, Céline. You always take things the wrong way. I mean Vaillancourt Builders." Gaston spoke slowly, enunciating the company name as if schooling a small child. "We're on the verge of going under," he said. "We have been for months. And that affects everything. I mean, it all comes down to cash flow. It's true. I don't think about stuff the same way I used to, back when we had all the work we could handle. Be honest—do you? I don't know how you could."

Céline no longer knew what she thought. Her thoughts were all jumbled together and raging in her head and didn't make sense anymore. She couldn't believe they were talking about this, that they were having this conversation. It sounded like something she'd heard about, a rumor, or gossip she wasn't privy to that had already been settled and was over, at least for Gaston. But she wasn't over *anything* yet. Why was he? She felt a knot form in her chest, the blunt edge of panic. *He* had been the one to dismiss the recession she had seen coming; *he* had been the one to reassure her, to dismiss her unfounded fears.

Now it was settled.

"He said he's going to pay us this spring, when we get the foundation rebuilt," Céline said. "We'll be okay then. We can get by."

"Yeah."

"Well?"

"I don't believe him. I don't *know* if I believe him. Why should I? Look at what he's done already."

"But he's a doctor. He's got plenty of money. We have a contract."

"We haven't got anything, Céline. I signed off on the damn contingencies. I needed the money. *We* needed the money. It was a mistake but now I got to do it anyway because we have no other choice. None."

Céline sat in silence, the wool throw drawn tightly around her neck. Gaston folded his arms and stared not at the distant lake beyond the window but below, at the windowsill, at the floor, at nothing that was beyond a future he could not see. A small roll of fat had begun to creep over his belt and he self-consciously zipped up his coat to cover it. But the muscles in his shoulders and arms were still thick and strong, as were the corded neck and strong jaw and the day's growth of blue-black beard flecked with gray, and in this Céline saw how the two of them had aged in tandem, the air around one dissolving in the breath of the other. He was forty-one years old.

"We still have the rentals no matter what happens," she said.

"We only got three of them rented. We still can't get that one on Maple Street rented."

"I know," Céline said. The Maple Street tenants had left in the middle of the night and they'd had no calls on the ads Céline placed on Craigslist. The abandoned deposit had paid for two months' service on the mortgage, but the deposit was gone and the mortgage would be due again soon. Gaston had made a half-serious suggestion to sell it. "Maybe we should rent it to Edmund," he said, joking.

"If he makes it in the big leagues, he can afford it," Céline said.

Gaston smiled a little. "You know, not to change the subject, but I was thinking about what he said, that stuff about wanting to be a contractor or a baseball player? Because I can remember being like that when I was his age. You look up to the people you idolize, your coaches, movie actors, famous baseball players. But they're not like real people; they're like these cardboard cutouts of real people, perfect like cardboard cutouts always are. Photoshopped. That's why you look up to them, because they're perfect. That's the problem. But you don't know that when you're a kid. You think perfect is how grown-ups are, how you're gonna be when you grow up. That's what I thought, anyway."

Gaston suddenly pressed his palms against his eyes and shook his head, hard, and said, "Oh." He wiped his eyes.

"Sometimes I think he's just like me, Céline. I see it in how he struts around, like nothing can go wrong. It's like anything I tell him is automatically the gospel truth, just because it's from me. Isn't that crazy? Sometimes I try to tell him how the world really is, like everything isn't peaches and cream, like there are bad people out there and bad things and all kinds of shit going on. I feel responsible for that, like it's my job as a parent to tell him about the things he doesn't want to hear, even if he's too young to understand."

Céline gazed past him and into the kitchen, where Edmund would, she hoped, be returning for supper at any moment. She'd hear his boots stomping the mud off on the back porch and the excited, staccato clicks of Breeze's nails on the back porch and then he'd burst inside, the door banging off the doorstop on the base molding. Edmund never *entered* the house; he *threw* himself into it, as if his compact body simply couldn't contain the thought of staying outside any longer.

She smoothed the throw with her fingers, pulling out the folds covering her legs, then remembered a cotton throw she'd once owned, that memory: *When he was very small.* When he was very small he had watched his father at a ball game, enraptured, lost in a reverie. Gaston had been on deck swinging a weighted bat, ignoring the pitcher on the mound, his focus on his swing, which slashed through the cool, humid air like a scythe. The batter had singled and Gaston selected a bat from the rack and strode to the plate. He rocked back on his heels and let the first pitch go by.

Then Céline, the light cotton throw across her knees, had spied her son. Somehow, he had scrambled out of the bleachers, made his way to the deck and found Gaston's weighted bat, and with his father's fierce concentration on his four-year-old face, had picked up the bat and was trying to swing. But he was barely strong enough to lift the weighted end off the ground and it dragged through the dirt and banged into the fence beside him. Over and over he tried, never quite able to get the bat all the way around, which made him more determined than ever to complete a full swing on his next try. He had caught the attention of the other wives and mothers in the stands, who had quietly begun to cheer him on. Gaston heard the commotion and called for a time out, then walked to the deck and stood before his son with his hands on his hips.

"You think you about got it?" he asked.

Edmund gazed up at his father. "Nope," he said. "But I will."

* * *

Gaston arose from the recliner. "I'm gonna take a shower," he said. "I got concrete dust in my eyeballs. God, I hate this."

"Gaston," Céline said, and he turned. "Maybe he understands more than we think."

Chapter Sixteen

S HE STOOD ON the back porch and put her hands on her hips and stared at the orchard, as if a force of will would part the trees and reveal her son, who had not returned for supper. It had begun to sleet. Microscopic ice crystals slanted across the low sun, glittering cold and white. She shivered and fashioned her throw in a hood about her head, clutching the folds beneath her neck to ward off the cold. Why did he always do this? He was never home in time for supper. She tried to remember the last time he had been on time and couldn't. He was too young to comprehend the danger of being outside in this kind of weather. The forecast called for temperatures in the thirties and sleet throughout the night, a predictable lake-effect cold front. Yet the weather seemed to have no more ameliorating effect on her son's poor judgment than on her husband's, who, exasperatingly, did not seem concerned that daylight was almost gone and his only son was alone in the woods in an approaching and potentially deadly storm.

She walked back inside, loudly shutting the door behind her. Gaston was where she had left him, sitting at the kitchen table.

"You see him?" he asked. He didn't look up.

"No."

"He'll be back. He always comes back. Right? Sooner or later. Don't worry about it."

Céline was in no mood for a debate. She ignored him and walked into the kitchen. If Edmund didn't show then he wouldn't eat. Those were the long-established rules. There were consequences for stupid behavior.

She knew all about stupid behavior. Her girlfriend's husband and son had been fishing on the lake when a storm came up and their undersized boat swamped in the waves. They were close enough to shore that someone saw them and called the Coast Guard, who plucked them out just in time. After a harrowing night in the ER, both had been fine. Gaston said they were fools for going out in a boat that small. She hadn't disagreed. But wasn't that beside the point? Stuff happened out there. People got lost, got their boats swamped in storms, broke legs, ran into bears. Hadn't Gaston shot a bear that very summer? He hadn't tried to dismiss *that*.

Céline had potatoes roasting in the oven and a thick stew in the crockpot that she'd been simmering since morning. Winter meals— or what would soon be winter meals—called for hunter's stew made with last year's venison which she didn't particularly care for, but Gaston and Edmund loved. At least in a stew the distasteful gaminess was masked by vegetables and tomato paste. She lifted the lid, ran a wooden spoon around the inside of the crockpot, then knocked it clean and set it on a plate. Then she flicked her throw over her head and walked back outside.

She stood on the back porch and wondered if she should call out, if he would hear her voice above the soft rustle of sleet striking the dead leaves and frozen earth. It was now nearly dark, and a thin sheet of ice was encasing the decking and rails, gleaming and black like a newly applied coat of varnish.

"Edmund," she said. "Edmund!"

She saw a flash of red dart across the light from the kitchen window and knew what it was and a second later felt Breeze shove her nose into the back of her leg. The little dog gazed up at her, swishing her tail, unable to contain her delight. Edmund emerged from the trees. He had pulled the hood of his parka over his head, but his daypack was covered with a brittle rime of ice. He stomped and scraped the mud and ice on his boots against the porch steps. Breeze pranced between the two of them.

"Crazy weather, huh?" he said.

* * *

Céline was amazed that Breeze was minding her manners and remaining on the mat inside the back door, just as Edmund had commanded her to do. She stared into the kitchen, intently studying every morsel of food they ate, until finally Edmund arose from the table, put several spoonfuls of stew in a napkin and fed it to her. Céline reminded him to wash his hands.

Sleet had begun driving into the side of the house, pinging against the windows in a muted tattoo, but her relief at Edmund's return had greatly diminished the anger she felt at his childish irresponsibility. It wouldn't kill her to let Breeze sleep in the kitchen tonight, not in weather like this. She wondered, briefly, if the dog had anything to do with her son's safe return. Weren't horses supposed to find their way home if you gave them the reins? She'd never had to try that with Sir Lancelot or Dutch, but maybe dogs were like that, too. It was a comforting thought, even if technically it might not be true.

Edmund seemed oblivious to the fact that he'd been snatched from the jaws of death and was in a chatty mood. He'd found a live porcupine, he told them breathlessly, balled up and motionless under the boughs of a balsam tree. Breeze wanted to attack it, but he'd caught her just in time. Then they'd watched a muskrat clamber onto the shelf ice rimming the irrigation lake.

Céline was struck, as she had been many times, by the notion that the orchard and the woods and all that *out there* were as familiar to Edmund as her own back yard was to her. How many hundreds of days had he spent traipsing through the woods, his only companions his dogs? He knew the game trails and the land they traversed with the same quotidian intimacy with which she knew the soft topography of their front yard. Did he even use the trails anymore? She didn't know. Gaston had given Edmund a cheap machete for his ninth birthday and she thought, perhaps, that he hacked his way through jungles of growth, like she saw in some of the classic movies she watched on Netflix, back when they'd still had a subscription. But where did the trails he hacked out of the jungle lead? It seemed reasonable to assume that they went someplace.

Then Gaston was telling Edmund about the last porcupine *he'd* seen, except that at the end of the story, he shot the porcupine.

"Why?" Edmund wanted to know.

"Why? Because they kill trees. They girdle the bark and then the trees die."

"Yeah, but … maybe they're just hungry." Edmund didn't like killing things. He still remembered the rabbit.

"Doesn't matter what they are," Gaston said. "You can't have animals like that running around killing trees all over the forest."

Edmund frowned and nodded. Gaston had convinced Céline their son was old enough to carry the antique .22 rifle Gaston had inherited from his Grand-père and Edmund had subsequently been schooled in safe gun use at DNR hunter-safety classes, but to Gaston's disappointment, he seemed to have only a passing interest in guns and rarely took the rifle with him on his hikes.

"How's your stew?" Céline said, trying to change the subject. "It's venison."

"It's really good, Mom."

"Ah!" Gaston said. "Venison!"

Céline caught her husband's triumphant grin. "Edmund doesn't want to talk about that stuff anymore, do you Edmund?"

"Nuh-uh," Edmund said.

Gaston rolled his eyes, which likewise did not escape Céline's notice. She pursed her lips.

"Oh, c'mon you guys," Edmund said. "Grow up."

"*What?*" Céline put her palms flat on the table.

Edmund ignored her, clearing his throat dramatically. "I've kinda made a big decision in my life. I know I'm still just a kid, but it's sort of a big decision? I want to get married. I mean, not, like, *now*. But someday when I'm old. Like you guys."

Céline stared. Gaston whooped.

"Who?" she said. "Anybody we know?"

"Melanie."

"You mean Melanie Aldrich? Who came to the funeral? That Melanie?"

Edmund nodded. He was suddenly shy again, his cheeks reddening beneath his dark skin.

"I've been thinking about it a lot," he said. "That's why I was walking around up there, you know, thinking? But I mean it's like, *someday*. Not today, you guys."

"No, I get that part," Céline said. "*Someday* you want to marry Melanie, but not right now. What does she say?"

"Well, we haven't exactly talked about it. But it's like, she *knows*, Mom. You can tell."

"Oh!" Gaston said, raising his hand. "Can I jump in here? Let me give you some good advice, son. Never assume *anything* when it comes to women. Do that and you'll live long and prosper. You heard it here first."

Céline reached across the table and pushed his hand down. "I'm not sure that's the kind of advice he needs at his age," she said.

"It's okay, Mom. I was wanting to talk about some stuff like that, anyway. You know, how you do it. How do you do it being married to someone else. You guys have been married for, like, forever and in love and stuff so you gotta know something."

What could she tell him? In love? Lately, Céline hadn't the time to think about *love*, not in the romantic way her son meant it. For months, her worry about making ends meet had pushed every other thought and emotion to the back burner. What was love, anyway? The truth? Or just a meaningless euphemism? Perhaps—this thought, like a lost sock discovered under a pile of laundry, surprising only because it was so emphatically mundane—it was nothing more than forbearance and faith in light of an uncertain future, the willingness to take one more step, one willing step at a time.

Gaston stared out the window at the dark. The sleet had been replaced by snow, small wet flakes that flashed like sparks in the yellow light from the kitchen and stuck to the glass.

"It's not like what you think, Edmund," he said. "When you're a kid everything looks all one-dimensional and shiny. But when you grow up, things look different. Things aren't supposed to change, but they always do. You know what I'm saying?"

"You mean like, your friends die and stuff, like Cloud?"

"Yeah, sort of. That's one thing that can happen. But it's more like, you're two different people. So your mom and I are two different people. That's why it's so hard." He glanced at Céline and lowered his eyes, as if embarrassed to have made such a personal admission.

Céline thought, *but it didn't used to be.* They'd been married when she was just twenty-two. It hadn't been hard at all, then. They both knew what the other wanted. They had reasonable plans for each other's lives. Even Edmund's arrival hadn't fundamentally altered that. He'd wanted a son and she'd been proud to provide him with one. Now it was as if she were listening, really hearing, for the first time in months. She'd been listening all along but not really hearing and he had returned the favor by not hearing her. They addressed separate failings, outwardly courteous but secretly adamant that something the other was doing was wrong; they lay awake nights worrying about separate futures. Their conversations had been reduced to lecturing to different walls in the same room.

Céline didn't want to believe that circumstances as pedestrian as not having enough money, something she had been woefully unprepared for, could have this kind of emotional fallout. What was a marriage for, if not to man the same lifeboat in stormy seas? She'd read the magazine articles: Issues around money and sex were the two leading problems cited by marriage counselors. But they'd never been to a marriage counselor; somehow it hadn't seemed appropriate. It had been months after the recession was officially labeled as such before she would admit to herself that their marriage *hadn't* been working ... for months.

But then, she certainly wasn't convinced it was beyond help. What was Gaston's analogy? Like a truck running on seven cylinders? It was like that. That's what their marriage was like; a truck running on seven cylinders. It needed a tune-up. A major tune-up to be sure, but nothing that couldn't be fixed.

She touched Edmund's hand. "You have to talk to each other," she said. "That's what your father and I do, we talk." She looked at Gaston hopefully. "Because you just naturally will have different ways of looking at the world, so you have to sort of smoosh them together and find something you can both live with. Isn't that right, Gaston?"

Gaston nodded.

"And, um … you have to, you do that a bunch. Every married couple does. But that's probably more than you need to hear right now, kiddo. That kind of talk is for grown-ups. I think it's nice that you like Melanie. I like Melanie, too."

"Melanie's cool," Gaston said.

Edmund seemed pleased.

"No, seriously," Gaston said. "She's cool. I remember her from the funeral. I like her. All I'm saying is, just don't be in such a big hurry to tie yourself down. Stuff changes every day. You'll see."

* * *

Edmund could barely look over the dash. Gaston wondered when his son would begin growing, if ever. A few of his mother's genetics wouldn't kill him, but he didn't seem to have them, or at least, not the tall, lanky ones. At some point in a boy's life, he was supposed to become taller than his mother, but Gaston wasn't convinced that was ever going to happen.

"I don't think I'm being unrealistic, Dad," Edmund said, as if reading his father's thoughts. "I know I'm not very big. You weren't very big, either."

Gaston drummed his fingers on the steering wheel. "Yeah, but I didn't play pro ball, either," he said. "Look, having goals is good. But in the real world it's pretty tough to go from Port Landing to playing for, like, Detroit or something. There are a lot of good ball players out there, Edmund, millions. Only a few hundred of them ever make it to the majors."

"But didn't you almost make it to the majors?" Edmund gazed at him expectantly, wanting to hear the story again. They were sitting in Céline's Subaru; Gaston could no longer rationalize the gas it cost to drive the company truck anywhere other than to the job site. Céline had dispatched him to the grocery store and Edmund had invited himself along. They put Breeze in the back seat. Gaston, as always, was amazed at the manners that had been painstakingly drilled into the little dog by his son. She lay quietly on a wool blanket, her ears pricked, intently listening to their conversation but unwilling to move until given permission to do so.

"More like semi-pro. More like a*lmost* semi-pro. I mean, I just wasn't gonna be big enough, even for a shortstop," Gaston said. "It was tough enough in college. Which, by the way, you're going to."

Edmund nodded distractedly. "Some guys go to the pros right out of high school," he said.

"Who?"

"I don't know. Some. I've seen them on TV. C'mon, Dad, you know there are. I don't have all the stats in my head like you do."

Gaston grinned. "You're a little shit, you know that?"

Edmund beamed. "Goddamn straight," he said.

"Okay. Assuming you get out of high school and go to college on a scholarship and then assuming you get drafted, where do you want to go?"

"Los Angeles." Edmund folded his arms triumphantly.

"The *Dodgers?* Really? Man, you don't know what that place is like. I was in LA once and it ain't like Port Landing, I'll tell you what. You might want to think about a backup plan, you know, something closer to home, so you don't have to miss out on your mother's cooking."

"Nope. I've already thought about it. That's where I want to go." Edmund thrust out his jaw. "You asked."

Gaston turned on the engine. Why quash his son's dreams? He'd had dreams, too. He wanted to tell him that dreams didn't always come true, that sometimes, no matter how hard you worked, the dream was always just beyond your outstretched fingers, that dreams, held too tightly, too close to the heart, could still suffocate of their own infinitesimal weight. Would he understand? He still wasn't sure *he* understood. Grand-père had taught him that hard work and persistence and sheer will would always prevail and his grandfather had lived what he believed, even if his son had not. But Gaston was no longer sure that will and persistence were enough. It was as if he, Gaston, were frozen in a photograph whose background had faded beyond recognition.

He gazed out the windshield at the barn and the orchard above the barn, bare limbs stark against the blue sky that good weather always brought: clear and cold and blue. He could not remember when his view of the world had been anything other than a distillation of this: house, barn, sun, orchard, leaves, snow; his future spinning out from his past, unchanged and unchanging. Today would be no different. Today, perhaps, it was not so cold for December; today it was *nice*—Céline's favorite word. Today would be a nice day.

"Hey," he said, lightly punching Edmund in the shoulder. He touched the accelerator and began pulling out of the driveway. "Your mother wants us to get a tree."

"You mean, like, a Christmas tree?"

"I mean, like, a Christmas tree," Gaston said. "They got trees down at the hardware store. Your mother finally trusts us enough to select one without her expert advice."

Edmund frowned. "How much do they cost? The ones at the store."

"How much? I don't know. Too much. But you gotta have a tree for Christmas."

"I know where there are free trees," Edmund said. "Lots of them. Millions and millions of them, Dad." He was grinning, unable to resist telling his secret. "I bet you don't know where, either."

Gaston didn't know.

"Up there!" Edmund pointed past Gaston's nose. "There are tons of Christmas trees up there, Dad. *Tons.*"

"In the orchard?"

"No! Shit." Edmund gave him a patronizing look. "Don't be so dumb, Dad. In the forest. I mean, I see them every time I hike. There's a whole bunch of little trees growing up around the lake up there. I can cut one down and we'll have a free tree. It'll save us money big time!"

"Big time money, you say?"

Edmund nodded. "I don't know why I never thought of it before. They're like, everywhere. Better than the ones they got in the hardware store. I mean, some of those aren't even *real*. They're white with sparkles and stuff."

"I kind of like sparkles and stuff," Gaston said. "That's what I was thinking of getting. Lots and lots of sparkles."

Edmund snorted. "This is getting embarrassing. We need a *real* tree, Dad. A real, *free* tree. It's stupid to spend, like, millions of dollars for a free tree. I'm afraid I'm going to have to put my foot down on this."

"Well," Gaston said. "Then I guess that's that. You got something to cut it down with? Take the bucksaw in the tack room."

Edmund nodded. "I'll run up there when we get back."

"You think you can drag it back down by yourself? That's a long ways."

"Not that long," Edmund said. "I'll tie a rope to it."

They were nearing town and last night's scant snowfall had done little more than frost the brown leaves in people's yards, a white patina on frozen earth, winter nearly upon them, the dusting received as a promise of more to come. Without snow, dragging a tree was going to be a little more work than Edmund bargained for. But why not? He had a point: It would save them some money.

"Don't get one that's too big, okay?" Gaston said. "You get one that's too big and you won't be able to get it back down. So don't chop down a real big one." The top of Edmund's head was barely even with the top of the seat. "Get one a foot taller than you are, your mom will be happy with that. A foot taller will be perfect, okay? Two feet, absolutely max."

"Don't worry, Dad. I can handle it. This will be, like, a personal mission."

Gaston presented his fist and Edmund punched it. "Dude," he said.

* * *

Céline gazed at Gaston from the kitchen, her hands on her waist, a pot of chili on the stove and the steam's thick pungent aroma rising up. "What happened to Edmund? He ran out of the house so fast I didn't even get a chance to talk to him."

Gaston thrust his chin toward the orchard. "Up there," he said. "He's on a mission." He made quotation marks with his fingers.

"Before lunch? He couldn't do this secret mission after lunch?"

"He was too excited to wait. Plus, it's not a secret. He's gonna cut us a tree. He took the dog and the bucksaw and split. The kid has a mind of his own."

Céline shook her head. "You just figured that out? Why couldn't he wait twenty minutes and go after lunch? He needs food, Gaston."

Gaston shrugged. "Because he's all fired up to save us some money. That's what he said. You know how he is. I told him you'd be pissed off. But then I got to thinking about it … it's gonna be a little bigger project than he thinks. Cutting down the tree's the easy part. Then he's got to drag it home. That irrigation lake's a good half mile from here. It's all downhill, but still, he'll be wishing he had some food in him by the time he gets back. Maybe it'll soak into his thick head, I don't know. I told him to go ahead and get it over with. So I guess you can blame me."

Céline frowned and balanced her wooden spoon on the edge of the pot and carried bowls to the table, including one for Edmund, just in case. She wasn't blaming anybody. She'd long ago become accustomed to her son's absence at meals, but it still irked her. He could train his dog, why couldn't he train himself?

"So you decided not to buy a tree. You and Edmund."

"I didn't decide, he did," Gaston said. "I mean, he's got a point. You see what a Christmas tree goes for? It's a royal rip-off. We have about four hundred thousand of them up there growing wild for free. Makes perfectly good sense to me."

"Don't you have to have a permit from the Forest Service or something? I read that someplace. I'm pretty sure you do."

Gaston snorted.

Céline fixed her gaze on the air above Gaston's head. "Okay," she said. "He'll be back by supper? You at least told him that, didn't you?"

"He should be. I mean, he will. But I mean, realistically, it could turn into a two-day project. I'll run up there tomorrow and give him a hand if he can't get it all the way back today. He *should* be home by supper. Figure forty-five minutes to get up there and then ten minutes to cut it down and then however long it takes to drag it back. So I'd say, yeah, he should be done by then. That would be my guess. My guess would be late afternoon."

Céline returned to the kitchen and grunting lifted the heavy pot of chili with both hands and carried it to the kitchen table and set it on an iron trivet. She rested a moment, catching her breath and gazing out the window.

"At least it's kind of nice," she said. The previous evening's dusting of snow glinted from the metal roof of the barn, sparkling in the sunlight. "He'll work up a good sweat. He may have to shed a layer. He knows about doing that, when he's sweaty." The dial on the thermometer outside the kitchen window had nudged into the low thirties.

"He knows," Gaston said.

Chapter Seventeen

S HE COULDN'T FIND the ornaments. The lights and the tree stand, the one with the red water bowl underneath it, were gone. The wreaths, the candelabra, the porcelain nativity scene, the wrapping paper: gone.

She leaned against the counter and folded her arms under the sweater she'd thrown over her shoulders and tried to think. This was irritating. She hadn't misplaced them; she'd put all the Christmas decorations in the same place in the basement, in the same closet beneath the stairs, since they were first married. Where were they?

Then it struck her: the garage sale. She must have sold them.

She didn't remember selling them. She couldn't believe she would have knowingly sold the Christmas decorations she'd spent all these years collecting, but maybe Edmund or Gaston had carried them into the yard, and not knowing what was in the boxes they held, placed them on the shoe rack or on a bench with something else, tools maybe, where they wouldn't be noticed. And perhaps—there had been so many people—perhaps someone had thrown them in a pile on the folding table she'd set up as a counter and that someone had made an offer on everything, take it or leave it, and without thinking she had taken it; her mind had been elsewhere. She had sold her horses that day.

The memory of Sir Lancelot and Dutch made her belly twist in a small painful knot around the emptiness they had filled, as they had filled the barn with their warmth and eager affection. Gaston had his work and Edmund had his dogs, but the two horses had been hers. Even now, a month after their departure, she rarely visited the barn. The stalls seemed cavernous and empty, and the air, washed of its warm animal musk, seemed astringent and cold. The memory of her horses' scent made her put her hand to her eyes. When she stood close and put her face beside his and snuggled her nose against his neck, Sir Lancelot had smelled like freshly baked bread. She'd loved the barn then, when she could spend hours in the tack room cleaning and oiling her saddles and bridles and listening to the soothing cadence of her horses munching hay a few feet away in their stalls.

She'd missed them terribly at first, but then those feelings faded as Gaston had told her they would and they had gone on with their lives and it had all worked out and the money had come in handy and she had accepted her loss as the manner of painful things. The barn changed from being an extension of their home to just another outbuilding, like the garden shed Gaston had retrofitted into a work space for grafting seedlings. Now, without the horses, there wasn't much reason to visit the barn, other than to feed Breeze and refill her water bucket, but that was Edmund's job.

Hidden under some blankets she found a single coil of colored lights that apparently hadn't been packed away with the rest of the ornaments. She tucked it under her arm and began climbing the steps back upstairs. It would be enough for Edmund's tree. She still hoped he'd be home by dinner but knew better than to expect him. He and Breeze seemed able to survive on each other's company for days, as if the exhaled breath of one were sustenance inhaled by the other, and he lost track of time and where they were and any promises he might have made to his mother.

The previous evening's dusting of snow had burned off in the sun, even though, on this day, it was yet below freezing. But her son and her husband seemed immune to cold weather. She'd watched Gaston work in the orchard in twenty-degree weather wearing little more than a flannel shirt and insulated gloves and Edmund seemed cast in the same impervious mold. Still, she had insisted for so long that he carry a pile vest and extra socks in his daypack (she felt vindicated when Gaston had adamantly backed her up on this) that he'd finally begun carrying them automatically, although she suspected he did it as much to avoid an argument with her as from any sense of necessity.

Gaston had helped him compile a survival kit, which Edmund was constantly rearranging and adding to on the floor of the living room. It was beyond Céline's comprehension that anyone would find "survival" enjoyable. It made a lot more sense to her to get home early so you could sleep in a warm bed in a warm house, but she'd given up trying to figure out why boys did the things they did.

Still, Edmund would be hungry by now and therefore more likely to return in time for dinner, so she decided to plan accordingly. She pulled out a package of frozen chicken and set it in the sink to thaw and another package of frozen peas and carrots; she'd figure out what to do with them later. The chicken would keep if Edmund was late and if he didn't show Gaston would finish the vegetables and she would swallow her anger at their spoiled dinner and her husband's indifference and the thoughtless manner of boys.

* * *

This was wrong. The little red dog stayed behind him as he slowly picked his way across the thin ice on the reservoir, looking around anxiously, touching her nose to the back of his leg for reassurance and whining under her breath. She felt the ice flex and pop beneath their feet, the soft, muted reports sounding as if they came from a great distance away. They were approaching the far shore now, moving toward the trees. She could see the trees.

She felt the ice give way beneath them. She barked to warn him and he spun halfway around and then they were both plunging into the water. The shocking cold burned her lungs in searing gulps. She paddled frantically to the edge and clawed her way out onto the ice, shaking violently and staring back at the boy. He was saying something to her, his voice on the edge of panic, his arms spread to either side to balance himself, the burning water halfway up his chest. He put his hands on the ice and tried to pull himself out but the ice broke beneath him and he failed and he tried again and he failed. He took off his daypack and hurled it as far as he could toward the trees and tried once more but the ice would not support his weight and he got no further than before.

"Oh no, oh no," he said. He pounded on the ice with his mittens to break a pathway to shore but the ice which had broken beneath him would not break under his hands. He pushed off from the bottom and tried to fling himself over the ice and onto his elbows, but the ice snapped off in useless shards beneath him.

"Breeze!" he said. "Come to me!"

She edged closer and put one paw in the water, whining. Did he want her back in the water with him? The boy said something and she sensed the urgency in his voice and then he had grasped her collar with one hand and begun pushing off the ice with the other. Instinctively, she began pulling him back, toward the trees, toward safety. She pulled until his chest was flat on the ice, then his legs, and then, with a final, violent frog kick, he was out of the water and lying flat on the ice and free. He slithered away from the hole and then, carefully, unsteadily, rose to his hands and knees and crawled to his daypack and she walked just in front of him as if leading the way.

When he reached his daypack he looped one arm through the shoulder strap and crawled to the trees, dragging it beside him. Only when he was several feet up the bank did he try to stand. He was shivering so violently it was hard to find his balance. He gave up and sat down and opened his daypack and turned it upside down and a stream of frigid water poured out onto the frozen ground, followed by a sodden wad of wet clothing entwined around his baseball glove.

"Fuck! I can't believe this is happening," he said. He kicked the daypack in disgust. Then he was talking to her again.

"We still got waterproof matches," he said. "We still got a space blanket. We got to make a lean-to like Dad showed me."

She cocked her ears and listened while he pulled apart the pile of wet clothing at his feet. He found his machete and again tried to rise, this time making it shakily to his feet. With both hands he hacked the limbs from a small pine tree with the machete and then hacked half-way through the trunk two feet off the ground, pushing it over to form a crude frame. He pulled off one of his mittens with his teeth to get a better grip and unfolded the space blanket slowly, his exposed hand numb and nearly frozen from the water and the cold. He draped the space blanket over the pine tree and staked it taut and took the branches he'd cut and placed them beneath the lean-to for insulation and looked around for firewood.

A dozen yards beyond lay a blown-over oak tree; a stroke of luck. There was no better firewood than oak. He broke off what branches he could and clutched them to his chest and dragged them to his lean-to and stomped on the smallest branches until they broke into kindling. He made several trips, his uncovered hand now wooden and useless. He tried to pull the wet mitten back over his hand with his teeth but couldn't and he cursed and threw the mitten on the ground. He began doing jumping jacks, and when he had warmed up a little he made several more trips to the oak tree, breaking off the smaller branches by stomping on them and hacking off the larger branches with the machete he held in his good hand.

The exertion brought some feeling back into his frozen hand and he was able to light a match and touch it to the pile of tinder he had placed under the lean-to. The flames took and he carefully fed them with twigs and branches until he had a small but steady fire. He was still violently cold and shaking so badly his ribs ached but the heat from the fire felt good. He lay on his side and tried to squeeze the water out of his pants and coat and then, remembering what his father had told him, got his baseball glove and put it under his shoulder for insulation.

She watched from just outside the lean-to, wet and shivering in the cold, brittle light of late afternoon, uncertain he wanted her closer to the fire until he called for her and she came to him.

* * *

Céline stared at Gaston across the table until finally he looked up. He held up his hand, palm out, ending the conversation that had not yet begun.

"I know," he said.

"He always does this."

"I know. Believe it or not, it pisses me off, too."

"You'll talk to him then? That this is not acceptable? He does this constantly, Gaston. It's bad enough that you're late half the time."

Gaston put his knife down. "You know where I was. Dick's got weekends off. We're not even halfway through yet. That foundation ain't coming down by itself, Céline. I don't get that concrete out, we're gonna have a lot worse things to worry about than what time our stupid kid decides to come home for dinner."

Céline studied her plate. She'd baked a chicken casserole in cream of mushroom soup with lightly steamed vegetables, seasoned with lemon pepper. Nothing particularly fancy, but Edmund liked it this way and Gaston would eat anything.

"He'll be back," Gaston said. "He's dragging a tree so it's gonna take him a while. I'll go up and help him tomorrow; he doesn't get it back pretty soon, like I said. I mean, he's trying to do the right thing. Just for the record, I checked out the trees at the hardware store." He held up one hand, his fingers spread wide. "Fifty bucks," he said. "That's what a Christmas tree goes for. And that's for a little one. I didn't even check out the big ones like we used to get."

Céline took a small bite of her casserole and set her fork on her plate. A dollop of mushroom soup dripped on the table and she dabbed it up with her napkin. "It's almost dark," she said.

"I know."

Céline set the napkin beside her plate and rose from the chair and walked to the back door and went outside. She listened for a moment, cocking her ear toward the dim outline of trees in the orchard. Then she cupped her hands around her mouth and yelled. "Edmund!" She heard nothing and yelled again and again heard nothing, only the brief rustle in the leaves of an animal startled by her voice, a deer or perhaps a rabbit. She went back into the house, shivering from the cold and immediately wrapped a throw around her shoulders.

"Is he there?"

"He's not there."

* * *

She listened. She did not understand the words but she lay against his chest and licked his face and tasted the salt in his tears. He told her he couldn't feel his feet. He told her they should get up and try to walk but he couldn't make his legs move. She wagged her tail to encourage him.

He said, "I'm cold."

He moved a little and she tried to crawl closer. When he spoke again, his voice was distant and garbled, as if he were speaking from within a dream, from a longing.

"Dad says ... you don't want to drop down on one knee," he whispered, his tongue thick and slow. "You stay on both feet then you can move if the ball takes a bad hop. My friends, they all drop on one knee. But not me." Slowly, he reached for the pile of wood beside his head and dragged a broken branch into the fire. It caught and for a moment the flames licked up the wood and lit their faces: the small red dog and the boy. He held his exposed hand to the fire, but he could no longer feel the heat and withdrew it, not in panic but in resignation.

He could see the stars now. He found the Big Dipper and traced the handle to the North Star, as Gaston had shown him on countless warm, summer nights, and in that way knew that their house was less than a half mile downhill, between the lean-to and Lake Superior. He knew the way. But they would not make it home tonight. In the morning, when the sun had warmed them both a little, they would make their way home.

He tried to point out the North Star to her, but now his good hand wouldn't move. He pulled his mitten off with his teeth and held his fingers to his face and in the light of the fire they were white and waxy looking, as if they belonged to a mannequin, but the realization that he had lost his good hand no longer bothered him.

She licked his face again and tasted his cold skin on her tongue. She whined and growled under her breath and pushed her nose under his chin, but he did not respond nor did he try to push her away.

They lay in silence for a long while and then again he spoke.

"I let them down," he said. "Dad showed me how to do this." She cocked her head, straining to hear. The words seemed to come from within, for the boy's lips would no longer move. The words were like ghosts and she could feel the shape and the texture of them, and she wagged her tail furiously against the frozen earth, wanting him to understand that she'd heard.

* * *

Céline could see that Gaston was worried. Why wouldn't he just admit it? She had stopped being impressed with his machismo decades ago. Now she just thought it was stupid. He had not finished his casserole and instead had turned his chair toward the kitchen window, facing the orchard. But the night was black and he could see nothing, only the shadow of his face in the reflection.

"Are you finished?" she said.

"Yes." He pushed his plate across the table. "I guess I'm just not that hungry tonight."

"I wonder why that is?"

He shot her a look and rose to his feet and walked to the living room and hit the remote for the TV, then turned the sound down and watched her take their plates to the kitchen. She hadn't finished her meal either.

"Maybe we should save some of that for Edmund," he said.

"When he decides to come home," she said.

"He'll get here. I told you. Dragging a tree all the way down from the reservoir is hard work. Harder'n he thinks. Obviously."

"Obviously."

"Yes. Obviously." He watched her some more. "Can we just cut this shit out? You're acting like this is all my fault."

"Whose fault is it then? Edmund's eleven."

Gaston's face grew dark and he jabbed the volume control on the remote. "I know how old he is," he said.

* * *

He had wrapped his arms around her and his wet clothing soaked through her fur and made her wet and cold but she refused to leave, to lie closer to the dying fire, where it was warmer. She shivered and then licked his face and nipped his chin but he had not responded in over an hour. She felt his chest rise and fall under the soggy parka but the cadence had changed; it was shallower now and she sensed something wrong. She growled a little under her breath and then barked at him but he had stopped talking to her. He had not been able to get his mitten back on his good hand and he had shoved it between her warm belly and the earth, but it had eventually slipped out from beneath her and now lay exposed, pale and chalky looking, in the flickering shadows thrown off by the fire. He made no effort to put his hand back beneath her.

The fire had nearly gone out and the coals glowed dimly from under a thin gray shroud of ash. There was a stack of branches just a few feet away. She didn't understand the connection between the branches and the fire, but earlier that night—it seemed a long time ago now—he had crawled to the stack and then back to the fire and it had been warmer then and he had spoken to her. But he had stopped doing that and what little heat there was from the fire no longer warmed her and he had stopped talking.

She felt him breathing.

* * *

"It's almost ten," Céline said. "This isn't right, Gaston. He's not this late even in the summer."

Gaston slammed his fist into the sofa. "Goddamn him! I'll kick his little ass when I get him back here!"

"Will you go look for him, then? Please? You said he went to the lake or something. I don't know what he was talking about, do you?"

"Yeah." Gaston was still angry. "There's an old irrigation reservoir up there that's mostly filled in, they put it in before Grand-père bought this place. You can't hardly see it anymore because it's covered up by trees. You got to know where it's at." He walked to the coat rack behind the back door and put on his heavy work jacket and gloves. "Where's my flashlight?"

Céline pointed to the shelf above his head. Gaston put the flashlight in his pocket.

"What's gonna be tough is, there's almost no snow left for tracking. He might of wandered off in a completely different direction. Or Breeze got on a rabbit and he took off after her. That would be just like him."

"Should you take some energy bars with you? I mean, he might be hungry by now."

Gaston snorted. "Yeah, that's probably a good idea, seeing as how he missed supper. He's gonna be *real* hungry after I kick his little French ass."

Céline stood in the doorway and watched Gaston disappear into the night, his shoulders in an angry set, the beam from the flashlight bobbing like a firefly on the ground before him. When she could no longer hear his footsteps she walked out onto the back porch, shivering, cold in her cotton sweater despite the throw, a bare sliver of moon above and the stars glittering like pinpricks of life beyond this earth. Then she returned to the living room and turned on the TV and lay on the sofa and watched a detective story that she had no interest in so she walked into the kitchen and got a glass from the rack under the cupboard and poured a glass of white wine from an almost forgotten bottle in the refrigerator. She thought about going to bed but what was the point? She went back to the living room and turned off the TV and stared at her reflection in the bay window and beyond at the lake she couldn't see: Superior, vast, silent and eternally patient in the cold dark night.

She thought then of the people in town. The residents of Port Landing loved Superior, they loved the north woods, they loved the snow. She didn't love any of it, she could finally be honest with herself about that. The farm was wonderful in the summer but autumn was better; that's when the leaves turned and the presses were running and the air smelled like apple cider with cinnamon and the days were still warm, even if the nights were cold, and the cold nights gave the days a delicious urgency, a longing for the summer passing. One of her girlfriends had been a Nordic racer in Madison and she loved the snow but the rest of her girlfriends didn't. They had moved to Port Landing so their husbands could live in the woods during deer season or spend their summers on the lake fishing for salmon and walleye. She had hoped to stay in Minneapolis but Port Landing was the only home Gaston would consider. He was born here.

They hadn't had a warm day in over a month. It was a miracle there wasn't already two feet of snow in the yard, as there had been every December as far back as she could remember. And she thought about Edmund in that much snow: how much better it was to be lost in a dry landscape of leaves on frozen ground.

She heard Gaston's boots before he opened the back door and then he was inside and his eyes were scared.

"I can't see anything out there," he said. "I think we better call the sheriff."

Chapter Eighteen

THE SHERIFF'S CREW parked two squad cars in the driveway and within an hour had assembled a team from county rescue, young men and women with radios and North Face parkas. She and Gaston briefed them on what they knew: when Edmund had left, where they thought he might have gone, what the dog Breeze looked like, the approximate location of the irrigation reservoir. They listened tensely, nodding. No one smiled.

Gaston wanted to go with them but the sheriff gently suggested otherwise and then stood in his way when he insisted, his gloved hand on Gaston's shoulder, restraining him. He was a big man with a big gut. Gaston glared but when Céline put her hand on his arm he backed down. Céline spoke to him and he reluctantly followed her into the house, beside himself with frustration and anger. One of the women detached herself from the group and caught up with Céline and squeezed her hand. "We'll find him," she said. She smiled and Céline smiled back.

Céline put a pot of coffee on the stove and stared out the window at the squad cars in the driveway. "We might as well," she said. "We're going to be up all night one way or another." When the pot whistled she jumped in alarm and hurried into the kitchen. She filled two heavy mugs and set one before Gaston, who took it numbly. He rolled the mug slowly back and forth in his hands, as if it were clay shaped by his thoughts. She set hers on the table and sat beside him. The lights from one of the squad cars pulsed like a heartbeat on the walls in the dark kitchen until one of the deputies reached through the open window of the car and shut them off. In the sudden darkness of the kitchen they could not see one another and for a while they were alone, each with the other.

The rescue team sent back a squad at one-thirty in the morning. Two men and a woman emerged from the woods and politely knocked on the back door. Céline opened it and waited for them to speak, unable to ask. They were still searching. There was very little moon on this dark night but they were making encouraging progress because of the lack of snow, which they all agreed was unusual for December, as if that were a thing noteworthy and good. They had been sent back to reassure them in person and to call for additional men. A few minutes later another squad car pulled up, and within minutes vehicles began lining the road below the house. The big sheriff unfolded a map on the hood of his car. They all trained their headlamps on it and were briefed as before. They set coordinates on their GPSs and then they too disappeared into the orchard above the house. Céline watched the lights from their headlamps flicker through the trees until the last of them winked out and it was dark again.

The darkness of night in the north woods is as deep and as black and as silent as dreamless sleep, a presence unseen but as overt as if it were a hand blocking the light. From that dark and quiet place, sound is strident and quick and given meaning. Céline stood in her open doorway in that black night and listened to the rustling in the dry leaves and the leaves whispered to her that her son was dead.

They found him just before dawn. They called for a litter and strapped his small body into the litter and covered him with a sleeping bag and carried him out, six at a time, back through the orchard, back through the trees the way he had come. They told her that the dog had found them and wouldn't stop barking and had led them to the lean-to he'd made with the space blanket and the cold ashes from the fire and the stack of unused firewood, and that the dog had crawled back into his frozen arms and they could see then that the boy had been holding her to his chest for warmth when he died. They found where he had fallen through the ice. Céline listened and said nothing, her grief beyond consolation. They set the litter down and gently pulled away the sleeping bag and Edmund lay as if sleeping, his eyes closed and his arms encircling the space where Breeze had lain against him. She followed them out and sat beside Edmund's body, protecting him, keening softly in the way that dogs mourn their lost masters. Gaston collapsed sobbing to his knees and one of the men bent over him and put his arm around his shoulders.

Céline asked if they could take him into the house. For a little while, for the night. Please. The sheriff glanced at one of his deputies and seemed uncomfortable and looked away.

The deputy spoke. "We can't. It's against the law. We can't do anything about it."

"But he's my son."

"Mrs. Vaillancourt … the law … The body belongs to the coroner. That's the law. We can't. He'll be in the funeral home in the morning. They open at ten. I think ten, right, Dez?" The sheriff nodded. "Call them first, it's Dokken Funeral Home. It would be better if you called first."

Céline said she would call first.

An ambulance pulled into the driveway with its lights flashing and then had to back out and turn around because of the squad cars. They lifted Edmund out of the litter and put him on a gurney and covered him with a yellow blanket and slid him into the back of the ambulance. The ambulance drove out of the driveway with Edmund's body and down the road from the house the driver turned off the lights and then the rescue crews left, walking to their parked cars and driving away. The sheriff told her they should call the sheriff's department if they needed anything at all. He said he was sorry.

Then it was quiet as it had been before. Gaston, Céline and Breeze stood on the back porch. Céline went inside and Gaston and Breeze followed. Breeze stopped in the open doorway and watched them.

"I'm going to let her sleep inside tonight," Céline said. "In Edmund's room. She always did, anyway. I never told you that. She used to sneak inside at night and sleep with Edmund."

Gaston looked at her and said nothing and began walking up the steps to their bedroom.

Céline said okay and Breeze scooted into the kitchen. Céline opened the door to Edmund's bedroom and the little dog leapt onto Edmund's unmade bed. She turned once and lay down. Céline sat beside her and Breeze pushed her cool, wet nose into Céline's hand. Céline began sobbing and lay down on the bed while Breeze licked her hand.

* * *

Gaston arose before daybreak not having slept. Céline found him sitting at the kitchen table looking out the window toward the barn, the untouched cup of coffee she had made the previous night before him on the table. The sun poked feebly through light cloud cover and it had begun to snow small hard flakes in the sere, brittle air of the winter now upon them.

"Are you ready?" she said.

Gaston nodded and looked at his hands and smiled weakly. He put on his work jacket and stuffed his black hair under the collar.

Céline put some dog food in a bowl and gave it to Breeze but she wouldn't eat. She walked to the door and swished her tail back and forth. Céline put the bowl with the food in it on the kitchen counter.

Gaston said, "Did you call?"

"After you got up. They want us to sign some papers. We can go whenever you're ready."

Gaston rose. They walked out onto the back porch and Céline closed the door behind them. It was very cold and there was a skim of new snow covering the railing and porch decking. Their boots left crisp, sharply delineated tracks in the snow. Breeze trotted into the yard and then stopped and turned partway around.

"Here girl," Céline said. "Let's go to the barn."

Breeze wagged her tail and averted her eyes and took a step toward them but would not come.

"Come here, Breeze. Let's go to the barn." Breeze lowered her gaze as if embarrassed by her own refusal but wouldn't look at them.

"Breeze!" Céline said.

The little dog turned and ran into the orchard. She stopped once in the trees and looked back over her shoulder. Céline shouted, "Breeze! Breeze!" but then she was gone. She was not back when they returned from the funeral home that afternoon, nor that evening, nor the next day or the next. A front had moved in. It was bitterly cold and the long-anticipated storms that had been absent earlier in the month began rolling in off the lake every few days and the snow around the house and barn grew deeper and crept up the sides of the barn in windblown drifts. Two weeks later Gaston shoveled the doorway clear and went inside the barn and in the dust filtering down in the dim light and the cold in that unheated place he kicked apart Breeze's straw bed and fed it into the burn barrel, then tossed in the well-chewed stick he had found under the straw and watched the flames for a few minutes before returning to the house.

Chapter Nineteen

IT WAS SLOWER now, as if each exhalation in the rhythm of their lives were shallower than the one before and took a little longer before the ensuing inhalation began. There had been a boy, there had been horses and dogs, and the friction of living in proximity to one another had brought meaning and life and warmth to the farm they shared. Now, no matter how far she dialed up the thermostat, the house was cold. Gaston had stopped taking off his work coat when he returned from the job site, keeping it on until just before he undressed for bed. His work demolishing the foundation was eternal.

In February they ran out of money and he had to let Dick go, so it was just Gaston, on every day that wasn't so dangerously cold she wouldn't let him out of the house, pounding away by himself at the frozen concrete with his sledgehammer, his face contorted in a grimace of anger and pain, his strength and his fury and the concrete exploding under his blows a reminder of the rage and the doubt he could neither forget nor escape.

On the bitterly cold days that she insisted he stay home, he said little. They had barely spoken in months other than to reply to each other's questions, noting the bad weather, nodding politely while the other spoke.

She had thought they would talk it out. It came as a surprise to her that she had so little interest in doing so.

The Gurney catalogue arrived in early spring and she thumbed through it dispiritedly, knowing that she needed to order soon if she wanted to have a garden this year at all. They could still afford *seeds*.

And they'd save money by not having to buy produce at the farmer's market, which had become trendy of late, and because of that, expensive. But did she even want the bother? Gaston didn't care all that much about vegetables other than sweet corn and potatoes, although she liked them all. There was no Breeze or Cloud to keep the rabbits out, no Sir Lancelot and Dutch to feed the discarded greens to. No tanned little boy to help her eat the sweet carrots and grilled asparagus she loved. At the thought of Edmund she squeezed her eyes shut and put her hand to her mouth and for a few moments gave herself over to her grief, alone and cold at the kitchen table, her heaviest sweater not equal to the task of keeping her warm in this cold house, in this coldest of winters.

Two or three days a week she drove to town and ordered coffee at a little shop on the docks while Gaston was at work. Occasionally she had a glass of wine. They sold fresh pastries and once in a while she had an apple Danish. There was a free-standing wood stove in the middle of the room and she liked to pull her chair up close and take off her boots and prop her stocking feet on the warm limestone hearth surrounding it. She rarely spoke with anyone because there was rarely anyone to speak to. The Port Landing coffee shops were bursting at the seams in the summer but operated on reduced hours during the long tourist-free winter months. One day a woman she thought she recognized pulled up the chair beside her. Céline caught her eye and the woman smiled.

"Céline?"

"Oh. Yes. I'm sorry but I don't remember your name. I'm so bad with things anymore."

"Madeline Aldrich. We've met before but it was a while back. I'm Melanie's mom."

Céline tapped her forehead. "Of course. I remember you now. Of course. I'm sorry, Madeline, it's just … I'm sorry."

Madeline waved her hand dismissively. She was perhaps a year or two younger than Céline.

"Pooh. I can't remember anything anymore. It's my advanced age."

Céline grinned, rolling her palms up in supplication, as if she too were helpless against the ravages of age. "Who'd a thunk it?" she said. It was good to talk to someone.

"Listen," Madeline said. "I'm going to get right to the point and if I'm out of line just say so, okay? You won't hurt my feelings." She touched Céline's arm. "The funeral ... Melanie wanted to come. She asked me if I'd take her. I said no."

Céline didn't know how she was supposed to react.

"She and your son were, well ... not really dating, really, they were too young for that, but I guess you could say they were friends. But you already knew that."

"We knew," Céline said, nodding. "He told me. He liked her a lot."

Madeline tugged at the hem of her coat, straightening the wrinkles. "Melanie liked *him* a lot. When, you know, we got the news, she cried all day. He was over at our place a couple times, once just the weekend before, just visiting, and he was such a nice boy." She gazed over Céline's head. "God, this is so horrible." Céline put her hand on Madeline's arm and Madeline put her hand on top of Céline's hand and squeezed it. "Melanie told me he was popular with the other kids in school, that everybody liked him. God, I don't know why I'm rambling on like this."

But Céline ached to hear. She and Gaston had barely spoken of Edmund since the funeral, a bleak service that Gaston had nearly been too distraught to attend. She had stopped talking about their lost son in deference to Gaston's crushing remorse, but their silence had grown into an unspoken barrier, a wall between the two of them that had accumulated stone by stone until neither could reach over the top.

"No, no. It's nice. *This* is nice," Céline said, encouraging her. "Everybody liked Edmund. He almost never got into fights, the stuff that other kids his age usually do. Maybe once. Gaston—that's my husband—Edmund was so different in that respect from his father. I guess we always knew that, but it's still good to hear it from you, kind of an unbiased source." She beamed.

She had almost forgotten that everybody liked Edmund and Madeline's confirmation of what she'd long taken for granted was an unexpected consolation and all the more precious for its earnestness. He had been good in school and was a pretty darn good baseball player. His circle of friends never included more than a couple boys his own age and she'd worried about that, but then, who else was like Edmund? Even the kids he didn't know knew of him and seemed to like him. While the rest of the kids in Port Landing lived in a world whose parameters were defined by computers and smartphones, Edmund was a throwback, a kid born in the wrong generation who wanted only to hike through the wild country beyond the orchard with his dogs. Maybe, she thought, that's where he was now, in the woods he loved, the right place. She squeezed her eyes closed, wiping them with a napkin.

"I knew it," Madeline said. "I should have just shut up. This was stupid of me."

"No, no!" Céline said. "It's just that ... I haven't talked about it like this, not for months. Please don't stop. I'm just ... I'm fine. This is good." She took Madeline's hand.

At the time, Melanie had been a shock. A girlfriend? Edmund had always been so shy around girls, so temperamentally different that way from his father. He had told her he wanted to marry Melanie. The irony of that—that he was so unlike what she thought she knew of her son—made her wonder what else she had missed about him, what else she might have learned had he lived—or that she might learn from others who had known him, like Madeline.

Madeline was staring at the flames in the stove. She leaned forward, closer to the heat, her elbows propped on her knees, the shadows flickering lightly across her face. Then she swung in her chair to face Céline.

"But here I go getting sidetracked. I want to get back to elaborating on what I was saying. Melanie told me she wanted to go and I wouldn't let her. I think I owe you an explanation."

"You don't owe me anything," Céline said.

"No, I do. Please. I've thought a lot about this, and now I don't know what to say. I remember thinking she was too young to be exposed to that, maybe that's all it was. You want to protect your kids from everything, you know? Including hurt feelings."

Madeline was near tears. "I mean, nothing like that has ever happened in Port Landing before, and I've been here all my life. Everybody lives in this picture-perfect little fairytale town sticking out into Lake Superior, where bad things never happen to kids and la-dee-dah. Not in Port Landing. I was born here. People's children don't ..." She looked at Céline suddenly and her mouth formed an embarrassed "oh" but Céline smiled and squeezed Madeline's knee.

Madeline's eyes glistened. "I just don't know anymore. Maybe it's like I wanted to keep it that way for Melanie a little longer, like a fairytale. As long as I could. But I don't think that's all of it. I think now that I kept her home because it just wasn't fair. It just wasn't fair what happened to Edmund. I didn't want her to be exposed to the world the way it really is, the unfairness of it. I mean, I know how this must sound to you, me telling you of all people how unfair it was. I don't even know what I was thinking that day. It was stupid. I told Eric and he said I should have just let her go. He was probably right. God, I'm just so sorry."

Céline had once believed that there was a reason for everything. There was a reason for her carefree childhood in Minneapolis, which had led to the good years of her marriage to Gaston, and had ultimately given her a reserve of strength to keep going despite their declining fortunes. But Edmund's death *hadn't* been fair, there was nothing to be gleaned from the pain, from the ache in her heart that she woke with and wore like an ill-fitting shawl through the long hours of each day, to escape only in fitful sleep. There wasn't going to be a do-over, another boy to get right the second time around. There had been no lesson learned. There had been only Edmund, once.

She liked this woman. She found Madeline's hand and held it on the table. "I would have done the same thing," she said. Madeline closed her eyes and then opened them and wiped the tears from her cheeks.

Céline said, "Hey! Do you come here very often? I mean, to this place?"

Madeline shook her head. "Not really. I was just up the street and I saw you come in. I knew I had to say something, even if I didn't know what."

"Well, maybe next time we should plan a date. I need to get out more. I'm dying for some girl talk. Let me get your number."

* * *

That spring Céline started a garden with the seeds she'd bought from Gurney's. She used a quarter of the space she'd used in years past and rototilled the black earth until it was receptive and fertile. She planted the seeds in short rows marked with the corresponding package stapled to a wooden stake at each end. She put up a chicken-wire fence to keep the rabbits out but some of them got in anyway. Even at a quarter of the original size, the garden would supply both of them with all the produce they could eat.

Gaston had begun demolishing the last few feet of the foundation. His hands were blistered and claw-like from months of swinging a sledgehammer and his shoulders and back ached so much he couldn't sleep at night, tossing and turning fitfully, wrenched and haunted by violent dreams. Céline finally retreated to one of the guest bedrooms down the hall. It was better that way.

They shared breakfast, in unspoken acquiescence to habit.

"He's gonna do it," he told her one morning. "Like he said he was going to. I never knew if he would. He's gonna cut me a check for getting the foundation out plus some extra to repour the new one, which he didn't have to do but I can live with that. I told him I had to get a crew together but I could probably start in a couple weeks when it warms up. I took a bath on that foundation, but at least I'll have something, at least I got enough to start on the house. I guess I should be happy but mostly I'm just relieved. I didn't think he was gonna come through."

"I didn't either," Céline said.

"We'd have been shit out of luck," Gaston said.

Céline nodded and sat opposite him with a bowl of oatmeal. She hadn't thought the doctor would live up to his word not so much because she doubted his word (although she had), but rather, because she'd stopped thinking that the foundation, as an entity, was in any way directly connected to her life. The foundation had long ago become the province of her husband and the doctor he worked for whom she had never met. She knew in the abstract that their being able to keep the business depended upon his paying them for the work Gaston had destroyed his health to complete, but the foundation's completion did not occupy her thoughts. So where did that leave her? Maybe, like Gaston, she was simply relieved. There were no further projects, no final hills to die upon. It was over.

At the beginning of the following month, on a warm Saturday morning in May, she loaded her Subaru with the last of her clothing and a few cardboard boxes of odds and ends and moved out. Gaston said goodbye and gave her a hard, quick hug and then pulled back and seemed not to know what to do with his hands. Then he got in his truck and drove to the job site, which was now in full swing. She drove north on Highway 13 around the peninsula, the mute expanse of Lake Superior flashing like frames in a silent movie through the gaps in the budding trees off her right shoulder, through Cornucopia and Port Wing and then east on 2 to Superior.

She stopped at a restaurant and ordered a salad and asked if they had something other than iceberg lettuce but they didn't. When the waitress came back with her salad she decided to order a glass of red wine, whatever they had was fine, and picked at her salad but finished the wine and then took I-35 to her mother's home in Minneapolis.

Chapter Twenty

"IT'S OKAY, MOM. It's not what I learned in school, but I like it okay."
This was part of her mother's routine monthly interrogation, implied, never spoken, about what she was going to do with her life. Céline had moved into her old room, a room she'd last slept in while in college. There were pictures of her in her high school and college volleyball uniforms. Pictures of her on graduation day from Concordia, proudly displaying her degree. Pictures of their cabin on Mille Lacs Lake. Missing were pictures of her with Gaston, the collages of Vaillancourt family photos plucked from the walls as if they had never been there.

Her mother had hung framed photos of Edmund on every wall of the house and Céline finally had to ask, tearfully, if temporarily they could be put somewhere else. She'd find her own place soon and then she could put them back. But that had been eighteen months ago, and she hadn't found a place of her own. She found little comfort in the thought of living alone.

Céline took a job as an office manager in a Downtown West financial services firm, which she leveraged from her years managing the books for Vaillancourt Builders. The recession was bottoming out and they had offered good pay and benefits. She marveled at the twenty-one-story elevator ride to her office and the view of skyscrapers all around and the relentlessly green city parks far below. It seemed too pat, too common a trope, to dismiss her sixteen years in Port Landing as a dream, but downtown Minneapolis was a world apart from the small town she had lived in on the tip of Lake Superior. The web of relationships she had fostered with her family and the people and the animals and the shops and their farm had shaped her as indelibly as the footprint of her genes.

In the same manner that the aged reflect upon their youth, she hadn't really understood until there had been a reckoning of the sum of things. In her flight she had taken with her the largest and least noticed of these: the memory of a vast inland lake which continued to haunt her dreams. For sixteen years, Lake Superior, always in the background, had been as much a constant in her life as the silent rise and fall of her breath, as unremarkable as death and as profound as the chirp of a cricket. It had defined her and everyone else in Port Landing, while etching invisible parameters around their lives that a change of location would not erase.

She found herself continually explaining to her mother that the job was okay. The pay was more than fair. They treated her very well. There was a career here if she wanted it. But she didn't.

She occupied her mind with work and when she was through working she came home. Occasionally Madeline drove down from Port Landing and the two of them would go to a nice restaurant, and for a while Céline was able to let her thoughts drift away and enjoy the growing friendship they shared. Madeline told her that Melanie was now a cheerleader in middle school and Eric was doing quite well and they were building a home on the lake on land her parents had bought in the early eighties, before prices went through the roof, and wasn't she blessed to have that? Of course, Céline agreed that she was, because it was genuinely true, and because she now knew that blessings were distributed unequally and often without merit and that misfortune, too, was distributed unequally and without merit and there was no balance between the two in this life.

She finally agreed to a date with a stockbroker she'd met at a conference across town, but they talked in superficialities while he drank single malt scotch and she told him she was separated, not divorced, hoping he would take the hint but he didn't and she finally stopped replying to the messages he left on her cellphone. He was ten years older than her and she preferred to spend her nights reading or watching television.

Her mother belonged to a garden club and had the zeal of all those who become converts to a hobby late in life. She had gardening books and magazines scattered about the living room in their expansive brick tri-level and Céline enjoyed sharing what she knew and occasionally lending a hand. She marveled at the abundance of rabbits in the neighborhood, which waited until she was nearly upon them before disdainfully hopping out of the way, their whiskers twitching with annoyance. Her mother had bought a Havahart live trap at a garage sale that she didn't know how to use, so Céline took it upon herself to trap the rabbits, only to be confronted with the problem of where to put them. She finally released them in a private park on the far side of their gated subdivision, only, she was certain, to have them return within a day or two.

She heard from Gaston. Not often. He had another project under contract and he was doing well enough. Madeline had driven by once and told her the farm looked like the lawn hadn't been mowed in a month. Gaston spoke in business-like platitudes, as if he were selling a bid on a remodel job. Port Landing was good. Business was coming back, not booming but steady. There was another bear hitting the orchard and he'd taken his rifle and laid up for it one night but it hadn't turned up. They'd had the Fourth of July father/son game but of course he hadn't played, and while he was thinking about that he had something for her, he'd give it to her when he saw her again. If he saw her again.

"What?" she said.

"Nothing. I just don't, you know, need it anymore and I thought maybe you could use it. Not use it but you would want it. I don't know. It's his glove. His mitt."

Céline put her hand to her eyes and squeezed and then took her hand away and spoke into the phone.

"I thought it was lost," she said.

"I did too. The funeral home guys called. It was after you left. They had some stuff of his they'd misplaced or lost or something that they said belonged to me. They apologized all over themselves. They had his red daypack and the glove was inside it. I put it upstairs and then downstairs and then in the basement but it's like everywhere I go I'm looking at it, like it follows me around or something, like those eyes that follow you around in a painting. And then I ran into one of the guys that was on the rescue team that night."

Céline heard a quiet inhalation and for a moment the line was silent.

"I didn't recognize him, but he remembered me. Conversation got around to the baseball glove. He told me Edmund had it under his body. He was using it as insulation in the lean-to to stay warm. He had the daypack under his head. I always told him you had to have insulation between you and the ground, that was the only way you'd survive in the winter. I told him that would protect him from the cold in the ground."

Even in summer Minneapolis was warmer than Port Landing. The breezes wafting off Superior had kept their farm cool and pleasant. Céline had become accustomed to the hum of the air conditioner in her mother's home, but now it seemed louder, almost intrusive. Her mother refused to open the windows, afraid the cool air of the house would escape outside. Céline listened to the air conditioner hum and then she walked across the living room to the beveled glass windows that gave onto the back yard. There was a rabbit in the garden.

"I want it," she said.

Gaston said okay. He cleared his throat and mumbled something under his breath but she couldn't hear him and he said okay he'd try again.

"I'm sorry," he said.

* * *

She agreed to meet Madeline Friday after work at Bistro Ernie's downtown. Céline looked up the address so Madeline could plug it into the GPS in her car. Madeline would stay for the weekend and leave for Port Landing Monday morning. They'd run over to her mother's house afterwards and she could throw her suitcase in one of the guest bedrooms. It wasn't like there was a lack of guest bedrooms.

"They let you off on a Monday, just like that?" Céline asked after they met in the parking lot and exchanged hugs. Céline's two and a half weeks of paid vacation were strictly delineated.

"I'm self-employed, or self-unemployed, depending on how you look at it," Madeline told her. Madeline was in the real estate business. She tapped her phone. "Have phone, will travel."

"How's it going? The real estate business."

"The real estate business," Madeline said. "The real estate business is … real. A couple years ago I couldn't sell a house if I included a Puerto Rican maid and a German shepherd in the back yard. I've been doing this since, let me think …" She began ticking off the years on her fingers. "You count the time I worked in the office for Mom and Dad in college it's been, like, twenty years. And it was always like this. It booms for a while and then it crashes for a while. When it booms everybody thinks they're going to get rich and it's going to last forever. And when it crashes they think it's the end of the world and the market will never come back again and they want to shoot themselves. But it always does, especially in Port Landing. Port Landing's pretty touristy, so it gets these crazy swings in the market. I would imagine it's a lot more stable down here. That's what I've been told, anyway."

Céline had no idea what the real estate market was like in Minneapolis. It seemed like it was doing fine, according to what she'd heard from the finance people in her office. Her mother had made some noises about her inheriting the house when she was gone, but hadn't said much beyond that. And her mother was only seventy-one.

"Maybe I should buy a house down here or something," Céline said. "I mean, Mom's not charging me anything, she's been great, but I really ought to find a place of my own. You can't live with your mother for the rest of your life. I'm forty. I just can't decide if this is where I want to make a stand. I mean, I grew up here. Minneapolis is great, but, you know."

"You could always move back to Port Landing." Madeline was watching the bar. Friday evenings were always packed at Bistro Ernie's. Waiters in white shirts and black pants and white aprons scuttled back and forth from the kitchen carrying trays of free-range roasted chicken and mixed baby greens over their heads and bottles of French Cabernet under their arms. Bistro Ernie's was expensive, but Madeline enjoyed it and Céline figured she could afford it on the occasions Madeline drove down to visit. There was a row of tables outside on the flagstone terrace fronting the street and throngs of people scurried past, as fit and trim as swimwear models, their cotton blazers open to the warmth of the summer evening. Minneapolis, Céline thought, must have the healthiest people on the planet.

Céline shook her head. "I don't know about that," she said. "Port Landing's pretty teensy when you're trying to, you know … Well, I guess I just wouldn't feel all that comfortable running into Gaston. Still. You can't avoid your ex-husband in a town that size."

Madeline swung back toward the table. "I thought you guys were only separated. Last time we talked you were just separated, right?"

Céline frowned. She hadn't touched her wine, but now she reached for the glass and brought it to her lips. She took a sip, looking at Madeline over the rim of the glass, then put it back on the table. She shook her head.

"We are. But not for long. He wants a divorce. He called me last week. At least he didn't send an email. He wants to sell the farm. He says it's too much to keep up by himself anymore. I'll get half of the money, of course. I think he's being fair about it. He already got it appraised. If we both agree to the terms we won't have to hire a lawyer."

"Is that what *you* want?"

Céline stared at her glass. "I'm not going to fight it. I guess I kind of knew when I left that I was never going to live there again. I just couldn't. It would be too hard. It would be, just, really hard." She took another sip of her wine and let it linger on her tongue, enjoying the taste, enjoying the warmth spreading through her body. She'd finished half the glass.

She was still a casual drinker, preferring to share a glass with good friends. Except when she didn't, when she was still up and she couldn't sleep and her mother had already gone to bed. Nights in her mother's cavernous home were hard. Céline found no solace in sleep; her dreams offered no escape. At night, alone in the four-poster bed she'd slept in as a child, she dreamt of Lake Superior and the orchard and the harvest and the colors of the leaves on the apple trees, their lamp-like incandescence just before they fell. She did not dream of Edmund. But she sensed him there, as if he were standing in the wings just off stage.

"Have you been back at all?"

Céline shook her head. "I thought about it a couple times. Really thought about it a lot. I've still got people up there I'd like to see again. It seems like a long time ago now, Port Landing and the farm and all, like a life I lived long ago and far away, like they say in the movies. Everything is fuzzy around the edges and shiny and pretty. It's like the Land of Oz, that's the way I remember it. Isn't that silly? But I know it's not like that and maybe I'm afraid I'll be disappointed. Or maybe I'm just afraid."

Their waiter had been standing at a polite remove and when he sensed a lull in the conversation he darted in and took their order, quickly and professionally.

"Should we get some more wine?" Madeline said. She had already finished her first glass.

Céline studied her half-empty glass. She'd had so little to drink over the course of her life that a single glass of wine left her loopy and almost afraid to drive. She shook her head.

Madeline frowned. "Party pooper," she said. She ordered another glass for herself.

The waiter closed his book and smiled and walked away. Madeline watched him go.

"He's cute," she said.

"He's half your age," Céline said.

Madeline arched her eyebrows. "So what? I love Eric, but sometimes ... But there I go again. How about you? Seeing anybody?"

Was she *seeing* anybody? Of course she wasn't seeing anybody. She wasn't even officially divorced, not yet.

"No," she said. "Nobody. I've been asked out once or twice. You know." She shrugged. "Nothing."

"Girlfriend, you need to get out a little more. Look ... I know I shouldn't say this, but when has that ever stopped me? It's *time*."

Céline reached for her glass.

"Why not?" Madeline said. "Okay, I know why not. I'm being out of line. But ..."

Céline looked at her.

"But ... except ... I guess I think everybody should be, you know, in the swing of things. While you're young. While *we're* young. While you can."

"I can't do that here. It just doesn't feel safe yet," Céline said. She touched her wine glass with the tip of her finger. "Maybe that's not the right word."

Madeline screwed her mouth into one of her puckish grins. "What, is there a plague of ED in Minneapolis?"

Céline loved Madeline. But Madeline was like this, she said things that left her no place to hide. It was as if she asked questions and answered them at the same time.

She picked up her glass of wine, swirled it around and took a small sip.

"So what are you going to do?" Madeline asked.

"Well, I wanted to talk to you about that," Céline said. She touched Madeline's hand. "Can I stay with you and Eric for a couple days? I was thinking maybe the end of the month, I've got some time off coming up. It would be just for the weekend."

Chapter Twenty-One

PORT LANDING HADN'T changed. She found the thought surprising. What, exactly, had she expected? High-rises like in Minneapolis? A new shopping mall? Port Landing was everything she remembered and all that which she had forgotten she valued: its unchanging character. Rows of shops and art galleries and small restaurants bordering the docks. Sailboats still plied Chequamegon Bay, and on a wooded hill a half mile above town was the farm where she'd raised her family, the barn and the orchard beyond the barn and beyond that everything that was beyond that, as it always had been and always would be.

Madeline and Eric's new home was tastefully modest and just a few dozen yards from the shore of Lake Superior. Her bedroom had a view of the Apostle Islands, which Madeline had proudly pointed out, as if she were offering the view to a personal client. Madeline had floor duty at her real estate office so they'd caught an early breakfast at LeMond's—redecorated by the new owners—and then Céline was on her own until dinner. She sipped a cup of coffee and nibbled on a buttery croissant. Gaston would be meeting her at the farm in an hour; he had told her he'd have all the papers with him. It would be simple and quick.

She'd taken her mother's advice and spoken to a lawyer who'd suggested some small changes to the copy Gaston faxed her shortly after his phone call several weeks earlier. The lawyer had thoughtfully pursed his lips, crossed out a couple sentences with a ballpoint pen, then handed it back to her.

"It's not bad," he said, shrugging. "I don't see many like this. Mostly they're out to exact revenge, if you know what I mean. But no, it's all legal. If his lawyer agrees to the minor changes we discussed, and he should, since your ex appears to be a reasonable man, then yeah, this will fly. Go ahead and sign it."

She'd taken it home, set it on the dresser beside her bed and avoided looking at it for two weeks. The night before she left, she signed it, folded it in half and put it in her purse without reading it.

* * *

Gaston met her in the driveway, planting himself in front of her Subaru, his arms held stiffly at his sides, smiling awkwardly at her through the windshield. She waved with a gaiety she did not feel, as if she were imposing upon an estranged friend, and he walked around to her side and opened the door for her and when she got out they gave each other a hug at arm's length, patting each other's back as if anything beyond that formality were an unwanted commitment.

"Long time," he said.

She hadn't seen him in almost two years. They had talked on the phone. He'd put on some weight, not much, but enough that she noticed, and he'd tied his long hair back with one of the elastic bands she'd bought him. She saw the new strands of gray in his hair. They walked side by side to the house.

"You want to look inside? That would be okay if you want to," he said. "Realtor says it's gonna go pretty quick."

Céline nodded. Looking inside the house was fine; she would want to remember. They went inside and sat at the kitchen table as they had always done and she gazed around at the kitchen and at the door to Edmund's bedroom and at the living room and the windows overlooking the bay and beyond that Lake Superior but that was as far as she got. She did not ask to see the rest of the house. He had cleaned the kitchen before she arrived. She pulled the papers from her purse and put them on the table and he didn't look at them and then they sat across from each other and spoke a little about the weather and wasn't it a nice summer so far.

"You think you'll be here long enough for the harvest?" she said.

Gaston shook his head. "I'm not planning on it. I've gotta let it go, I don't have any other choice. I can't do it by myself and I'm getting too busy at work. I've got two projects going and I'm working six days a week. It's like before." He was sitting upright in his chair, his hands folded awkwardly on the table, his back not quite touching the chair. "You working for a real estate company? Isn't that what you told me? How's that going?"

"Financial services. They do investment planning and stocks and things. I'm the office manager, which is what they used to call a secretary. It's okay. The pay's pretty good and the benefits are pretty good. Everything's pretty good." She smiled and he immediately smiled back.

"They contribute to my 401(k)," she said.

"That's great!" Gaston said. "We don't have much to do with 401(k)s around this place. As you know."

"I'm thinking I might buy a house down there," she said. "Something small."

"You like Minneapolis, then?"

"Yeah. It's nice. There's lots to do. You forget how much when you live in a small town. I grew up there but, you know, all the time I spent here … You forget."

"I never was a city guy," he said.

"I know."

"So anyway, I'm thinking short-term I'm gonna move into that rental on Maple. It's still vacant. I might as well use it. When we get all this taken care of I'll figure out my next move. I may build something smaller, I don't know. I don't need all this space. Maybe build a storage unit someplace where I can store my equipment and put in a grandmother apartment upstairs. I know of guys did that."

Céline agreed that it was a good plan.

"So that's what I'm thinking, anyway." He looked at her and then looked away. He said nothing for a while. Then, "I have that stuff I told you about. I'll get it for you." He rose from his chair and walked into Edmund's bedroom and returned holding Edmund's red daypack in one hand and his baseball glove in the other. The baseball glove had brown water stains across the pocket. He placed them on the table beside the papers, the glove resting on top of the daypack.

"You don't want these, I guess," Céline said. Her hands had begun to tremble and she was embarrassed so she put them in her lap and forced a smile.

"I can't, is more like it," Gaston said. "It's like they shouldn't be in this house anymore. Not now. Like they don't belong here with me."

Céline's breath caught in a little hiccup and she put her hand to her mouth and swallowed.

"Can I have a glass of water please?" Gaston jumped to his feet and filled a glass from the sink and put some ice in it from the ice maker in the refrigerator. He set the glass in front of her, which immediately began to sweat in the warm air. She took a sip and set it back down in the ring of condensation it had left on the table and the cold water cooled her throat and made her feel better. She heard a truck rumble along the gravel road below the house. In the hazy blue distance beyond Madeline Island and far out across the open water of Lake Superior, a tanker moved so slowly and silently as to appear to be not moving at all, as if it had been captured and embedded in a painting trailing a silent and unmoving white wake.

"I think he would have wanted you to have this stuff, even the glove," Gaston said. "Especially the glove. I know that sounds weird, because we both loved baseball so much, you know? But it's like I don't feel I have a right to it anymore." She caught his eyes but he couldn't hold her gaze and he stared at the baseball glove and the divorce papers on the table.

Céline touched her glass and the condensation wet her fingers. "It wasn't your fault," she said. "I never thought that."

* * *

She pulled into the parking lot, gravel popping beneath the tires of her Subaru, and sat listening to the PBS station, gazing at the manicured baseball diamond through the windshield. She'd passed a half dozen cars as she drove in, all with boys in baseball uniforms leaving practice for the afternoon. Now the place was deserted save for a father and son in the outfield, who were taking turns throwing a Frisbee for a dog. She killed the engine and put Edmund's glove under her arm and walked to the bleachers and put the glove on the painted wooden plank beside her. She heard the father giving instructions to the boy but they were at the far end of the outfield and she couldn't make out what he was saying.

She had the discomforting thought that, for the first time in her adult life, she was homeless. Not homeless like the people she saw flying cardboard signs on the streets of Minneapolis, but homeless in the sense that she wasn't living in a home she owned. She'd signed the papers Gaston had asked for and returned them and with that small formality had walked away from the home she'd known and loved for sixteen years and the place she'd raised her only son.

Gaston had fallen apart after Edmund's death, spending days at a time in bed, but her grief had stolen upon her slowly, like the tide across the sand on a beach, hollowing her out a few grains at a time with each passing month. On the nights she took the Pilates classes her company paid for, she was able to push her sorrow away with exercise, but that small hard kernel of pain was never entirely absent; it was always there like a stone under a rug, beneath the smile, beneath the cheerfulness, beneath the chatter with her coworkers at the restaurants they visited during their lunch breaks. She was tired of the pain, tired of remembering.

It had not been difficult to accept the divorce and the sale of the farm. She had thought it would be even though she had known it was coming but it hadn't been, and this surprised her. She didn't know what she would do next, but she assumed she would buy a home somewhere in Minneapolis and live there, perhaps indefinitely. Maybe that's what it meant to be open to taking an unknown road in your own life: the willingness to face uncertainty, to embrace a future of not knowing.

Or perhaps, she thought wryly, she'd read too many pop psychology books in college.

She lay back against the bleacher behind her and gazed at the sky, then rolled onto her elbow and looked around. Abutting the baseball diamond was a soccer field, and, as with the diamond, the Jaycees kept the grass fertilized and meticulously trimmed. On the other side of the parking lot was a small cinderblock shed that sold pop, candy bars and popcorn during the games, and drilled and tapped into the wall under the eave was a copper plaque inscribed with the annual winners of the Fourth of July father/son baseball game. Somewhere on that plaque was the name of the team Edmund and Gaston had played on.

The father and the boy and the dog were working their way closer to where she sat, and now she could hear his instructions to his son. "Make her sit before you take it from her," he said. "Don't let her drop it at your feet, okay?" She watched the boy flip the Frisbee out in a low, flat arc and the dog raced out beneath it and caught it in mid-air and ran back to the boy with the Frisbee in its mouth, only to prance around his feet, teasing him with an impromptu game of keep-away. She heard the boy laughing.

"No," the father said again. "Remember? Tell her to sit. Make her put it in your hand."

"Sit!" the boy said. The dog crouched and spit out the Frisbee and waited for another throw. The boy walked to the Frisbee and pointed at it and said "Fetch!" but the dog responded only by furiously wagging its tail.

She thought then about what Madeline had said, about Port Landing being on the verge of another real estate boom. Madeline had offered her a job in her real estate office.

"It's harder than people think, but it's not *that* hard," she'd told her. "Getting in right now when the market is strong is, like, perfect timing. It's the best thing you can do. You get a few sales under your belt and it builds up your confidence. All you have to do is get your license. Besides, everyone in town already knows you and in this business, it's who you know that pays the bills. Eric and I own some rentals and we can give you a sweet deal on one if you decide to move back up. You should give it some thought."

Céline told her she would think about it and she had. She knew nothing about real estate, but then, she'd known nothing about financial services either until she'd been hired by a financial services firm. So maybe she would do that; move back to Port Landing and become a real estate agent, despite her reservations. She knew about half a million realtors in Minneapolis. Did it really matter how she put bread on the table?

She lay back once more, enjoying the warmth of the sun. She'd always loved the summers in Port Landing. Warm, but never hot, and cool at night. As green as Minneapolis was, it wasn't as verdant as the hills around Lake Superior, which glowed with life, the leaves on the maples and oaks waxy and full and ripe, like the glowing faces of an infinitude of young mothers. She felt something beside her leg and she sat up and saw that the dog had buried its nose in Edmund's baseball glove and begun a soft, quiet keening. The father and his son began trotting toward her and she reached out to stroke the dog's side. It took its head out from inside the glove and turned toward her, meeting her eyes. It was Breeze. She put her nose to Céline's hand and in that moment of certainty leapt onto her lap and licked her face and whined and barked and pawed at her wildly and Céline could not contain her own joy.

The man arrived first, breathing from his jog across the infield, and stopped a few feet away. "Oh man," he said. "I'm really sorry. I don't know what's gotten into her. Come here, Rojo."

"Rojo?" Céline said. "That's what you call her?" Breeze had wriggled under her arm and was licking her face. Céline had both arms around her neck and made no move to stop her.

"God, she's gone crazy," the man said. "Rojo, get over here." The boy walked up and snapped a leash to her collar and Breeze reluctantly sat by his side but gazed at Céline and whined and would not stop.

"It's Spanish for red," the boy said.

His father nodded. "Preston's taking Spanish in school," he said.

"That's a really good name for a dog," Céline said.

The boy said, "We got her right here, right, Dad?"

His father nodded again. "Yeah. She was hanging around the in-field one day during practice. She kept going into the dugout, checking out everybody like she was looking for somebody, you know? Nobody knew who she belonged to. She was covered with burrs and dirt and she didn't have a collar on or anything. But then she saw Preston and just latched on to him. He'd been wanting a dog anyway so we took her home but we told him we had to do the right thing and try and find out who her owner was. We put an ad in the paper but nobody called so she became Preston's official dog. She sleeps on his bed every night. Jeez. It's like we adopted another kid or something." He grinned. "She sure seems to like you, though."

Preston unsnapped her leash and Breeze cast about for the Frisbee and picked it up and delivered it proudly to Céline. She took it and Breeze pressed her nose against Céline's leg, snuffling happily.

Céline said, "How old are you, Preston?"

"Nine." He was tall for his age, taller than Edmund had been, with a smattering of freckles on his sunburned arms.

"Did you ever know my son? His name was Edmund. He was a little older than you and he had black hair. He loved baseball."

Preston thought and then shook his head.

"He would have been thirteen this summer," Céline said. "He had a dog, too."

"Your son is ..." the man said.

"He died the winter before last," Céline said. "It was one of those things."

"I'm very sorry to hear that," the man said. Preston said nothing. The man put his hands in the pockets of his jeans and then took them out again. He whispered something to Preston and the boy clapped his hands and said, "C'mon, Rojo, let's go."

"His mom's got supper waiting," the man said. "Are you from around here?"

"Not anymore," Céline said. "I used to be. I live in Minneapolis now."

"Well, maybe we'll see you around again. I'll bet Rojo would like that, right Preston?"

Preston nodded but his eyes were on his dog. He clapped his hands and Breeze cocked her head but didn't move.

"C'mon son, let's go," the man said. He began walking away.

Reluctantly, Preston turned and followed, gazing at his dog over his shoulder. Breeze had crawled into Céline's lap again and pushed her head under her arm and was making soft, happy sounds under her breath. Preston clapped his hands once more and called her by name and the little red dog watched them depart and then she sprang suddenly from Céline's lap and ran to the boy. Preston threw the Frisbee and she brought it back to him as he watched her glancing back, watching Céline.

* * *

She was speaking to Madeline. "Did I ever tell you we had dogs?" she said.

Madeline thought and then shook her head. They were on the back deck overlooking the lake; below them a small boat with two fishermen was trolling close to shore, trailing lines over the outboard. She was close enough that she could hear them talking. One of the men spied her watching and saluted. Céline waved back. She leaned over the railing, dangling her wine glass from her fingers. Madeline was already halfway through hers.

"What kind of dogs?" she said.

From across the lake Céline heard the deep bellow of a freighter, faint but clear.

"Border collies, a brother and a sister. The brother got killed by a bear. His name was Cloud. It was an adjustment, really pretty bad. I'd never really had a dog growing up so I didn't know how hard it could be to lose one."

"I didn't know that, that you had a dog," Madeline said. She was fiddling with the flame adjustment on the grill. Eric, who normally did the grilling, was out for the night with his poker buddies.

"What happened to the other dog?"

"She was really Edmund's dog. Always was. They were inseparable until he was gone."

"Did you take her to Minneapolis?"

"No." Céline swirled her glass around and set it on the railing. "I gave her to a boy who loved her the way Edmund did. I think she's happy with him. I think she's very happy."

"Do you ever miss her sometimes?"

Céline picked up her glass and took a small sip, then set it back down and gazed down at the lake. She tried to find the fishermen that she could still hear but they had motored around a wooded bend and she couldn't see them. A breeze was coming in off the water and it was nice, a Port Landing summer, warm during the day and cool at night, the way she'd always remembered it. She turned toward Madeline but Madeline had walked through the sliding glass doors and into the kitchen.

Acknowledgments

To Cynthia ("Bob") Gage I'd like to express my sincere thanks for your insightful first reading of this book. To Mark and Kathy Wendling— thanks for putting me up all these years in the town that would become the fictional setting for this novel (and for supplying me with the best bird dogs I've ever owned!). Finally, I'd like to thank my editor at Guernica, Margo LaPierre, for her professionalism, superb line editing, and dedication to improving this book.

About the Author

Dave Carty finished a three-year stint at the Colorado State and University of Colorado Schools of Journalism before dropping out two semesters shy of graduation. During his early twenties, he worked, reluctantly, at a succession of largely blue-collar jobs: waiter, bartender, carpenter, door to door geodesic terrarium salesman (really), wallpaper hanger, ski instructor, convenience-store clerk, and others too numerous to mention. In his late twenties, he returned to writing and began a thirty-year career in freelance magazine work while writing a succession of novels set in and around the west. He has lived for many years in the small home he built for himself in southwestern Montana.